ASKING
for
MURDER

ROBERTA ISLEIB

BERKLEY PRIME CRIME, NEW YORK

THE BERKLEY PUBLISHING GROUP
Published by the Penguin Group
Penguin Group (USA) Inc.
375 Hudson Street, New York, New York 10014, USA
Penguin Group (Canada), 90 Eglinton Avenue East, Suite 700, Toronto, Ontario M4P 2Y3, Canada
(a division of Pearson Penguin Canada Inc.)
Penguin Books Ltd., 80 Strand, London WC2R 0RL, England
Penguin Group Ireland, 25 St. Stephen's Green, Dublin 2, Ireland (a division of Penguin Books Ltd.)
Penguin Group (Australia), 250 Camberwell Road, Camberwell, Victoria 3124, Australia
(a division of Pearson Australia Group Pty. Ltd.)
Penguin Books India Pvt. Ltd., 11 Community Centre, Panchsheel Park, New Delhi—110 017, India
Penguin Group (NZ), 67 Apollo Drive, Rosedale, North Shore 0632, New Zealand
(a division of Pearson New Zealand Ltd.)
Penguin Books (South Africa) (Pty.) Ltd., 24 Sturdee Avenue, Rosebank, Johannesburg 2196,
South Africa

Penguin Books Ltd., Registered Offices: 80 Strand, London WC2R 0RL, England

ASKING FOR MURDER

A Berkley Prime Crime Book / published by arrangement with the author

PRINTING HISTORY
Berkley Prime Crime mass-market edition / September 2008

Copyright © 2008 by Roberta Isleib.
Cover illustration by Brandon Dorman.
Cover design by Judith Lagerman.
Interior text design by Laura K. Corless.

ISBN: 978-0-425-22331-4

PRINTED IN THE UNITED STATES OF AMERICA

10 9 8 7 6 5 4 3 2 1

continued . . .

DEADLY ADVICE

For my teachers,
especially Joel, Joan, and Mort

Acknowledgments

My warmest thanks go to Chris Falcone, Ang Pompano, Cindy Warm, and Chris Woodside for their careful reading and insightful comments. Thanks also to Susan Hubbard and Hallie Ephron for brainstorming fever, and to Cathy Cairns and John Brady for helpful comments on later drafts. You've got to have friends!

Thanks to Sally Sugatt, a teaching member of Sandplay Therapists of America, who walked me through the details of Annabelle's work.

Thanks to the talented and enthusiastic crew at Berkley Prime Crime, especially my two fine editors, Katie Day and Shannon Jamieson Vazquez (who picked up without skipping a beat), and my reliable, cheerful, and dogged publicist, Catherine Milne.

Chris Falcone graciously gave up her day off to provide a hospital tour, and Dr. Dennis Spencer took me through the ICU and answered many questions about head injuries—thanks to both. Mistakes are all mine.

Thank you to Lyn McHugh and Terry and Martha McGuire (on behalf of Howdy Phipps) for the generous use of their names to benefit the Guilford Art Center and the Shoreline YMCA.

I'm beyond grateful to have Paige Wheeler and Folio Literary Management in my corner!

A tip of the hat to Sisters in Crime: Pressed firmly into their ranks, I never feel alone on this crazy journey! And my deepest gratitude and affection goes to all of my family, and of course, to John.

Roberta Isleib
February 2008

- A Whitfield Street man reported his wife missing for several hours. She was found shopping at the Guilford Green.

- A Sugarloaf Road woman called 911 to report a stranger in her house. Moments later she called back to report the stranger was her husband.

- A Durham Road woman called police to report two women walking behind her house wearing red boots and coats.

- A Grist Mill Circle man reported that his soon-to-be ex-wife was taking his mail.

- A Boston Post Road mattress store reported that there was a cat in the showroom that refused to leave.

- A cabdriver summoned to a Copper Hill Drive home reported hearing someone crying inside the house.

- Police assisted in the pursuit of a man who had reportedly assaulted someone with a hammer.

From the
SHORE LINE TIMES
Police Log,
January and April 2007

Chapter 1

Spring, and a young woman's fancy turns to Louis' Lunch: broiled square hamburgers on toast, loaded with cheese, tomato, and onions.

I all but skipped the blocks from my psychotherapy office on Orange Street to the downtown New Haven, Connecticut, green, where my friend Annabelle Hart practices sand tray therapy in an aging brownstone off Ninth Square. In order to celebrate the crocuses and daffodils and robins and the general hopefulness of the season, we decided to suppress our anticipatory worries about future middle-aged spread and trek to the home of the best burger on the East Coast. Possibly the whole United States. My mouth had been set on a slow drool all morning.

I climbed three cement steps, pressed the buzzer next to Annabelle's name, and tipped my face up to the sun, admiring the small red buds on the maple tree that was causing the sidewalk to heave as it grew. If that wasn't a great metaphor for therapy—ha! No answer.

I hissed a small sigh. She was probably chatting with Dr. Frazier, the therapist down the hall. That young woman soaks up as much of Annabelle's advice as my friend is willing to dish out. She took up residence in her office last fall with an attitude. With the subtlety of paper over rock or scissors over paper, she managed to communicate her certainty that psychiatrists have more status and skill than social workers, especially social workers who encourage their patients to play with little rakes in their miniature sandboxes. Rock over scissors. Bam.

But when the reality of handling a solo practice full of psychiatric patients without the safety net of one-way mirrors, case conferences, and close supervision hit home, Dr. Frazier—Dr. Frantic, as we call her in private—got a lot more friendly. Annabelle has a wealth of experience and a kindly way of sharing it, as I knew first from a year under her careful supervision, and through our friendship since.

I leaned on the buzzer again. Nothing. I fished the cell phone out of my purse and speed-dialed her number. Her voicemail picked up. Feeling a little prickle of annoyance, I tried her office number—the line no one uses except her patients. Annabelle's pleasant voice assured me that though she wasn't available *exactly* at that moment, she'd get back to me as soon as she *possibly* could.

"It's Rebecca," I said. "Butterman," I added, just in case. "Where *are* you?"

I perched on the brick wall beside the steps for half an hour, more annoyed by the minute—and hungry to the point of feeling nauseated. This was not at all like her. We'd confirmed our lunch date by e-mail only yesterday. A dark-haired woman in a black trench coat trotted up the stairs and poked Dr. Frazier's bell. She pulled the door open when the doctor's buzzer squawked. I grabbed the heavy door before it slammed shut. After waiting a decent interval so as not to spook Dr. Frazier's patient, I slipped in after her. So much for the upgraded security the landlord had promised Annabelle and the other tenants after a recent rash of break-ins on this block.

I paused on the second-floor landing outside Annabelle's office. She sometimes complains that in spite of the double doors she and her colleagues paid to have installed, the offices aren't adequately soundproof. I listened for voices. Maybe she'd lost track of time. All quiet.

It would be uncomfortable if I interrupted a session she was conducting with an emergency patient. On the other hand, even if one of her patients had shown up unexpectedly, full of angst and suicidal ideation, Annabelle would have taken the time to warn me that lunch was off. She knows how I get if I don't eat. So I knocked, first a quiet tap-tap, then a more robust rat-tat-tat. She didn't answer either one.

I trooped back down the stairs and checked my cell phone again for a message. As I pushed open the door, I heard a dull buzz. A tall woman with a fringe of blond bangs and a slight baby bulge at her middle was stabbing at Annabelle's doorbell.

"Did you come from Annabelle's office?" she asked, a frown on her face. "She's not answering."

"She doesn't appear to be in," I said, not responding to the woman's barely unspoken question: *Are you one of her patients too?*

"Crap!" she said with a small stamp of her foot. "I hope she didn't forget. I hope she's okay. I really need to talk with her today." She ripped a page off the pad hanging near the doorbell, scrawled a note, and tacked it to the mini-bulletin board screwed to the wall beside the door. She glanced at her watch. "Retail therapy instead," she said, brightening. "Even better."

I smiled tepidly and watched her stride down the sidewalk toward the New Haven green, trailing tendrils of perfume in her wake. Carrying a caseload of therapy patients is a little like having small children. Even when they're concerned about you, they are most worried about the effects your problems may have on them. Psychology types call this transference: buried childhood feelings rippling forward and settling into the current therapeutic relationship. New therapists find it curiously uncomfortable when grown adults relate to them as if they were a parent. Their parent. But it's the nature of the beast—transferring conflicts from their past to your present—and it's what allows therapy to work. As Annabelle is forever reminding her office neighbor, Dr. Frazier, if you need nurturing, look outside your practice.

I scribbled my own note. *A: was here for lunch. Hope you're okay—call me! R.* I no longer had time for the trek to Louis' Lunch—besides, it wouldn't be the same alone. So I stopped at Clark's Dairy Restaurant on Whitney Avenue and picked up a cardboard container of pea soup and a grilled cheese on rye that shone with grease through its waxed paper wrapper. Then I left the restaurant and returned to my office. Sigh. This was winter comfort food, not a spring splurge, and not nearly as satisfying as that burger would have been.

I used the remaining minutes of my aborted lunch hour to choose a question for my advice column and rough out an answer. I'm a clinical psychologist by day, but in the off hours, I whisk on my advice columnist cloak and write the *Ask Dr. Aster* column for *Bloom!* e-zine. Sometimes the column feels downright silly; other times, profound. I love it most when it evolves into a Greek chorus of my life that I didn't consciously intend. This month, my twelve-year-old (a slight exaggeration) editor, Jillian, had asked for columns that fit the category "Bloom! In spring!" In other words, no downers, no freaking stages of grief, no miserable housewives in housecoats abandoned by their freshly vital, chemically driven husbands. The advice should be uplifting, encouraging, bursting with new life and new possibilities. Sigh again.

"Happy people don't ask for advice," I told her.

"You'll come up with something!" she chirped back. "I'll check in with you later in the week."

Dear Dr. Aster:

I volunteer at a local charity that fights mental illness. I got involved because I believe in the cause, but I also hoped it might be a way to meet a nice guy with similar interests. (Isn't that what you always recommend to your readers?) The people on my committee are smart, caring, dedicated—and all married, except for one widower who's slightly older than me, though smart and attractive. Lately the married folks take every opportunity to push us together. There's a lot of winking and elbowing going on, and it's very embarrassing. He's a nice guy, but there's no chemistry between us— certainly not on my side! What can I do to stop the matchmaking? I'd hate to ditch the committee to escape the man.

Yenta's Volunteer Victim in Vermont

Dear Yenta's Victim:

Gold stars are in order—I do recommend exactly the path you've taken. But oh dear, I had not anticipated this particular roadblock. One question: Does Mr. Wonderful seem to feel the same lack of chemistry that you do? If so, it might be easy enough to enlist his help in shrugging off the well-meaning nudges. However, if he appears to have feelings for you, you'll need another tactic. How about dropping a few not-so-subtle hints about the recent social whirl your new BOYFRIEND has swept you up in?

And here's one more thought: Since you signed your letter "Volunteer Victim," don't overlook your possible contri-
bution to the drama that's unfolded. Your fellow workers
might be reacting to your subtly sawing violin strings. Check
to be sure you haven't been moaning about your single status without being aware of it! If that's the case, dost thou
protest too much?

                    Keep up the good works and Happy Spring!

I saved the document—obviously Dr. Aster shouldn't be
in the business of recommending imaginary boyfriends.
And the snippy finale would need a little honing. I walked
out to the waiting room to collect my two o'clock patient, a
serious, plain woman who almost always dresses in scrubs.
Ariana is a Yale undergraduate struggling with her family's
expectations about her becoming a doctor. For weeks,
we've been nibbling around the edges of what it might be
like to try another field—like art history, her one true love.
It's slow-going with four generations of doctors in the family tree and no siblings to deflect the heat.

After Ariana's appointment, I headed across town to the
Connecticut Mental Health Center to supervise a psychology intern who was treating a patient suffering from chronic
depression and a borderline personality disorder. She—the
patient a little more than the psychologist—manages to alien-
ate every mental health worker she sees. Including me, and
I've never met her in person. I parked in the lot across the
street, locked up the car, and set off at a near-trot. Yale New
Haven Hospital sits just on the fringe of some of the poorest
sections in the city, resulting in a jagged juxtaposition of the
haves and have-nots and a steady string of minor muggings
and car radio thefts.

By the time I emerged from the meeting, my mood had
sunk lower. Nothing about that case was going well. The

patient was hysterical and my student was too. Then I hit two red lights in two minutes along Frontage Road and sat fuming at the intersection in front of the hospital. A homeless girl thrust a ratty cardboard sign toward my open window. *"Instead of pointing a finger, why not lend a hand?"* the childlike scribbles read.

Up close I could see she was more woman than girl, in spite of the dirty jeans, pierced lip, and bare midriff. A thin, sour-smelling man hovered close behind her. Looking straight ahead, I rolled up the window, thinking a decent human being could have overcome their nervousness and at least offered one lousy crumpled dollar bill. I comforted myself by thinking about the item on the adult IQ test we psychologists often use. Question: "Why is it better to give to an organization instead of a beggar?" Acceptable answer: "The organization has vetted the victims." I still didn't feel that great about shutting them out.

As the light turned green, I pressed on the accelerator and sped away. My cell phone rang. I glanced at the screen—Bob—then pressed the little green phone icon.

"How's your day going?" he asked.

"Not that great. Some days greeting customers at Wal-Mart sounds pretty darn good."

He laughed. "Poor girl. How was your burger?"

"That's the other thing: Annabelle stood me up."

"And knowing you, you're thinking the worst," said Bob, his words the equivalent of a chuck under the chin. "Lighten up a little, sweetheart, I'm sure she's fine."

Which annoyed me even more. Bob and I have been seeing each other since Christmas—if "seeing" describes a series of long-distance phone calls between me in Connecticut and him in Atlanta, and two weekend rendezvous when he was up visiting his parents. He's relentlessly optimistic and cheerful—fine qualities, but perhaps not always a great match for me: Dr. Rebecca Butterman, queen of the worried, the sad, and the angry, with enough baggage of my own to load a large freighter. Bob was born equipped with rose-colored glasses; on good days, mine shift to pale gray. I'm still working on that.

"I am concerned," I said firmly. "In fact, if she doesn't answer me this time, I'm going to break into her office."

"Whatever you need to do," Bob said without even a trace of sarcasm. "I'm so looking forward to seeing you Friday. And meeting Annabelle and her friend too," he added. "Call me later when you find her, okay?"

I pressed *end*. While reveling in the hamburgers at lunch, Annabelle and I had been supposed to hatch plans for this Friday night—the public unveiling for both of our new boyfriends. The evening had to be handled delicately. What if one of us didn't care for the other's choice? A reasonable concern. What if the two guys went at each other like rabid dogs? Not that good old Bob would ever pick a fight. Good Old Bob. Gob, Annabelle had started to call him, just teasing.

I checked my cell for messages again, but she'd left no word. Maybe she'd taken the day off for a last-minute trip to New York City to see her beloved Metropolitan Opera. But then why confirm lunch with me yesterday? Maybe she'd come down with the stomach flu and rushed home. I dialed her home number and left a message there.

Maybe a friend had shown up in big trouble. Annabelle would never turn someone down. More possibilities swirled forward: a car accident, a robbery, a murder. Ordinary people don't leap to those kinds of conclusions, but I'm a little jumpy after stumbling across two murders in the last year. I felt myself slipping into Dr. Frazier's frantic range, something Bob would never understand.

I drove back to my office, dashed up two flights of stairs, and crossed the room to pull open the top drawer of my file cabinet. Taped to a white postcard in a folder filed at the back of the drawer, I found the key to Annabelle's office. We had exchanged keys six months ago and signed notarized statements giving each other official permission to exchange professional help as needed. She was designated to take care of things at my office should anything happen to me. And I would take care of loose ends for her. This is important in our business. If a therapist has an accident or falls unexpectedly ill, or God forbid, dies, someone has to catch the patients left pinwheeling through psychological black holes without a net. Someone has to list the notices required by state law about the practice closing.

I forced myself away from that line of thinking. There would be a logical explanation. And we'd laugh over a drink, hopefully tonight. I could use a glass of wine about now.

I tucked the key into my purse, shut off the lights and locked my own office, then inched back over to Annabelle's through the rush hour traffic. I parked illegally and trotted down the block to her building. A woman with a half inch of gray roots growing out of her faded auburn pageboy sat hunched on the stoop, crying quietly. I couldn't just step over her.

"Anything I can help with?" I asked, my voice coming out a little brusque.

She raised her face, streaked with tears. The purple bruising around her left eye had been badly disguised with foundation that was too dark for her pale skin. "I had an appointment with Ms. Hart," she said. "I'm sorry to trouble you." She struggled to her feet and limped to the bottom step, brushing a smudge of pollen off her expensive slacks. "I'm sorry."

I pasted on a sympathetic smile. "I'm a friend of hers," I said, touching her elbow. "Would you like to leave her a note?" I gestured to the corkboard.

Her eyes widened and she shook her head. "No!"

Understandable. Not everyone wanted other therapy consumers with poor boundaries perusing their private business. The pad had been Dr. Frazier's idea.

"If you want to give me your name and number, I'll gladly call you if I hear anything," I said.

"No," she said quickly. "Thanks anyway."

I extracted a business card from my wallet and handed it over. "Just in case," I said.

She tucked it into her pocket and scuttled down the walk.

I climbed the stairs for the second time today, took a deep breath—my pulse was pounding harder than one flight of stairs could explain—and unlocked Annabelle's door.

Chapter 2

At first glance, the room was in perfect order: no cryptic notes, no sign of a struggle, nothing out of place. My gaze swept the space again; a curtain of multihued blue beads hung across the window. They tapped gently against the sill, refracting the sun into flashes of sapphire. Annabelle's rock garden fountain burbled softly against the nearby wall. I crossed the room to the shelves on the far side, partly hidden by a rice-paper shoji screen. They were crowded with miniature figurines and objects—people, animals, buildings, gravestones, emergency vehicles, and more. Two large rubber trays filled with sand stood on legs, with wooden chairs beside them. On the other side of the screen sat Annabelle's rocking chair and the comfortable wing chair in which I'd spent many hours talking about my patients and hers. The coffee table in between them held Kleenex and a clock, the therapist's standard tools, and a small bottle of Purell, for the germ phobic.

The soft trill of the phone startled me. I walked over to

my friend's desk and listened to her recorded voice: "You've reached Annabelle Hart. Though I'm not available *exactly* at this moment, please leave a name and number and I'll get back to you as soon as I *possibly* can." Then came a pause and the caller hung up without leaving a message. I noticed the red light of the answering machine blinking.

I hesitated. Normal people don't listen in on their friends' private messages after they've missed a lunch date. But then normal people haven't been exposed to two murders, escaped a kidnapping, and foiled what could have been another, leaving them suspicious and edgy.

I pressed *play*. Five patients had complained, with varying degrees of sympathy to outrage, that Annabelle had missed their sessions.

"Excuse me," barked a voice from the hallway. I startled and took a step back from the desk. "I'm Dr. Frazier," said the petite woman framed in the doorway—about my height, but tiny bird-boned. She had on dark-rimmed glasses, slim black pants, and a stylish white tuxedo blouse that looked freshly pressed. And pinched lips. She would have been a knockout if she wasn't so severe. "And you are?"

"Dr. Rebecca Butterman," I said, striding across the room with my hand outstretched, emphasizing the "doctor" part of my name. "I got worried about Annabelle when she didn't show up for lunch. It's not like her." I laughed and hunched my shoulders. Dr. Frazier tapped her lip with a Bic pen and shrugged her own.

"She hasn't been in all day as far as I know. Though I generally end on the hour on Tuesdays," she added, "so we don't always connect."

I suppressed a grin. Annabelle had recently switched to seeing her Tuesday patients on the half hour in order to avoid a mini-consultation with "Dr. Frantic" in between each session. "If you see her later," I said, "will you ask her to call me?"

She nodded, and moved into the hallway to let me lock the office. At the bottom of the stairs, I glanced up. Still watching, she offered a small salute. Dismissed.

I drove the ten miles home to Guilford, the voices of NPR's *All Things Considered* a pleasant drone in the background. As if any news is pleasant these days. I pulled off the highway, drove through Guilford, and zigzagged on the narrow road through the salt marsh. I crossed over the railroad bridge leading to Annabelle's neighborhood, Mulberry Point. *Danger: Live rails underneath bridge. Keep out.* The spring sun had slipped under a bank of clouds, almost the same steel-gray as the Long Island Sound. I parked in Annabelle's driveway. The bungalow with its weathered shingles looked deserted and undisturbed.

I got out and knocked on the door. No answer. I pulled my lower lip out over the upper, knocked again, and waited, straining for sounds of activity inside the house. Nothing. I retraced my steps across the bluestone path and peered into the wavy glass panes lining the top of Annabelle's garage. Her red Prius was there. My heart pounded faster. Should I call the cops right now? And say what?

Crossing back to the stoop, I picked up the pot of maroon and yellow pansies perched there and slid out the key tucked beneath it. I knocked a third time, and then unlocked the door and pushed it open.

"Annabelle?" I whispered, then cleared my throat and tried again, louder this time. "Annabelle?"

She didn't answer. The hallway seemed undisturbed. I took a few steps in and startled myself with a glimpse of my frightened face in the mirror hanging over a narrow oak table. *Breathe, Rebecca.* I heard the cheerful chirping of birds at the back porch feeder and the languorous ticktock of Annabelle's grandfather clock.

I turned on the living room light. The drawers of the cherry desk against the far wall had been yanked out and thrown to the ground, papers scattered and dotted with loose change, pencils, and pens. The lumpy ceramic vase that Annabelle had made for her mother in kindergarten was shattered into pieces.

"Annabelle?" I gasped.

I hurried down the hallway, past the guest room, to her bedroom. And stopped short in the door.

She was crumpled on the floor beside the bed. One arm was twisted awkwardly underneath her. Blood had soaked the torn neckline of her pink-flowered flannel nightgown. Worst of all, her face had been beaten to a pulpy mass. The colors reminded me of a rotting log. My heart hammered with shock and horror. I darted over to her and crouched down to see if she was breathing, relieved at the soft rise and fall of her chest.

"Annabelle," I whispered, touching a curl of her hair with my shaking finger. "It's Rebecca. You hold tight. I'm going to get you some help." Gulping the tears back, I ran to the bedside table, snatched up her phone, and dialed 911. I grabbed the fuzzy purple afghan from the chair near the window and tucked it around her body. Then I took one bare undamaged foot between my hands and began to stroke it gently.

"They're coming," I crooned. "They'll be here any minute."

Finally the warning howl of emergency vehicles blared over the sweet sound of spring peepers in her marsh. "They're here," I told her, letting go of her foot and rushing outside to greet the first police car. I showed the two cops to Annabelle's bedroom.

"Can you wait in the other room please," the older man growled, not really a question. Two husky emergency medical technicians pushed a wheeled stretcher through the front door and trotted down the hallway as I retreated to the living room. Their voices floated out from the bedroom: "You hold traction, I'll get the collar," said one man.

"I hope my relief comes to the scene. My shift ended half an hour ago," said the other. "Look at that. They must have had one doozy of a fight."

My fists balled, matching the angry knot in my stomach. Annabelle would never pick a fight: To use an old-fashioned term, she's a peacenik. I paced the length of the room and back, willing myself to stay in control. It is a rare situation where a hysterical friend improves the outcome of an emergency.

"Dr. Butterman?"

I whirled around, nearly slamming into the beefy form of Detective Jack Meigs.

He put one arm out to steady me. "What do you know about all this?"

A physical rush of relief shot through me. This was the guy who'd seen me through all the mayhem of the past months, the man who sets my hard-wires thrumming, despite his being married to a very sick woman. The man who'd seen me tear around in the last local emergency like a deranged and besotted Nancy Drew. But I was too upset to be embarrassed about the past.

"It's Annabelle," I said, my voice cracking. "Someone beat the hell out of her."

"I'm sorry to hear that," he said, looking at first like he might hug me, but then taking a step away. "Start at the beginning. How did you happen to find her?"

I clutched my neck and willed myself to breathe and speak in a normal voice. "She stood me up for lunch. We were going to get a burger at Louis' Lunch. We'd been planning it for months so when she didn't show, I got worried."

He scratched his head, took a Palm Pilot from his back pocket, and slid a pair of tortoiseshell reading glasses onto his nose. Were these new?

"Was there any particular reason you were worried, other than the sandwich? Anything unusual about her state of mind?"

"What does that mean?" I snapped, feeling a surge of fury that I was certain had more to do with fear and horror at Annabelle's attack than the detective's question. And maybe a little bit just the shock of seeing Meigs again, for the first time since he'd given me an unexpected Christmas present and then dropped off the face of the earth.

"I mean, was she having problems with anyone?"

"For God's sake, you can't think she brought this on herself?"

He grimaced. "Take it easy. I'm just trying to get a bead on what the hell happened."

"Sorry." I shook my head, slumped into the rocking chair next to Annabelle's fireplace, clutching my arms with my hands, and began to rock. "She has a tendency to let the state of the world get to her. But lately, she was happy," I said softly, worrying my grandmother's turquoise ring around my left ring finger. After my divorce, it hadn't felt right to leave that space empty. "She has a new guy in her life. She has such a tender heart. Who would do this to her?" I croaked.

"We'll find out," he said, striding across the room to pat my shoulder and then backpedaling around the coffee table. "Who's the new guy?"

Tears threatened to seep down both cheeks. *No.* I dashed them away. "We were having dinner with him on Friday."

"We?" he asked.

I blushed. "Me and Bob. You met him at the church supper last December."

Meigs scribbled in the Palm Pilot.

"Bob is my boyfriend, not hers," I said.

"Got it," he said, eyes blank. "And her boyfriend's name?"

"Russ something. I can't think of the last name. I'm sure she has it around here somewhere." I gestured at the mess on the floor, feeling myself winding tighter and tighter. "He was doing some carpentry for her. That's how they met." I gestured to take in the great room—the pickled ash bookshelves, the new floor-to-ceiling windows, the renovated powder room with its raku pottery bowl sink. "This part of the house is all new," I told him. "He finished up a couple of weeks ago."

"We'll find the name," Meigs said.

"I haven't met him yet. Friday will be the first time. Would have been." The tears threatened to push out again. I blinked hard to contain them. Maybe she'd still be able to make it to dinner.

"Let's go over a few more things," Meigs said. "The door was open when you got here?"

"Locked," I said. "When I saw that her car was parked in the garage, I took the key she keeps under the flowerpot on the porch. Something was very wrong. She had stood up an entire day's worth of patients without calling anyone."

Meigs shoved the PDA into his back pocket. "If you could stay put for just a couple more minutes, we might have more questions."

"Of course." I wandered across the room and studied the figurines on her bookshelf, recognizing some of the same ones I'd seen at her office. In the small sand tray tucked on the bottom shelf, someone—Annabelle, I assumed—had

placed a fairy on a leaf, with a monster lurking behind her.
On the other side of the tray, a baby had been half-buried
near a knight in full armor. I sank back down into the rocking chair and gazed out the back window.

Annabelle had chosen the bungalow on the basis of this
marsh view, even though she probably could have afforded
a home on the Long Island Sound just a block away. But she
adores the shades of green and gold the marsh grasses turn
with the seasons. And her spring peepers. And the Stony
Creek pink granite fireplace. She splits the wood herself—
she says it's the best way in the world to work off the tension generated by holding unhappy people in her heart.

The corner of a small maroon-covered book stuck out
from under the sofa. I pulled it out: Annabelle's day planner. I flipped through to the next day's appointments. She
was booked solid. Oh hell. I was responsible for all that
now, wasn't I?

I slipped the planner into my back pocket and reached
for the pile of cashmere wool in the basket by the hearth—
half an afghan crocheted in the colors of the salt marsh in
spring. I pressed the yarn to my face, inhaling Annabelle's
lavender scent, then folded over into the swirls of green
cashmere, my head resting on my arms. Annabelle's orange tiger kitten, Jackson, nosed out from under the couch.

"Oh you poor kitty," I said, tapping my fingers on the
chair rung and clucking to lure him over. He streaked under the glass coffee table and vaulted into my lap, burrow-
ing under the half-finished blanket, purring and kneading
my leg with his claws.

A voice floated out from Annabelle's bedroom. "Load
and go."

Detective Meigs appeared in the doorway again, the
halfhearted sunset backlighting his reddish curls. The cat's
claws hinged into my thigh. I sucked in a deep breath and

straightened my shoulders. The stretcher rattled down the hallway and out the front door, Annabelle's body strapped down under a blue blanket, a clear oxygen mask over her nose and mouth.

"News?" I asked in a panicky voice, standing and setting Jackson on the chair.

"They're taking her right to the Yale ER. You can follow them over."

"Thank you." I looked down at my hands. "When we're with our patients, we let them think that any problem can be shrunk small enough to let them feel safe. If only they talk things over, life improves. The truth is, we could all be flattened like bugs tomorrow. Today."

Meigs cleared his throat. "On first impression it looks like a botched robbery."

"Badly botched," I said. "Are you sure? Are you saying this was random?" I gestured to the wall containing her TV, DVD player, and sound system. "All her stuff is intact—it's only the desk. A robbery doesn't seem right."

"Looks like some jewelry is missing. The box on her bureau was ransacked. We'll be following up," he said, scowling. "She was a shrink, right? Could one of her patients have had it in for her?"

"I can't imagine that. I don't know that much about them yet."

"You'll let me know what you find out?" The kindness that had been in his voice earlier was gone.

"I'll tell you what I can," I said stiffly, remembering a case I'd just read about in the *APA Monitor*—a psychologist in California had been murdered. His colleagues refused to turn over the patient records. So I didn't mention the day planner—I'd need to contact Annabelle's patients first. They too deserved to have their privacy protected from the cops.

Meigs started to say something else, stopped, and frowned. "You won't be able to get back in here—the officers will be taping it off."

"What about the cat?"

Meigs shrugged. "Shut it in the basement with some food. We'll be finished in a day or less." His eyes narrowed, then dark brows arched toward the rust-colored curls on his forehead. "I know you're upset. But we'll handle this. You're not needed for canvassing neighbors, no interviews, no nothing. Do I make myself clear?"

Why did he have to act like such a bully? Even if I had stepped over the line a few times before . . . I swept the trembling tiger cat into my arms.

"I'm taking Jackson home. Unless you need him for an interview?" I started across the room. "She was my dear friend," I said, turning back to face him and trying hard to keep my voice strong. "She *is* my dear friend. And that means I'll do what I can. And that happens to include contacting her boyfriend and taking care of her patients." I stormed out, trampling the stand of crocuses beside the front stoop in my haste.

"For the love of Christ," he shouted out the door. "I'm sorry about your friend. Let me know if you hear anything. I'll be in touch."

Once in the car with the doors safely locked, I set the cat on the passenger seat, leaned my head against the steering wheel, and sobbed. I couldn't believe I'd crushed Annabelle's flowers—the same stand of slender stalks and purple flower buds she'd told me about last night. She'd be sick about it. Kind, but sick.

I blew my nose, leafed through the address section in the day planner, and punched in the number for Annabelle's sister.

Chapter 3

I dumped my purse and keys on the counter and set the orange kitten on the kitchen floor. Spencer, the gray cat I inherited from my neighbor last fall, crouched low to the ground and circled him, growling. Then he sprang forward, sank his teeth into Jackson's neck, and launched a series of vicious rabbit kicks. The little cat screamed and scrabbled for purchase on the polished oak.

"Dammit, Spencer! Cut it out!" I shrieked, grabbing a broom and sweeping them apart. Lunging for a handful of gray fur, I snatched up the big cat, stormed across the kitchen, dropped him onto the cellar stairs, and slammed the door. I briefly considered calling my neighbor, Babette Finster, and asking her to check on the kitten later this evening. But that would require a full explanation of where I got him, and probably fifteen minutes to calm her down after I told the story. Besides, she doesn't go anywhere without her little rat-dog, Wilson, who would not improve the angry cat mix. I poured a tablespoon of milk into a small

Pyrex bowl, showed Jackson the litter box, and promised them both I'd be back soon.

≈

I pulled into the parking garage next to Yale New Haven Hospital and spiraled up the narrow cement chute to the top level, looking for a space near a better-lighted pedestrian exit. The hospital's Air Rights garage can be downright claustrophobic and spooky, especially at night, especially for one woman alone, already frightened and exhausted. I jockeyed my Honda into a narrow space near a blue-lighted call box. The way this day was going, I'd come out and find dents on both sides of the car. I took the elevator to the Plexiglas skywalk that connects the garage with the hospital, and followed the signs to the emergency room. Somewhere along the endless walk around the outside of the building, I remembered that I could have parked in the ER lot.

The universal emergency room smell hit me as soon as I pushed through the revolving door: sweat, vomit, and antiseptic. I approached the harried-looking woman at the desk. "My friend was brought in a little while ago. Annabelle Hart?"

"Are you a relative?" she asked, still staring at her computer screen.

"She's my friend. I found her. She'd been beaten," I said, my eyes filling again. "Annabelle Hart. They brought her in from Guilford. I called her sister but I have no idea when she'll get here. I'm not even sure that she's coming," I added when the woman failed to look sympathetic.

"I'm sorry," said the clerk without taking her eyes off the screen. She unfastened the tortoiseshell barrette holding her ponytail, clamped it between her teeth, ran her fingers through her hair, and refastened the clip. "You can have a seat and we'll let you know when she's been transferred to a room."

She saw hundreds of desperate people each day, I was sure of it. How to break through and get her attention?

"I have information about her relatives," I said, veering around the ugly phrase "next of kin." I yanked Annabelle's day planner out of my purse and waved it in front of the computer. "And her insurance."

The woman finally glanced up.

I paged to the back of the book to find Annabelle's sister's name and phone number and fed the details to the clerk, along with her address and a string of insurance numbers listed under an entry labeled *Blue Cross/Blue Shield.* The clerk tapped and tapped and tapped.

"They have her stabilized. They've taken her for a CT scan," the woman said once she'd finished. "I didn't tell you this, but she's on her way back to number three." She pointed down the hall.

"Thank you, thank you!" I grabbed her hand and squeezed.

She reached for the Purell on the counter, squirted a dollop onto her palm, and rubbed her hands together briskly. "You're welcome."

I disinfected my own hands, then trotted down the row of cubicles and pushed aside the curtain around number three. A breathing tube pressed Annabelle's features into an ugly purple pastiche and an IV dripped clear liquid into her arm. Dried blood had matted her hair into spiky peaks. Her nose looked wrong, as though it had been pushed off center. Her eyes had swollen almost shut. The flowered nightgown had been replaced by a Johnny-coat, white with tiny blue flowers. I concentrated on filling my lungs with stale hospital air and letting it whistle out slowly.

"Annabelle," I said softly, watching for the slightest change in her expression. Nothing, not even a flicker. "I called your sister. She's on the way up from Greenwich. I think she was at a party," I babbled. "There was so much noise in the background, I could hardly hear. But she's coming and we're going to make sure you get everything you need." I patted her upper arm as gently as I could and slumped into the chair by the bed. "I'll be right here." I choked back my feelings. Not helpful to wake out of a coma and find a friend weeping over you as if you were a goner. Also not helpful to report that I'd practically had to beg her sister to make an appearance.

I must have dozed off—unbelievable when you factored in the noisy chaos of the ER that I glimpsed through the crack in Annabelle's curtain. These were the nonemergencies, based on the lack of urgent attention they were receiving—people puking into kidney-shaped containers, a raving man who reeked of stale alcohol and fermented body odor even from fifty yards away, and a moaning woman clutching her distended belly. Her husband offered her every food item in the cafeteria in return for her silence—here was a marriage that needed serious reconstruction.

"Dr. Butterman." A heavyset, gray-haired woman in blue scrubs touched my shoulder.

"Ms. Hart's sister is here. They're taking your friend up to the Neuroscience Intensive Care Unit." I bolted to my feet and crossed the room to a pale woman in a black silk pantsuit. She had Annabelle's freckles, but dimmed under a layer of makeup and streaks of bottled-blonde in her wavy hair. She wore a very tight expression on her polished red lips. Annabelle never wears lipstick.

"I'm Annabelle's friend, Rebecca Butterman," I said, as they wheeled her off.

"So kind of you to have her brought in and then stayed with her all this time. I'm Victoria White." Her handshake was efficient but cool. "You must be exhausted." Her tepid smile didn't reach past the red slash of her mouth. "I'll be sure to tell her you were here when she comes around."

Bitch, was my first thought. *She's in shock*, was my more charitable second. She surely must not realize how serious things were. I trotted behind her to the bank of visitor elevators, searching for the words that would connect us. "I love your sister to death," I said. "I'd love to stay and help you with this however I can."

"I appreciate that, I do," said Victoria, her eyes moist. She turned away and punched the *up* arrow on the wall beside the elevators. "I'm sure she'll need you in the days to come. But right now, if you don't mind, I'd rather wait alone."

But I did mind. And even factoring in the idiosyncratic weirdness that each of us exhibits when it comes to dealing with shocking events, I found this preference bizarre. I squeezed in beside her when the elevator door opened.

"Believe I'll just head up there too. I'd like to know that she's out of the woods. I won't bother you," I said stupidly, kicking myself as soon as the words were out. Couldn't I think of something more professional to say?

She dipped her chin once and we watched the lighted numbers pass without speaking until we reached the sixth floor. Victoria bustled off ahead of me. *Family members only beyond this point*, read a large sign on the wall of the small waiting room. Victoria identified herself to a speakerphone on the wall; the doors swung open and she disappeared into the ICU, leaving me standing uselessly in the empty hall.

I paced to the end of the hallway and back, then went into the larger of two waiting rooms and sank down on a worn blue couch. The nightly news blared from a television across the way. I popped back up and rustled through the pamphlets on the desk—articles on cancer, mental health, neurology. Nothing that would tell me what I was desperate to know. After five anxious minutes, I called my friend Angie Niehoff and described the whole rotten day.

"Oh you poor thing," she cried once I'd finished. I dabbed at my nose, smiling through the tears that had started as soon as I heard her friendly voice.

"And poor Annabelle! She's just lucky you found her. Have you eaten?" she asked. "Do you want me to fix you something and bring it over?"

Angie has a lot of strengths: She's a warm, loyal girl-friend who also happens to be in great demand for legal proceedings that call for an expert in forensic linguistics. And she's ten inches taller than me, slender, and naturally blond—none of which I hold against her. But she's definitely not known for her expertise in the kitchen. I'd stand a better chance of finding something edible in the hospital cafeteria.

"Aren't you flying out to Houston at the crack of dawn?"

"You're right. How could I forget the Hernandez trial?" She sighed. "What about Friday?"

"I was supposed to cook for Annabelle and the boyfriends." Would Annabelle make it? My doubt and fear hung in the silence. "Let's see how it plays out. She's a pretty tough bird." Angie started to point out that dinner would be unlikely, then switched over to noises of sympathetic agreement and signed off with promises to be in touch.

I walked across the room and down the rose-painted hall to peer through the small glass window in the locked door protecting the neurological unit. There was no one at the desk and no sign of Annabelle or her unpleasant sister.

I paced back to my seat in the waiting room and called Bob. "There *was* something wrong!" I announced as soon as he picked up.

"Whoa, whoa, back up a minute and tell me which disaster we're on," said Bob genially.

It's taking some time to get used to Bob after my ex-husband, Mark. Since Mark's father weathered the Holocaust in a prison camp as a young child, no one in his family has quite figured out how to complain about their ordinary life problems. Compared to the horror of prison camp, nothing weighs enough to be worth mentioning. So the family compromises with a pervasive gloominess. Cheerful Bob with his functional family, on the other hand, takes everything in stride; and he interprets any emotional blip from me as a potential overreaction, if not a sign of unfolding hysterics. Up until now I'd appreciated his level thinking. Tonight it felt like untrimmed nails on a chalkboard.

Teeth grinding, I explained about the attack and my present status as waiting room attendee. I skipped the part about Annabelle's sister—he'd come up with some reasonable explanation for why she'd acted so cool and then I'd feel like a jerk.

"I'm so sorry," said Bob. "I wish I could be there right now."

"Thank you," I whispered. "I wish you could be too."

A balding man with a closely cropped salt-and-pepper beard and a white coat exited the double doors from the ICU and strode down the hall. He poked his head into the room where I waited. "Department of Social Work, Yale New Haven Hospital" was written in blue script above the pocket.

"Miss Butterman?"

I dropped the phone to my lap. "Oh my God. Is she dead?"

"Oh no, sorry to alarm you," he said, holding both hands up, one clutching a clipboard. "I'm the medical social worker, Fred Polson. Ms. White asked me to keep you apprised."

Wasn't that Joan Didion's line—you know you're in trouble if they give you a social worker? It means something awful has happened and you're going to need counseling. I picked up the phone and got to my feet.

"I'll call you later," I said to Bob and cut the connection. "What's happening? How's she doing?"

Polson perched on one of the blue vinyl seats and patted the chair next to him. I stayed where I was. "She's in a coma, which is frequently the body's response to traumatic brain injury. Naturally, it will take time to determine what course her recovery might take."

"What does that mean exactly?" I asked.

He stood up and smiled. "Her doctor would be the one to provide more complete medical details. I'm the social worker on the case. I'll be dealing with insurance issues and aftercare treatment, that sort of thing. Rest assured that she's getting the best available care."

"Please, can you tell me anything? You know the doctor won't talk to someone outside the family. Anything at all?" Without even thinking, I'd grabbed hold of his forearm and squeezed.

He cleared his throat, looking down at my fingers. "There's a lot of swelling in the brain, some concern about a subdural hematoma. Her neurosurgeon is in the process of removing a trauma flap—a small piece of her skull. Then he will be able to extract the blood clot and monitor the pressure from the swelling."

My hands lifted to cradle my own head. My hair felt frizzy and tangled. "I'd really like to be in there with her."

He reached out as if to pat my shoulder and I backed away.

"I know. Ms. White mentioned that to me." He tapped his clipboard with a red pen, ran one hand over his beard, and smiled again. "You should understand that some people reach out to other folks in times of tragedy and others draw inward. She's the drawing-in kind of personality." He tipped his head and tapped the pad again. "It doesn't mean she doesn't care about your friendship with her sister. Or appreciate how you handled the emergency. It's just her way of coping."

I couldn't help it: I rolled my eyes. "I'm a psychologist," I said with as much dignity as I could summon after a Psychology 101 lecture from a hospital social worker. "I'll be taking care of Annabelle's patients as long as she's out of commission."

"Excellent!" he said heartily. "And I've suggested that Ms. White phone you as soon as there's news. Meanwhile, I'd suggest *you* get home and get something to eat and some rest. You can always call the front desk for an update."

And be put on hold by a cranky receptionist or told practically nothing, I wanted to scream. The guidelines about medical confidentiality have been tightening like a wet noose over the past decade. As they should be. Professionally, I understand quite well the need for this trend toward privacy. But the new guidelines feel punitive when you're frantic for information about a dear friend. Polson headed toward the elevators.

"Good night and good luck," he called back over his shoulder.

They'd assigned Annabelle to Edward R. Murrow in a white coat.

❧

My cell phone rang on the way home from the hospital. It was Jillian.

"It's your pesky editor reminding you the column has to be in tomorrow," she said. "How are things coming?"

"I can't do it." My voice was dead flat. It was either that or scream at her too. I summarized the horror of the day.

"It's a serious coma," I added for emphasis. As if all comas weren't serious. "The doctors wouldn't say whether or not she'll make it." Actually not true—I hadn't gotten through to a doctor, just that damn Teflon social worker. I swallowed an urge to blubber. "Worst of all, I was the one who called her sister, but once she got to the hospital, she refused to let me wait with her."

"Bummer," said Jillian. "Aren't people just so weird? Why wouldn't she think it was helpful to have someone with her? Now there's a question for our Dr. Aster." She laughed and waited a beat. "How far along are you with the column?"

"I have one of the answers roughed out. I haven't even chosen the other problem."

"Bummer," she said again. "Well, even Ann Landers kept writing in rough times. You told me the column she wrote when her husband left her was the most popular ever."

I *had* told her this: how Ann got thirty-five thousand letters from readers after that column and how the "golden age" of advice columns sparkled even though the two main stars were twin sisters who weren't speaking to each other. Once in a while, I should learn to keep my big mouth shut.

"Maybe I can get my assistant to finish it up," Jillian offered.

I groaned. Even if her minion's advice didn't turn out to be totally shallow, it would be peppered with "Awesome," "Dude," "Perfect," and "Chill." Things the real Dr. Aster would never, ever say.

"I'll try to dash something off," I said.

"That's the spirit," she chirped.

Chapter 4

The phone shrilled once, then fell silent. I slit open my eyes: six a.m. Spencer was stretched out along one side, with Jackson tucked under my armpit on the other. Pinned between the two warring cats and worried sick about Annabelle, I'd had a restless night. The phone rang again and my heart started to pound. Good news just doesn't come in the off hours. In my experience, good news comes between eight and eight, telemarketing hours. I fumbled the receiver to my ear.

"Hello?"

"Dr. Dutterman? It's Detective Meigs." He cleared his throat. "Jack. Meigs."

Meigs rhymes with *eggs*, I thought, trying to push my panic away.

"Is she all right?" My voice trembled.

"As far as I know," he said. "I haven't heard anything else."

I clutched my throat and stroked the big cat. "Oh thank God. I thought you were calling with the worst."

"Sorry," said Meigs. "I'd like to meet you over at Ms. Hart's office later today, look over a couple of files."

I sat up, pulling the down-filled quilt over my chest. Spencer batted the kitten, who yelped and retreated under the covers. Meigs began to list the free moments in his schedule.

"Wait!" I broke in. "One of her patients attacked her? You have a suspect?" Good Lord, was it someone she and I had discussed? I tried to conjure up the latest trouble spots in her practice, but drew a blank.

He cleared his throat. "We don't have any specific leads. Looking through the files will certainly help us narrow things down."

"So you'd like me to let you into her office?"

"Correct."

"To read through her patient progress notes."

"Right."

I desperately wanted the police to catch the person who'd attacked Annabelle, but this was the wrong way to go about it. "Those files are confidential," I snapped.

"And your friend was attacked by a lunatic," he snapped back.

"You're on a fishing expedition," I said. "There's no way you're going through Annabelle's confidential files unless you have a real suspect—and enough information to get a warrant." Not that I hadn't tried to worm confidential information out of him in the past myself, but patient privacy was different. Sacred.

"We'll see about that," he said. "What time are you going over?"

"I haven't set anything up."

"Let's get on it," he said. "I'll meet you over there now."

"It's six o'clock in the morning," I said. "If I find something related to the case, I'll call you." I slammed the phone down. What was the matter with that man? He was never one for touchy-feely, but in the last twenty-four hours he seemed to have developed the sensitivity of tooled leather.

It was one thing for me to look through the notes in the service of Annabelle's patients. But it would be completely unethical to send a set of bumbling cops rooting through them. What business did a small-town Guilford cop have pushing into a New Haven case anyway? I tried to think again about Annabelle's patient roster but came up empty. Honestly, we'd mostly talked lately about the scary, sorry state of the world, and then to cheer ourselves up, our boyfriend prospects.

I rolled out of bed, tightened a red flannel bathrobe around my waist, and jacked up the heat. It had started to rain in the night and the thermometer on my back deck read thirty-eight degrees. The potted tomato plants my next-door neighbors had optimistically set out last weekend and then neglected to bring in had been reduced to brown stalks by a late frost. Even the geraniums looked miserable. Some spring.

In the kitchen, I set my coffee brewing and called the hospital, asking to be transferred to the nurses' station on the sixth floor. After several minutes of my cajoling, a tired voice reported that there was no change in Annabelle's condition. Time to consider breakfast. Having skipped the cafeteria and scarfed down a handful of cheese and crackers last night when I got home, I was starving. Some mornings get launched just fine with cold cereal and blueberries or oatmeal sprinkled with raisins and maple syrup. Considering the day ahead, this was not one of them.

"We need bacon and eggs," I announced to Spencer, who began to purr and wind between my legs. Jackson bounded around the corner into the kitchen and Spencer hunkered down growling, ready to pounce.

I scooped the kitten up and set him on the far counter next to the answering machine and a stack of paid bills waiting to be filed and poured him a bowl of dry kibble. Then I pulled a package of smoked black pepper bacon out of the fridge and arranged the strips in the frying pan. Spencer hopped up on the bookcase containing my cookbook collection, dividing his attention between the kitten and the bacon. I extracted two pieces of homemade multigrain bread from the freezer and whipped eggs with a splash of water and a sprinkling of chives trimmed from the plant on the windowsill. The bacon spat and browned, filling the room with the irresistible perfume of rendered fat. I felt better already.

Over breakfast, I skimmed the *New York Times* and wondered how I would handle Annabelle's patients. Lucky for all of us, Wednesday is a day off in my own practice. And I'd taken Thursday and Friday off for an outing with my sister and my niece, and then to get ready for Friday's dinner party. Janice was going to have a fit if I stood them up for the trip to Boston, but right now, sticking close to Annabelle was more important. I clattered the dishes into the sink, booted up my computer, and opened Annabelle's date book. She had five appointments scheduled.

I copied their names and numbers onto a note card. Should I tell them Annabelle was in the hospital? That sounded inflammatory. I decided to say Annabelle was ill, and that she had asked me to contact them. Which she had, sort of, in the existential sense of "someday, if it ever comes to this . . ." I would offer to meet with them and if they pressed me for a time frame on their therapist's illness, I'd estimate she might be out for a week or two. I knew nothing really, since no one but the simultaneously obsequious and confident social worker would speak to me. If I couldn't reach her patients by phone, I'd simply be available at their appointed time and give them the news. I promised myself that at the end of the day, when I reached the hospital, no one would stop me from seeing my friend.

I hopped in the shower, realizing I needed to get to Annabelle's office early and read through her notes—the very ones Meigs was so desperate to see. Up until this minute, I hadn't given a thought to exactly how I would handle finding something suspicious. And what would constitute "something suspicious"?

There have been cases of therapists being killed by their patients, but they are few and far between. In the ones I could remember, an alert therapist might well have been able to spot trouble coming—a man who'd slept with his patient and then ditched her, for example. Wasn't that asking for trouble? Another whose patient had gone off his meds and was flagrantly paranoid and psychotic. Wouldn't you see that coming? Surely Annabelle would have mentioned any serious concerns. Not that we spoke about our cases every day. Not that I hadn't leaned on her more lately than she'd leaned on me.

What if the batterer showed up for an appointment? Why would Meigs ask to see the files if that wasn't a possibility?

"I'll wait and see," I told Spencer as I came back into the kitchen. I emptied the last inch of coffee into my mug and offered him the last edge of bacon. He crunched it down. "I'm not worried. What are the chances of someone beating up Annabelle yesterday and showing for their session today?"

Spencer headed into the living room, hopped up onto the coffee table, and began to wash his face with his paw.

My gaze caught on the vase of daffodils that Bob sent last weekend when I'd mentioned the rainy weather in Connecticut once too often. *Hope these bring a little sunshine into your day*, the card from the florist read. Sweet man. Which reminded me that I hadn't called Annabelle's new boyfriend, Russ. I found his number in her day planner, a little red heart drawn beside his name. A rumbling voice answered his line.

"Russ? It's Rebecca Butterman, a friend of Annabelle's?" I explained the situation.

He sounded stunned. "No wonder she didn't return my calls. When are the visiting hours?"

"None at the moment," I said. "Family only in the NICU. But I'll keep you posted. I'm sorry about dinner on Friday. We'll reschedule when Annabelle's up to it."

"We need our friends at times like this," I added.

I hung up, thinking of Victoria, who apparently needed no one at a time like this. Annabelle had never talked much about her older sister. Once or twice she'd mentioned that they weren't much alike. My sister, Janice, and I aren't much alike either, but we do have some basics in common—things our grandmother taught us, like be polite to strangers and generous with your family. Janice, oh Lord. She and my niece, Brittany, would already be putting the finishing touches on healthy snacks for the two-day junket to Boston and waiting for me to pick them up.

I called her home number and described what had happened to Annabelle. "I'm so sorry to disappoint you girls, but I have to cover her caseload. Besides, I don't dare leave town with her in intensive care."

"That's just awful," said Janice. She waited a beat. "Are you absolutely positive you have to stay? Brittany will be so disappointed."

"I know that," I said in a snippy voice. "I'm sorry too."

Janice sniffed. "It's not like you'll be doing the brain surgery. You could give them your cell phone number."

"Janice—"

"I understand." She heaved a theatrical sigh, as only my younger sister can. "She's lucky to have you as a friend. I'm just disappointed. And Brittany will be too."

"Me three," I said. "I've been looking forward to our girl time. Have a great trip and call me this weekend, okay? Love you."

I paced back into the kitchen, loaded the dishes into the dishwasher, and scrubbed the frying pan. The more I thought about it, for as open and welcoming as Annabelle is, her sister was a puzzle. I clasped one wrist with the fingers of the other hand and leaned to the right side and then the left. Sometimes stretching the physical kinks out helps when the mental side is knotted.

I dried my hands, returned to the computer, and typed "Victoria White" into the Google search bar. A page of links loaded quickly. Victoria appeared to be the society social climber of southwestern Connecticut. She was involved with several charitable organizations and showed up in many photos wearing full-length gowns, upswept hairstyles, and teetering heels. And, I discovered, she was the author of "Southern Connecticut Town Talk," a gossip column in an online weekly paper.

I cruised through the last two issues of her chatter. She specialized in the hanging innuendo—just borderline nasty—who'd been seen with whom instead of their wife or husband and whose droopy appearance suggested the rehab experiment had been a bust. It was funny and snarky and chockful of tips on how to make it in high society and when you shouldn't even bother to try.

Several pages into the Google search, I clicked on a link to the *New York Times*. Victoria had been married in De-

cember to a South American businessman by a justice of
the peace, with a party following at the Grammercy Tavern
in the city. The couple were to honeymoon in Greece, and
then return to homes in Greenwich, Connecticut; New York
City; and Argentina. The bride's two previous marriages
had ended in divorce. I clicked on the final link in Victoria's search page. A blogger speculated that this marriage
was in deep trouble before it had even been consummated.

I snorted. Marriage does take a certain commitment to
biting your tongue. Victoria may have missed that gene.
Which was a little mean, but she'd really pushed my buttons. All things considered, this was substantial and juicy
family gossip. Why hadn't Annabelle mentioned it?

An instant message from Jillian popped up on my screen.
"How's the column coming? Don't forget, something hopeful for spring! XXOO, J."

Victoria's story provided some inspiration. I made another cup of coffee, then quickly scrolled through my readers' letters until I found the right one.

Dear Dr. Aster:
*I've finally met my soul mate and we're getting married. Trouble is,
this will be my third walk down the aisle. As the weeks go by, I'm
getting more and more nervous. My friends keep making cracks
about how we'd be better off just living together. Especially considering my two teenagers and his daughter. Am I criminally insane
to consider taking plunge number three? Please give me your honest
opinion.*

Sincerely, Sheepish in Cheyenne

Dear Sheepish:
Let me start by offering congratulations and very best
wishes! Hopefully your friends have done the same. No
doubt you've heard the bad news—in fact, you've already

lived it! About 50 percent of all marriages end in divorce, 60 percent or higher when you're talking number two. And so few people go on to number three that it's hard to get an accurate number.

But lest you panic and rush off to cancel flowers and caterers, remember that not all marriages are created equal. Many things factor into success or failure. One of the largest is living with OPC—other people's children. Ask yourself: Have I learned from my mistakes? Have we discussed our feelings about money, child raising, dealing with exes? Am I prepared to respond to my new husband's teenagers—whom I may not even like, never mind love—with grace and kindness?

Above all, keep your expectations reasonable and talk, talk, talk. In the end, a third trip down the aisle might mean more than the triumph of dumb hope over experience— maybe your combined "rehearsals" and maturity give you a better-than-average shot at success. Good luck and have fun!

I e-mailed the file off to Jillian. With nothing left to distract me, I pulled out the note cards and called Annabelle's patients. Answering machines picked up at the first four numbers. I did not leave messages. You can't be too careful with the confidences of a patient—sometimes the family members they live with don't even know they've gone for help. The fifth patient, Mrs. Dillard, agreed to meet me at ten. Was this the woman with the black eye whom I'd seen on the steps yesterday? I'd find out soon enough.

The reality of Annabelle's injuries was beginning to sink in. I tried the hospital again, but no luck. I'd sworn to myself last night that I wouldn't grovel. But I called Victoria anyway: no answer. I felt shut out and helpless.

With an hour to go before I was due at Annabelle's office, I did what helps in almost any situation: I minced onions, garlic, celery, and carrots, sautéed them in olive oil, and dumped them in the Crock-Pot with chicken broth and a bag of organic split peas. Most problems recede a little over a bowl of split pea soup.

Chapter 5

In the lot next to Annabelle's building, I parked in the slot marked with her name, unlocked the outside door to the building, and trudged up the stairs, a cloud of dread settling in with each step I took. I fitted the key into her office door and pushed it open. The room was dim and quiet and smelled faintly of lavender, which I traced to a small bowl of dried purple flowers on the desk. I hung my jacket on a wooden peg in the closet and then perched on Annabelle's rocker. The other side of the room was strange territory for me: a U-shaped configuration of shelves crammed with miniatures, and two trays on legs, one filled with wet-looking sand, one with dry. I stood up and walked over, sifting a handful of white sand between my fingers and letting it run back into the nearest tray. More reality settling in: What the hell was I supposed to do with this?

I remembered my very first clinic patient in graduate school. She was a young mother with a set of mushrooming anxieties that were progressively crushing her life. I'd been near hysterics myself at the prospect of pretending to help when I knew so little.

"What if she asks about my previous experience?" I'd whimpered to my supervisor.

"You'll tell her the truth. That she is your first and that you are here to listen. And you'll get help if it's needed."

I eased out a breath, willing my shoulders away from my ears. I'd do what I did best for Annabelle's patients—listen. If they chose to show me their sand castles, we'd stumble through the meaning together. I slid open the top drawer of the file cabinet and found the folders marked with the names of today's patients.

Mrs. Dillard rang the buzzer at two minutes to ten and headed directly to the talk therapy chairs. She sat, patted her helmet of chestnut curls, then touched her cheeks and lips. This was not the woman I'd met yesterday.

"As I mentioned to you on the phone this morning," I said, "Ms. Hart is under the weather. I'm covering for her practice until she's back on her feet."

Mrs. Dillard nodded, her lips beginning to tremble. I braced myself: Some people do get very attached to their therapists.

"Joe filed the divorce papers this week," she began. "I told him I don't know how I'm going to explain this to my mother. She was unhappy for all her married life and she would never have considered divorce. It was a point of pride for her."

As far as I could tell, Mrs. Dillard was picking up exactly where she had left off last week—content to vent to me, whoever I was, with very little curiosity about Annabelle's absence. She patted her hair and face again, as if her head was going to lift up and fly away. Which seemed like something she might be feeling.

I floated a few tentative comments, "Your mother's

opinion means a lot to you" and "Your family feels it's important to stick something through" without much effect. I squinted my eyes, picturing her wielding a weapon. It was hard to imagine that she felt enough of a connection to her therapist to strike her even once, never mind beat her close to death. Her husband, maybe. After fifty minutes had passed, I broke in to tell her our time was up and that I'd keep her posted about Annabelle's condition.

The eleven o'clock patient didn't show. I skimmed through the case notes. This had been a pattern over the last few months. Then I noticed a CD in a paper jacket had been slipped into the folder. I switched on Annabelle's desktop computer and fitted the disc into the slot. It contained a series of photographs of arrangements in the sand tray—mostly the wet tray from what I could make out. Very few figurines had been placed. I went back to the patient notes. Best I could tell, the appointment no-shows and the sparse arrangements seemed related to this young woman's reluctance to commit to treatment. Again, not a good candidate for Annabelle's attacker.

After twenty minutes, I picked up the small green watering can beside the desk and crossed the hallway to the bathroom. I filled the can, then leaned over the sink to splash cold water on my face.

"What's going on here? What are you doing in Ms. Hart's office?"

I jerked up, banging my head on the faucet and wheeled around, face and hands dripping, to see Dr. Frazier. "I'm Dr. Butterman. We met yesterday," I said irritably, reaching for a paper towel and dabbing my skin. I picked up the watering can and headed back across the hall, palpating my head for telltale swelling.

"Can I help you with something?" she asked, planting her body in the doorway, her hands firmly on her hips, like a bouncer staring down an undesirable customer. Only bouncers don't wear houndstooth-checked pencil skirts, patent-leather heels, and cashmere sweaters.

"I'm helping out with Annabelle's patients." I carried the watering can over to the window and began to fill a tray of stones that held a small bonsai tree, then watered the fern dangling above it. They were both beginning to wilt under the relentless hiss of the radiator's steam heat.

"What's the matter? Is she ill?"

I motioned to her to step into the office and waited until she closed the door. "She's in the hospital. She was attacked at her home yesterday."

"Jesus, Joseph, and Mary!" She click-clacked across the wood floor and crumpled into Annabelle's rocking chair. "Oh my God, this is awful!" She reached for the afghan draped over the back of the chair and began to work the fringe with her fingers. "Who attacked her? Will she be all right?"

I shrugged, set the can down, and pressed my fingers against my cheeks, feeling the gathering ache in my sinuses. "She's in a coma. Of course, we're optimistic." Who was optimistic? Me and that social worker, I supposed. "Did she seem upset to you this week? Anything here at the office she was worried about?"

Her dark eyes shifted away, then back. She shuddered and pulled the afghan over her shoulders. "My God! The cops think one of her patients beat her up?"

"They don't know what happened yet."

"Was she sexually assaulted?"

I shrugged again, struggling to keep my composure. I hadn't permitted myself to consider that possibility. "I'm going over to the hospital when I finish up here. Maybe I'll have more news this afternoon."

Dr. Frazier leaped up and paced over to the bookshelves

behind the shoji screen. She selected a tiny freestanding brass mirror and moved it to the edge of the shelf.

"I remember we talked some about bipolar disorder." She fanned her flushed face with both hands. "She wanted to know about the latest pharmaceutical treatments. She wondered about the use of fish oil with someone who hasn't been compliant with traditional regimens. Fish oil!" She threw her head back and almost whinnied. "I explained that if the patient doesn't take the drugs as prescribed by the physician, it doesn't matter how effective they are. But fish oil—are we psychiatrists or shamans?"

Dr. Frazier seemed to be enjoying the opportunity to bestow me with a mini-lecture. I was sure she'd liked enlightening Annabelle on the finer points of medical treatment too.

"Did you get the impression that she was asking about one of her own patients?"

"She didn't request a formal medical evaluation, if that's what you mean." She set down the miniature coffin she'd been fondling and turned to focus squarely on me.

"Really, I'd be happy to take over Annabelle's caseload. She does use me for a medical backup whenever there's an issue of medication. And I've consulted with her on many, many topics." She tugged on one gold hoop earring with her perfectly manicured fingers. "She's a social worker, you know. What is *your* training?"

I just stared for a moment, swallowing a half dozen rude retorts. "I'm a clinical psychologist," I said. "She asked me to cover for her in case of any emergency. I'll certainly pass on your kind offer once she's able to receive it."

"Fine." She started to the door, then stopped. "We did have a conversation about abusive relationships just last week." She folded her arms over her chest and leaned against the door frame. "You know the 'friend of a friend of a friend has a problem' routine? It crossed my mind to wonder if she was looking for help with her own issues."

"Her own issues?" Nothing Annabelle had ever said would lead me to believe she'd turn to Dr. Frazier in a jam.

"The new boyfriend." The doctor squinted and jutted her chin forward. "I don't have any hard data to prove this, but I'm starting to wonder. Maybe she was feeling threatened. Maybe she'd gotten into a destructive relationship and was too embarrassed to come right out and say so."

I gaped. "You think she's being abused? Annabelle?" Annabelle is one of the more sensible, centered people I know.

"Wouldn't that be the logical conclusion here?"

"But—"

"Never mind." She waved her hand. "That conversation was confidential so I'm talking out of school."

Then she narrowed her eyes at Annabelle's desk, and strode over to peer at the computer, open to a photograph of one of the no-show patients' trays. I was still grappling with the idea of Annabelle in an abusive relationship. It was so not her. And so not like her to hash it out with Dr. Frazier. Or was it? I inhaled deeply. Maybe I shouldn't dismiss this young woman so quickly. Only one way to find out.

"Do you use sand tray therapy in your practice?" I asked. "I'm a bit lost facing the patients that were doing that kind of work with her."

She huffed and pushed a hank of glossy black hair behind her ear. "Sand*play* therapy, please. She has a fit if you call it anything else. Of course I don't use it. You can play with little dolls all day long, but if you don't talk about your family dynamics and then find the right structure for extricating yourself from them, you're going nowhere. And fast."

I had a feeling Annabelle had more empathy in her little rake than this woman did in her entire therapeutic arsenal.

As soon as Dr. Frazier's door banged shut behind her, Annabelle's one o'clock patient thumped up the stairs. We had a short meeting: This Yale student saw no advantage to talking with someone who knew nothing about sandplay therapy or her personal history. She hoisted her backpack over one shoulder and tromped back down the stairs. Maybe I'd been a bit too blunt about my ignorance, but no point in trying to argue her back in now.

I sank into Annabelle's desk chair and began to click through more sand tray images. I thought it would be simple enough to shift from talk therapy to sandplay, but the truth was I had no real idea how to use the damn things. Nor was I getting any closer to understanding what had happened to my friend. And altruistic urges to help Annabelle's patients aside, that's what mattered to me most.

I twirled the chair in a slow circle, stopping in front of the answering machine. The message light was blinking. I pressed the *forward* arrow and a shaky female voice issued into the room.

"I came for my appointment yesterday," the voice said, "but you weren't there. Did I get the date or time wrong? Could you please call me between three and five if possible? I'll wait by the phone. And please, don't leave a message if by any chance I'm not home."

She didn't leave her name. Was this the distraught and skittish woman I'd seen the day before on the steps? The voice sounded familiar. I flipped through Annabelle's day planner and ran my finger down the list of yesterday's appointments. "M" was penciled in for five p.m. Annabelle is always careful about patient confidentiality, but using one initial in her own book? Something was off. I reminded myself to call this woman later and try harder to connect.

Next came a voice I thought I recognized as the petulant pregnant lady who'd chosen retail therapy when the chips were down. I phoned and left a message offering to meet with her over the next couple of days.

I tipped back in the chair, thinking more about Annabelle's question to Dr. Frazier about the use of fish oil capsules. My friend is no crank when it comes to psychotropic medication. So why would she consider fish oil? This sounded like a desperate option. Really desperate. Not that I trusted "Dr. Frantic's" assessment on anything. The whole abusive boyfriend discussion confirmed my judgment there. Not that I should be referring to Dr. Frazier that way, even to myself. Sooner or later the nickname would slip out. I drummed my fingers on the blond wood desk.

My own therapy has helped me squelch errant urges to reconnect with my ex-husband, Mark—we were separated for almost a year and divorced since last fall and for God's sake it was time to move on. But he's a Yale psychiatrist who happens to be an expert in psychotropic medication. So I dialed his cell phone number, which I can't help that I still know by heart.

"It's Rebecca," I said when he answered. "Something awful has happened." I gave him the thumbnail: Annabelle in the hospital, her uncooperative sister, and finally, my day so far in the sandplay office. "I'm calling about a medication question."

"Hold on," he said. "Start with what happened to Annabelle."

Score one for Mark, who is not always high on the empathy scale himself. I told him just enough about finding her to keep the image of her battered face at bay.

"That's rough," he said. "She's a sweet woman. A little kooky, but sweet."

"Speaking of so-called kooky," I said, and described the fish oil capsule consultation. "Can you think of a situation where a therapist might consider that?"

"Hate to say it, but Dr. Frazier was on target this time," he said. "The biggest challenge with bipolar disorder is compliance. Because if you're on the upswing of the manic phase, you can feel very, very good—lots of energy, a sense that anything is possible. By the time you've gone too far along the continuum, your judgment is shot and medication no longer appeals. Fish oil has no place in treating this illness." He cleared his throat. "Why are you asking about this?"

"Honestly? I'm hoping to rule out her patients in the attack."

"She was beaten at home and you suspect one of her patients? That's a big leap."

"It's the only possibility I can do something about," I said. "And I can't deliver her records to the cops and let them tromp through confidential information."

"Agreed. But as soon as you turn up any reasonable suspicions, it becomes their job. Did Annabelle ever say anything about a dangerous patient?"

"Never," I said, my stomach sinking. "But I feel so helpless. She's critically ill and I can't do anything for her. At least if I'm looking . . . maybe I can eliminate some possibilities. I'll let you go—thanks for talking."

"I'm happy to help," Mark said. "Can I buy you breakfast on Saturday?"

"I'm busy," I shot back too fast, certain I sounded guilty.

"What's happening on Saturday?" he asked.

My heart dropped a floor. I had to tell him. Coming clean about another romantic interest should shut the door firmly on our defunct marriage.

"Bob's coming for the weekend," I mumbled.

"Bob?"

"I've been seeing him since Christmas. He's one of Angie's old Princeton buddies."

"He lives in Connecticut?"

"Atlanta, but he comes up to visit his folks in Old Say-brook fairly often. So far it's been mostly phone chats."

"That'll keep the sex fresh anyway," he said, striking me dumb.

"Don't be ridiculous," I said primly.

Sex had been damn good with Mark, right up to the last year of our marriage: We used it as a shortcut to hack through the bad feelings lingering after our quarrels. You might think two well-educated professionals who special-ize in human relations for a living would understand the dangers of that. Not always. For me, when both your par-ents are gone by the time you're six years old, you can't help expecting your other important relationships will melt away too. For Mark, his father's fears colored everything fragile. After a while, our intimacy issues just snapped to-gether like the last piece of an ugly jigsaw puzzle.

I'd left too much silence.

"Don't tell me you're not sleeping with him," Mark said.

"This is really none of your business!" I said.

"You're not!"

"We're in no hurry," I said stiffly. "*I'm* in no hurry. Dr. Goldman thinks I should take my time after the attack last fall."

"Dr. Golddigger's still on the payroll?"

Mark can't stand my shrink, who shored me up during the separation and divorce. But there's only so much un-happiness a marriage will bear, once the unhealthy patterns are brought to light. Mark knows better than to pin the blame on Goldman, when he was the one who had the af-fair. But the heartbreak and humiliation have to be laid at someone's feet. Hell, Annabelle herself always warns her patients that individual psychotherapy can be hazardous to marital health.

"We think I have post-traumatic stress disorder," I said, returning to a subject a little safer than our marriage—lack of sex with Bob.

"Could be," said Mark noncommittally. "Could also be your unconscious mind telling you this isn't the right guy."

"And you were?" I snorted.

"I'm just saying," said Mark with a chuckle. "I know you. When the right guy comes along you'll want to rip his shorts off."

Like an unwelcome slide show, the tired face of Detective Meigs flashed to mind, his broad shoulders under that hideous checkered sport coat. *Stop!* I ordered myself.

"When is Good Old Bob coming in?" Mark asked.

"Friday afternoon. And don't call him that," I said. I took a couple of deep yoga breaths, then managed to thank Mark and sign off before we spiraled into another fight. I hung up, horrified. How had I allowed myself to be sucked into discussing my sex life—or lack thereof—with my ex? Note to self: Next time, call another expert.

After twenty more minutes clicking through discs containing photographs of sand trays, I shut the computer down. I was dying to see Annabelle. And I wasn't going to draw any reasonable conclusions here: I simply didn't know enough about how this therapy worked. I gathered up my things and at the last moment, re-recorded the message on Annabelle's answering machine.

"You've reached the office of Annabelle Hart. She's out of the office and is unavailable to take your call. Please leave a message and she'll get back to you. If this is an emergency, please dial Dr. Rebecca Butterman . . ." I finished with my cell phone number.

As I emerged from the downstairs landing to the outside stoop, a woman rushed across the street. She was thin, dressed in a faded denim jacket, grubby jeans, and sneakers.

"Where's Annabelle Hart?" she demanded, her eyes wild in her chapped face. "Is something wrong?"

I stutter-stepped back, startled and a little afraid. Who was this woman? A desperate patient? "She's a bit under the weather," I said. "I'm covering for her practice for the next week or so. Would you like to make an appointment or leave a message?"

The woman turned and bolted.

Chapter 6

I drove across town to the hospital and parked on the top level of the garage, which is open to the air. This time, when I reached the security desk, I flashed my Yale ID and strode to the elevators before anyone could challenge me. The doors slid open silently on the sixth floor. The hallway was quiet too: no anxious relatives in either waiting room. I approached the locked doors to the unit and peered through the window. No one at the nurses' station either.

The elevator opened again, discharging a white-coated woman. She hurried past me and swiped her ID through the card reader on the wall. As any good Lance Armstrong fan would do, I drafted in behind her. I paused beside the vacant nurses' station to get my bearings. Patient rooms separated by glass doors fanned out from the desk in a half circle. The walls and floors were a cheery peach color, the desk a soothing blue. Mechanical beeps and squeals and raised voices came from the room on the right, which was crammed with medical people. I crept down the hallway in the other direction, passing a cluster of computers lit with brain scans. Did one of them belong to Annabelle?

I spotted my friend in the first cubicle on the left, her doorway marked with the unit and room number and her name. I hurried over to the window and peered in. It was hard to make out her face among the jumble of equipment—monitors, bags of fluid, tubes, and blinking lights. I didn't notice the nurse until too late.

She hung a chart on the end of Annabelle's bed and exited the room.

"Who are you? Can I help you?" she asked in a stern voice. She was a small woman with straight blond hair and huge blue eyes: "Lyn McHugh, RN," her name badge read. I briefly considered passing myself off as one of Annabelle's sisters. But the head shot of a fluffy white dog on her badge led me to think she'd be sympathetic to the truth.

"I'm a good friend of Annabelle's," I said.

"I'm sorry, but only relatives are allowed on the unit right now."

I pulled out my Yale ID again. "I consult here."

"With what service?" Nurse McHugh asked suspiciously, squinting at my card.

"Psychiatry," I said, sliding the ID back into my wallet.

"We didn't call for a psychiatric consult. I'm going to have to ask you to leave."

"Look, I'll be happy to leave if you'll just give me some answers—"

The nurse strode down the hallway and picked up the phone at the desk. "Could you send someone from Security to Six East?" she asked. Just then, Fred Polson, the social worker I'd met yesterday, burst through the entrance to the unit and started toward us.

"I heard your page. Is there a problem I can help with?" he asked when he reached the desk.

"This woman"—the nurse pointed at me—"came onto the unit without authorization and she refuses to leave. So I called Security."

"But I'm Annabelle's best friend," I said. "Look, I'm the one who found her and phoned her sister—"

"I'll be happy to show Ms. Butterman downstairs," said Polson, reaching for my elbow.

"Don't you dare touch me," I said, veering around him and starting down the hall.

Polson followed me out of the unit and held the door for the waiting elevator.

"I understand the hospital has to have rules," I sputtered as we began our descent. I waved my Yale ID in his face. "But not only am I on staff here, I'm a close friend of Annabelle Hart's. It doesn't seem right that you can't visit your own best friend when she's ill." Polson kept his gaze fixed on the numbers flashing by, a small smile on his lips. Which only infuriated me. "Besides, I'm the one who found her and had her brought in," I said. "And no one's let me see her since we came into the ER yesterday."

When we reached the ground floor, Polson gestured for me to step out. I crossed my arms and stood firm, way beyond annoyed.

"In the future," he said pleasantly, "it would be better not to try to visit that unit without permission and a visitor's pass." He patted my back.

"Get your paws off me," I snapped, jerking away and stalking off the elevator.

"Have a good day," he said and ambled down the hall.

"And what is really going on here?" I called to his retreating back. "It's not like she's a celebrity or something. She's my friend. I'm her friend!"

I blew out a puff of air, yanked my cell phone from my purse, and dialed Detective Meigs's cell phone.

"I need some help," I said when he answered. "I'm at Yale New Haven Hospital. There's something weird going on with Annabelle." I explained how I'd tried to visit and ended up evicted by the social worker. "Can you find out what's up here? Can you possibly call someone and intercede?"

"Sorry," said Meigs. "I have no pull at the hospital. No jurisdiction. Look," he added kindly, "it sounds pretty simple: Your friend's in critical condition and not allowed to have visitors outside the family."

I didn't answer. Annabelle *is* my family.

"I am sorry about your friend," he added.

I choked out "thanks" and asked if there was anything new on the case.

"I was just about to call you. Could you meet me at her house tomorrow morning? I need you to look something over."

"What? What did you find?"

"We really don't have much so far," he said. "So don't get excited. But you've spent time in her house, right? I thought you might see something I've missed."

I knew him well enough to know I wasn't going to worm anything more out of him. We arranged to meet at eight and I closed the phone. Then I collapsed into one of the waiting room chairs, feeling too exhausted to make it to the car, never mind forge through the rush hour out of New Haven, back into the shoreline suburbs where people move to be safe and cozy. Not beaten within an inch of their lives.

Maybe a cup of coffee first? Never mind—I'd be up all night. As if I wouldn't be anyway, worrying about Annabelle, wondering what Meigs had to show me, brain whirling with outrage about being thrown out of her unit. I hauled my tired body up and plodded across the room to the exit.

As I started into the revolving door, I noticed Annabelle's sister rotating clockwise in the triangle of space across from me.

"Victoria!" I shouted and rapped on the glass. She looked away and kept pushing. I circled around a second time and trotted after her. "Victoria!" I tapped her shoulder—harder than I'd intended but not as hard as she deserved.

"Yes?" she hissed, clutching her pocketbook to her chest.

"I'm wondering how Annabelle's doing. I tried to see her today and they won't let me in." I considered dropping to my knees and begging but that wouldn't probably do much to soften the wicked witch of Greenwich. "Don't you understand—I'm her friend and I'm terribly worried?"

She started to walk away. I stepped in front of her to cut her off. "Did you hear me?" I asked.

"Don't *you* understand?" she said, her voice thick with tears. "My sister is dying. I'm doing my best to take care of her. I can't take care of you too." She swirled away in the direction of the elevator and I just watched her go.

&

Use of cell phones without a hands-free device while driving is illegal in Connecticut, but I figured if I wasn't eating, reading, or applying makeup, one conversation was close enough to safe. I called Angie on the way home and spilled the whole mess, the three-minute version anyway.

"I'm picking up Thai food and bringing it right over," she said when I'd finished.

"I was thinking of going to yoga class." I pictured myself unrolling my mat and attempting to clear my mind enough to move through the poses and then relax. It wasn't going to happen. Not with Annabelle dying. I shoved that thought away.

"Forget the yoga, I do need Pad Thai," I said.

"I'll be there in half an hour."

"I have pea soup in the Crock-Pot," I said.

"Move it to the freezer," she said. Angie's not a fan of legumes.

❧

Our condo handyman, worth his weight in mulch, was planting pansies in the planters at the entrance to the complex. I rolled down the window.

"Hey Bernd, how are you? Everything okay?"

He nodded. "I saw that business in the paper about the woman over on Mulberry Point. Isn't that your friend?"

"Annabelle Hart." I swallowed the lump in my throat. "Wasn't that awful?"

"You have to be careful, a woman alone." He shook his head mournfully. I'm not sure he'll ever recover from being part of my kidnapping rescue effort last fall.

He wiggled the worn wallet out of his back pocket and handed me a business card. "I want you to have this. My cell number's written on the back. You call if you need me. I gave one to Ms. Finster too." Babette Finster is the other single "girl" in the complex. Unless you count Mrs. Dunbarton, resident battle-axe. She's definitely single—having worn Mr. Dunbarton to an early grave, by all reports.

"You're so sweet," I said. "Thank you very much."

Bernd's phone rang. "I saw your detective friend on a drive-through earlier. At least they're doing their job," he said as he answered the cell.

I smiled and waved as I pulled off, stopping at the mail center to extract a wad of what looked like solicitations and bills from my box. What the hell was Meigs doing in my complex? Then I pulled around the loop in front of the clubhouse and nosed into my garage. I'd completely forgotten about the cats. Poor Jackson had been shut in the cellar all day. His pitiful mewling echoed as soon as I unlocked the door. Spencer trotted to meet me. *What is that tiresome whining*? his disdainful expression said.

"Look, buster," I said, running my hand the length of his thick gray fur, "if you two can't get along, it's your turn in the basement tomorrow." He stalked off, tail twitching, and sprang up on the counter to observe. Jackson tumbled out of the cellar, blinking and mewing. I swept him up and nuzzled his head with my chin. "You poor baby. I bet you were scared, all alone in the dark."

I fed them both, admonishing Spencer to play nice, and listened to the messages on the answering machine. The first was from my sister, Janice, calling from Boston.

"Rebecca, it's me. We're having a wonderful time, but we miss you! And how is your friend? How are the dinner plans coming for Friday? Are you sure you don't want me and Jim to come too? I could pick up something from Four-and-Twenty Blackbirds for dessert, or you could bring Bob by the house Saturday morning." She lowered her voice. "Not too early. We don't want Brittany to think . . . you know. Call me as soon as you can. I tried your cell phone this afternoon but you didn't pick up."

Poor Janice. She'd be so disappointed when I told her the dinner was off. Honestly, she seems more interested in Bob than I am. And not necessarily Bob for Bob's sake. She barely knows the guy, having met him once after my niece's Christmas pageant. More to the point, I finally in her eyes—have a new husband prospect, someone who can make up a bridge foursome along with her and Jim. Or golf. Not that I play either game.

The doorbell rang and I hurried over to let Angie and her heavenly smelling take-out bags in. She kissed my cheek on her way to the kitchen.

"Rebecca, what have you done?" She dropped the sacks

on the counter and wiggled her fingers in front of Jackson. "You adorable little man," she said as he pounced.

"He belongs to Annabelle," I said, scraping the aluminum foil tin of Pad Thai into a ceramic bowl. It's one of my top ten rules about living alone: Never eat from the carton. You'll only feel more pitiful. Though I've been known to break that rule in an emergency. "I brought him over yesterday after the EMTs took her away."

"He's a doll," she said, snuggling him up to her face. I could hear the rumble of his kittenish purr from across the room. "I brought spicy chicken and eggplant too. Medium hot. It should stand up to that Beaujolais you keep for special occasions." She winked and set the kitten down.

I pulled a bottle of Cabernet from the rack in the closet and extracted the cork. We loaded our plates and glasses and carried them to the living room. Jackson spurted ahead of us; Spencer stalked behind.

I began to fill her in on the day. "Meigs told me yesterday they had decided it was a robbery gone sour, but I don't think he believes that. He wants me to give him access to her office so he can read her patient notes. Which I have no intention of doing, of course."

"Why doesn't he think it was a robbery?"

"Of course he wouldn't tell me that. But in my mind, robbery is about grabbing money or jewelry and then clearing out fast. It's not about beating someone up. This looked personal." I studied my plate, rearranging the noodles with my chopsticks. "And he wants me to meet him at her place in the morning."

She patted my hand. "If it was a random event, there's certainly nothing you can do to help." She speared a piece of eggplant and popped it into her mouth. "On the other hand, if Meigs wants to see her records, he must be thinking the person who did this knew her."

I nodded and sipped my wine. Feeling a little woozy after only half a glass, I pushed it out of reach. "That's my guess."

"Do you have any suspects?" she asked.

"I hate to say it, but Annabelle's sister has been perfectly awful—a witch. She's a society maven who thinks the world of herself. She seems to have the staff in the ICU unit believing I'm up to no good." I told her about the embarrassing eviction at the hands of the nurse and the social worker. "I'm sure she's upset, but why shut me out?"

Angie clucked with sympathy and refilled her wineglass. "She doesn't know you. She has no idea what a good friend you are."

"And I do wonder about the boyfriend. Not that I've even met him. Dr. Frazier, the shrink in the office next to Annabelle's, seems to have the idea Annabelle could be trapped in an abusive relationship."

Angie snorted. "Annabelle? Abused? I can't imagine that happening. Besides, she's hardly been dating him long enough to be trapped."

"If you could have seen her—" I put my fingers to my throat and reached for the wine again, forcing back the image of Annabelle's face, beaten and bloody.

"Does this Dr. Frazier know Annabelle well?"

"I didn't think so." I set my chopsticks on the plate, appetite gone. "She's slightly odd. She's been hovering for the last two days and she tried to get me to turn the practice over to her—as though she knows Annabelle better than I do; as though she could do a better job because she has an MD and I'm a psychologist."

"Did Annabelle ever talk about her?" Angie asked.

"Yes," I laughed. "Not too flatteringly. She switched her Tuesday patients around so they'd arrive on the half hour instead of the hour. Dr. Frazier was coming over to chat between every session and I guess it got to be too much. Annabelle needed a break."

I closed my eyes and pictured the conversation I'd had with Dr. Frazier in Annabelle's office. She had seemed honestly shocked about the news. I remembered her reaching for a miniature mirror and placing it on the edge of the shelf. I described this to Angie. "The only other thing she touched was a coffin."

"So you're diagnosing her as a sociopath because she fondled a toy mirror and a coffin?"

"It's a leap," I agreed with a chuckle. "I've got to figure a way to ask about her Tuesday morning schedule. If she was conducting rounds at the hospital or something, she'd be off the hook."

"Wouldn't that be Meigs's department?" Angie asked.

"I guess." I picked the orange kitten up, settled him into my lap, and stabbed a piece of eggplant with my chopsticks. "But it won't hurt to ask, if I see her."

Angie wiped her lips. "Tell me more about Annabelle's sister."

"She writes a society gossip column on the Web. Most of her victims are from southern Connecticut. Vicious," I added. "She's the anti-Annabelle, from what I can tell. No wonder they had a falling out."

"Did they?"

I shrugged. "I got that impression—mostly because Annabelle barely mentioned having a sister. And I looked her up online and saw that Victoria was married for the third time just a few months ago. Wouldn't you think that would make good conversation?"

"Unless she's ashamed of her," Angie said. "At some point, terrible family stories stop being funny. But I don't have to tell you that. I know a couple of lawyers in Greenwich. Want me to ask around and see what I can dig up?"

I nodded, resting my head against the couch and closing my eyes. "Can't hurt."

"You hardly ate anything. And you look exhausted," she said. "Let me help you clean up." We carried the plates to the kitchen and loaded them into the dishwasher. She dried her hands on a checkered towel and gave me a hug. "I'll be in touch. Call me if anything changes."

After packing the leftovers into the fridge, I started the dishwasher humming and settled back onto the couch. Jackson snuggled down on one side of me, Spencer perched warily on the other.

I fished Annabelle's day planner out of my purse and looked at her schedule again. She had four patients lined up for the next day, which I mentally added to my meeting with Meigs in the morning, Dr. Goldman in the afternoon, and hopefully a visit with Annabelle herself. Lucky thing I'd taken a couple days off from my own practice—I would have had to call in sick. If you can't take care of yourself when you need to, you sure won't be any good to anyone else.

This day had worn me down, flattened me like asphalt on a new road. It was discouraging to have such a poor grip on Annabelle's patients and her sandplay treatment—I'd charged into the morning like a white knight and straggled out like a captured pawn. I could use some expert guidance.

I leafed through the addresses at the back, then riffled through the past month's appointments, looking for a match. She had a standing appointment with Dr. Howdy Phipps in New Haven on Mondays. I typed the name into my computer: Dr. Phipps had a doctorate in social work, with a specialty in women's issues and sand trays. Was this her therapist or her supervisor?

I dialed his number, expecting to leave a message. Instead a warm voice greeted me.

"Howdy Phipps!" he answered, more cheerful than most shrinks I know. He'd clearly worked out any issues he might have had about his name—I would have been tempted to leave off the "Howdy" and stick with "Doctor."

"I'm wondering—this is Dr. Rebecca Butterman—if I could make an appointment for a consultation? I'm a friend of Annabelle Hart's." Best not to tell the whole story on the phone, I decided. I'd bring a copy of the agreement Annabelle and I had signed about caring for each other's practice in case of an emergency—it would sound better explained in person.

"I had a cancellation tomorrow at four," said Dr. Phipps. "Will that work for you?"

Same time as my appointment with Dr. Goldman. Which I wouldn't have made anyway if I'd gone to Boston. I hesitated only a nanosecond. "Thanks," I said. "I'll take it."

Chapter 7

A short length of crime scene tape had broken away and speared itself on a rosebush outside the home next to Annabelle's; the tape was the same warbler yellow as the house's stucco exterior. It snapped in the cold breeze that had kicked up over the salt marsh. I pulled into the driveway behind Meigs's white van and got out, feeling edgy and rattled. The tape gave me the creeps—it would bother Annabelle too. I hurried across the lawn to the neighbor's rosebush and tried to untangle it.

"Ouch!" I yanked my hand back. A globule of dark red blood welled up on my finger.

"What's the holdup?" Meigs barked from Annabelle's front stoop.

"Nothing," I said, reaching into my purse for a Kleenex and starting across the yard toward the sweep of her stone steps. He held the door open and waved me into the front hallway.

"My guys are pretty much done searching, but to be on

the safe side, why don't you put these on." He held out a
pair of white latex gloves.

"I'm allergic to rubber," I said. "I swear I won't touch
anything."

"For Christ's sake," he said, then glanced at my hands
and frowned. "You're bleeding."

"Just a prick." I pressed the tissue against the skin, then
noticed he was wearing a suit—dark gray, slightly snug,
lapels a tad too wide, smelling of cedar. "Off to a party this
early?" I teased.

"A funeral," he said. "Hartford cop, shot sixteen times
in the chest during a drug bust."

"Sorry," I said, my smile fading. "What's up? What did
you want me to see?"

"In here." He strode into the living room with its
panoramic view over the marsh. Among the reedy browns,
a tinge of pale green was beginning to emerge. Meigs
pointed to the sand tray on the lower shelf of Annabelle's
bookcase.

"Can you explain this?"

I glanced at the tray, then back at him. "She's a sandplay
therapist. This is the kind of work she does."

"I understand that." He rolled his eyes up to the ceiling,
muttering. "She thinks I'm an idiot." Back over to me. "I
want to know the meaning of this particular arrangement of
toys." He folded his arms over his burly chest and waited.

I crouched down and studied the tray, then reached for
the figurine of a child, half-buried in the sand at the far end.

"Don't touch!" he yelped.

"Sorry." How dumb could I be? I pressed on my cheek-
bones to push back a mist of embarrassment, then took a
deep breath and sank down to my knees. "A nonverbal
method like sand tray—excuse me, sandplay, that's what she
calls it—therapy provides a bridge between consciousness

and the unconscious. The images you construct can give meaning to unconscious conflicts and issues and bring them into consciousness in their own psychic time." I stopped, rather satisfied with this professional-sounding explanation, especially after my idiotic near-contamination of the crime scene.

"Wonderful," said Meigs, his voice bleeding sarcasm and punctuated with another eye roll. "What are the issues and conflicts in this sandbox here?" He pointed at the figures in the tray.

"Only Annabelle could really say for sure," I said. "I'm no expert on sandplay therapy. Even if I was, it's like dream interpretation—I might understand the theory, but I would need to hear my patient's personal associations—in this case, Annabelle's—to get clear on the meaning. And of course, if she was my patient—which she wouldn't be because we're friends—I couldn't disclose this anyway. It wouldn't be ethical. Unless of course it had some specific bearing on the case."

His eyes looped in another big arc. "In other words, you won't tell me anything."

"The eye rolling is not helpful," I said, sitting back on my heels. "Eye rolling projects profound disrespect."

"Fascinating," said Meigs. He lifted his brows, a dark line against his pale face. Didn't the man spend any time in the sun? He was a pasty, annoying bully.

"In fact," I said with a sniff, "studies show that eye rolling predicts future breakups."

His brows peaked again. "I wasn't aware that we had anything to break up."

Hot blood rushed to my face. Was it too early for menopause? Yes. This was merely another case of profound embarrassment. My gaze swept the photographs arranged on the bookshelf above the sand tray. Anything to avoid

meeting his eyes. I struggled to my feet and pointed to a picture of three women. "Okay to pick that up?"

He nodded. The photo appeared to have been taken at a
graduation. A younger version of Annabelle and a softer
version of Victoria stood with their arms around a third
young woman in cap and gown. I peered more closely at
the picture: The resemblance to Victoria was undeniable. A
niece, I supposed.

"This must be Victoria's daughter. Annabelle never mentioned her, but on the other hand, she barely spoke about
Victoria either."

Meigs sighed. "Look, the incident here was an attempted
robbery, not the result of a family vendetta. Some asshole
thought she wasn't home, came in looking for a quick score,
and she surprised him. Her very bad luck."

"If that's the official police conclusion, then why bring
me here to look at her sand tray? And why were you lurking
around my condo complex yesterday?" I planted my hands
on my hips, narrowed my eyes, and looked at him straight
on this time. "There's something you aren't saying."

"I'm doing my job," he said, staring right back. "Did
you meet with her patients yesterday?"

"Some of them," I said, "but you know I can't discuss
that. Do you think the robbery was committed by one of
her patients?"

He shrugged. "Did you come across a calendar, a day
planner, anything like that?"

"That would be privileged information as well. We've
been over that ground." I sounded snotty—an overcompen-
sation for the rush of guilt about holding back the damn
day planner. Or at least not telling him I had it. Was I interfering with finding the attacker by refusing to share?

Meigs clenched his teeth and let the air whistle through.
"We located a weapon. In the weeds. A hammer. We've

sent it out for testing and that'll take a while, but we're pretty confident about what we'll find."

"You mean you found it in the salt marsh?"

He nodded. We both looked out into the backyard, eyes skimming over Annabelle's yellow polyethylene kayak to the reeds behind. Steel-headed clouds were collecting ominously on the horizon. I blinked, imagining bits of skin and bone and lots of blood on the hammer's head. I felt myself begin to weave and grabbed for the back of the couch.

"Sit down," said Meigs, grasping the same elbow Polson had tried to pinch yesterday, and leading me to a chair by the window. He switched on the lamp, the white china base painted with blue figurines. I sat down and tried to focus on the scene. A slender woman dressed in a kimono peeked out from behind her fan; three men who looked like desperate suitors hovered behind her. Annabelle had gloated about finding this treasure at the antiques fair on the town green last fall. She loved the helpless geisha's hold over the men. I didn't see it the way she did, but—

"The other day you told me she'd had some work done by a carpenter," Meigs said.

Hammer—carpenter? My shoulders crept up toward my ears and I tried to ease them down.

"Russ Wheeler," I said softly. "Shoreline Carpentry. He was here working most of the fall and winter. Or at least it seemed that way to me."

"Were there problems with the job?"

"Aren't there always?" I sighed. "Especially right here near the water. The conditions can be brutal, with sheets of rain blasting in sideways during our nor'easters." I felt my cheeks pink up again. Meigs had lived in Guilford his whole life. He didn't need a weather report. "I'm just saying if you don't get someone who really knows how to handle it . . ."

"And apparently this Russ Wheeler didn't. Did they have any serious disagreements or arguments?"

"No, no. He came back five or six times to fix the leaks that cropped up. He said it was part of his job and he'd see it through until it met her standards."

"But he finished the work and moved on to something else?"

"Yes. Except then she started seeing him socially. We were supposed to get together on Friday." I felt sick to my stomach. Annabelle was a little infatuated with her carpenter—her golden boy, she called him. I informed her the glow was sawdust—once he took a bath he'd look like all the other guys. She said I was jealous; that my snarkiness was a symptom of delayed Post Traumatic Divorce Disorder. None of which Meigs needed to know. "I did call to tell him Annabelle was in the hospital. He sounded normal—or as normal as you can, hearing that kind of news."

Meigs made some notes in his PDA.

"If you guys think it was a robbery, why are you asking me these questions? Why am I here?"

"Covering all the bases," he said brusquely.

I felt a stab of panic as the facts hit home at gut level, no longer just words. Annabelle. Hammer. Weapon. Russ. "It wasn't random then. This is sick. You have to bring him in!"

"We believe it started out as a robbery," he said again. "If he was here working for months, he would have known exactly where to find her valuables. And her schedule." He glared. "Which is why I need her date book. Then we would know for sure whether or not he intended to arrive after she'd left for work."

I looked away, massaging my temples.

"From what you're saying, this guy would have known the neighborhood well—including exactly when it was safe to show up. In fact"—he rubbed a patch of whiskers on his chin and made another note in his PDA—"no one would have thought much about it, seeing as he was working here all winter and came back six times for redos."

"Did anyone see his truck here that morning?" I asked.

"We haven't had much luck with witnesses. Some of the neighbors are summer people only; the rest had already left for work when the crime was committed. At that time in the morning, nobody saw anything. I shouldn't even be telling you this, but there've been a couple of other break-ins over the winter."

"This doesn't make any sense," I started.

He held his hand up—as if he sensed my anger welling, ready to spill out and surge over him. "A few pieces of silverware and jewelry that belong to a woman down the block showed up in a New Haven pawnshop. Should be easy enough to track down this Russ and get him printed. It won't be long before we know."

"Then I don't understand why I'm here," I said flatly.

Now it was his turn to color. But he said nothing. Something wasn't making sense, something he was embarrassed to tell me. Good time to ask a favor.

"Can you help me get into the hospital to see her?" I pleaded.

"I told you, I have no connection with all that." He waved one hand, hitting the pleated shade and nearly knocking the lamp off the little table. I straightened the shade and took another full breath.

"Please," I said. "You could promise to escort me while I visited . . ."

"That's a medical decision," he said, his gaze dropping to his cell phone. "Let me give it a try. I'll call you later today."

I left the house and sat a minute in my Honda, observing the homes on either side of Annabelle's. These were middle-class families in what was evolving into a high-rent district, not part-time vacation homes. Most likely, these were the folks who'd been at work while my friend struggled with her attacker. Russ? I had yet to meet him, but I didn't want to think so. Annabelle had gushed about him, which wasn't like her.

I heard a chorus of faint, high-pitched barks from across the street and glanced in my rearview mirror. This house was smaller than Annabelle's, its yard busy with wind chimes, birdhouses, and an old-fashioned, claw-foot bathtub planted with pansies. I thought I saw a slight bend in the slats of the blinds, a flash of movement, and felt the spine-shiver that comes from being watched. I looked again. Nothing.

I backed down the driveway, stopping at Annabelle's mailbox painted with shorebirds and draped with twirls of dried conch shell egg cases, and gathered the stack of envelopes and catalogs beginning to build. Then I glanced one last time at Annabelle's house: Meigs's hefty shape was framed in the doorway. He seemed more prickly than ever. Why had he asked me to come? It would have been easy enough to confirm the identity of the workman without my help. In fact, he probably knew it before I arrived.

Only one conclusion came to mind: He wanted to see me. Which didn't really make sense, except in the land of fairy tales. And lately my life seemed to come directly from the Brothers Grimm.

Chapter 8

My cell phone rang on the way to Annabelle's office as the traffic on the interstate ground to a halt. My purse fell over, dumping its contents, including the phone, onto the floor. I swore, braked quickly, and leaned over to scoop the loose stuff back onto the seat. "Dr. Butterman," I answered gruffly.

"Dr. Butterman?" a faint voice echoed. "Could I possibly come in and see you this morning? I'm one of Annabelle Hart's patients."

"Who's calling please?" I asked, negotiating a transfer to the right lane. Some knucklehead had screeched up behind me and begun to flash his headlights. Where did he think he was going in this stop-and-go? I pointed an imaginary, long-distance stun gun at his receding taillights as he wove between the lanes. Z-z-z-zap.

"I'd rather not say," she whispered. "Can we make an appointment and I'll tell you then?"

I rummaged for the day planner in the messy pile on the

passenger seat, paged it open, and peered at my notes, trying not to run off the road. I'd left messages for my friend's nine and ten o'clock appointments, telling them I'd be available if they liked, but eleven was free. "I can see you at eleven."

"Oh thank you," she breathed. "I'm sorry for the James Bond act. I'll explain it all when we meet."

I made it to New Haven just before nine, found a parking space on the street with a two-hour meter, and vaulted up Annabelle's stairs. The nine o'clock patient was waiting. She had curly blond hair, full cheeks, and a baby voice.

"I'm really mad at Annabelle for missing the session," she squeaked, as soon as we were settled. "My mother is coming to visit this weekend and we planned to role-play."

"No reason we can't work on that together," I assured her. I spent the next forty-five minutes defending the woman's housekeeping, child rearing, and husband against the vicious attacks of the patient role-playing her mother, all rendered in her unlikely high-pitched voice. No wonder she dreaded the visit.

Annabelle's ten o'clock patient didn't show. Leaving the door ajar in case of a late arrival, I switched on the computer. I would have liked to review the patient notes for the eleven o'clock appointment, but she was coming incognito.

Flipping through more photos of sand trays built by Annabelle's patients, I formulated questions for the session with her sandplay expert this afternoon. At the top of the notepad, I sketched a drawing of Annabelle's personal tray, feeling intrusive and guilty. But wasn't it most important to find out what happened to her and who did it? Of course that's what Detective Meigs would insist. This was different. I had permission. Not exactly permission to poke in her personal business, but definitely permission to handle her professional concerns. Besides, I was her friend. Confidentiality versus finding the attacker—my mind whirled miserably between the two.

As I shuffled through the papers on her desk—insurance forms, professional journals, to-do lists—I massaged the cable of muscles in my neck. Near the bottom of the stack was an article called "On Treating the Hated and Hateful Patient." Annabelle had made notes in the margins.

"Demanding, critical, ungrateful patients challenge what you'd like to believe as a therapist," she wrote.

People who aren't in our profession don't like to hear that their shrinks might have these thoughts—especially about *them*. But why shouldn't it be true? Why wouldn't an angry or nasty patient have the same impact on a therapist that she does in the outside world? The difference is the therapist tries to use these feelings in the service of the work, rather than just react.

"Winnicott and Young say own and take responsibility for extreme feelings," Annabelle had written. "Survive insulting attacks, must retain ability to think under fire"—she'd underlined this three times—"detoxify, interpret, and hand it back in a helpful way."

Dr. Frazier stuck her head in the door.

"I thought of something else," she announced without any preliminary greeting.

She didn't seem to have a grasp on the small social graces, such as saying "hello."

"We also discussed the ethics of assisted suicide. For us physicians, it's clear enough," she added, her voice growing shrill, "or it used to be under the auspices of the traditional Hippocratic oath, which pretty much said don't give or suggest deadly drugs. The modern version is a lot more ambiguous." She cleared her throat. "It goes like this: 'But it may also be within my power to take a life; this awesome responsibility must be faced with great humbleness and awareness of my own frailty.' Not exactly a user's manual, if you see what I mean." She frowned, the vertical lines in her forehead creasing in a way that she'd regret when they settled in for good after forty.

Had Dr. Frazier wrestled with someone very suicidal in her own practice? Maybe she had raised this question with Annabelle, not the other way around, as she'd told me yesterday. Then why bring it up with me now, as though it was my friend's concern? Maybe the subject said a lot more about her inner demons than Annabelle's. She was hard to warm up to, Dr. Frazier. I should overlook her personality and try harder to listen to her theories.

"Did Annabelle have an opinion on assisted suicide?"

"Not exactly. She had an annoying habit of quoting from her favorite advice columnist. Can you believe it?"

Dr. Frazier clearly couldn't. I smothered a giggle. "What did her advice guru say in this case?"

"Most people have a pretty good idea of where they're already headed when they ask for advice. A wise friend simply shines a flashlight on the path."

I snickered out loud this time, recognizing the excerpt as something I'd written last month. And understanding Dr. Frazier's frustration: Dr. Aster wasn't real. Like most advice columnists, she was a made-up character who gave sound-bite answers in three paragraphs or less and let the real people finish up the dirty work.

Annabelle's door buzzer rang. I crossed the room to the intercom and pressed the button releasing the door, then turned back to the psychiatrist. "Thanks for the help," I said. "I hope you'll excuse me. One of her clients is here." Dr. Frazier backed into the hall and headed to the bathroom.

The footsteps coming up the stairs were deliberate and practically soundless. No joy in this entry. The small woman

I'd seen on the outside stoop two days ago rounded the corner into the office. She wore a cerulean blue linen suit, a strand of pearls, sensible pumps, and Jackie Onassis sunglasses. She'd had her hair color retouched so the gray roots I'd seen the other day were covered.

"Come in, come in," I said, smiling warmly. "I'm glad you called. Where would you like to sit? You'll need to let me know how you want to work today." I pointed first to the traditional seating area and then to the sand trays—a therapeutic Vanna White.

"Could we just sit and talk today?" Her lips quivered. "We can do the trays if you'd rather. It's just that Ms. Hart . . ."

"Certainly, whatever makes you comfortable," I said, dropping into Annabelle's rocker. Would anything make her comfortable? The slightest twitch from me might be interpreted as disapproval. "How can I help?"

"You gave me your card on Tuesday," she whispered. "And then when your name was on her answering machine . . ." She trailed into silence, then removed her sunglasses and set them on her lap, blinking nervously.

"It's not easy to talk with a stranger," I offered, trying not to stare at the swelling and discoloration around her eye.

She crossed her arms and squeezed them in little bursts from shoulders to biceps to elbows, then back up the other direction. Checking to see if she was all there, I couldn't help thinking, At least one mystery was solved: This had to be the woman in an abusive relationship whom Annabelle had discussed with Dr. Frazier.

"We've been talking about my marriage," she whispered, even softer. "Ms. Hart felt that maybe I should consider leaving my husband." One tear escaped and began to creep down her cheek. "I'm just not so sure. And now she's not here . . ."

I flashed on how difficult it would have been to leave Mark if Dr. Goldman had disappeared in the middle of the process. Really, really hard.

"Can you tell me a little more about your history with your husband?" I asked gently. "What kinds of things have been going on that led up to this point? Breaking off a marriage can feel like a very big step."

I wasn't about to tell her how big it had felt to me. And how badly Mark behaved before I could even consider it, though he certainly never hit me. But I was being paid to help her sort out her problems, not compare and contrast them to mine. Which looked rather minor after listening to hers.

"He loves me so much," she said, another tear leaking from the undamaged eye. She took a Kleenex from her purse and patted her face. "He's a wonderful man, so smart and so handsome. It's just that he gets frustrated sometimes."

I touched my own cheekbone. "Did he do this?"

She froze, the tissue on her lips. "He didn't mean to. He gets so impatient with me and he has a very stressful job and then I set him off . . ." Tucking the Kleenex back into her purse, she said, "I don't think I can do this." Her hands were shaking so hard she couldn't work the clasp. She pushed herself up from the chair.

"Please don't hurry off," I said. "I know this is hard."

"I'm so sorry to have wasted your time. I'm going to be late for lunch. Please tell Ms. Hart I'll call her." And she bolted from the room and scurried downstairs. I leaped up and called after her, but she was already gone.

I groaned softly, wondering how I could have handled this better. Most abused women are frightened—for good reason. Emotional and physical battering drains the life out of a person's self-esteem. So often the abusive partner reflects the blame for any violence back onto the victim. What would Dr. Aster say? I glanced at my watch. Two hours until my appointment with Dr. Phipps. I could pound out a column and get Jillian off my back for the week. Using Annabelle's computer, I connected with my e-mail from *Bloom!* and found just the right letter.

Dear Dr. Aster:

I've recently left my husband of twenty-seven years after many years of considering the move. On the one hand, I'm relieved—no more waiting up to see what mood he'll come home in and whether he might take it out on me. On the other hand, I'm desperately lonely. And poor. Cliché or not, I worked as a secretary to help put him through law school. At his insistence, I stopped once the children came and now my skills are strictly Stone Age. Who wants to hire a washed-up housewife who freaks out at the happy sound of a computer turning on?

Doctor, he calls me every day to apologize and beg me to come home. Honestly, the idea appeals. Would that be a mistake? He says he loves me so much that it hurts.

Sincerely, Frozen in Framingham

Dear Frozen:
I may be short on words of wisdom, but I do have some thoughts about your dilemma. You mention you've been thinking about leaving for years. Taking the leap must have been enormously difficult. "Moodiness" aside, your husband sounds very bright. And twenty-seven years working together to raise a family is nothing to sneeze at.

But when I read "moods" and "take it out on me," I hear warning bells of possible abuse clanging loudly. Abusive spouses have intermittent reinforcement down to a science— meaning you've probably experienced a period of loving attention and sincere regret following any episodes of bad behavior. Unfortunately, the cost of abuse is most often taken out in the woman's self-esteem. Low self-esteem coupled with earnest apologies often lead to a repetition of the entire cycle, sometimes with escalating violence.

Of course you feel lonely and helpless. You've depended on this man heavily for many years. Before you go back home, please take the time to breathe and stretch. Like a plant that's been kept in a dark basement and suddenly moved outdoors, you're experiencing a shock to your system. But with some nurturing and professional support, you may find yourself bursting with new growth. And then your answers will come.

Good luck and keep us posted!

I saved the file and sent it off to Jillian, wondering how long Annabelle's patient had been married to this battering man and wishing she'd stayed long enough for me to raise some of these questions. I still didn't know her name. Glancing at the clock, I gathered my sweater, purse, and Annabelle's notes about the hated patient and headed out to see her therapist, whatever.

Outside, the sky had turned gray. It felt cold, almost like snow. Couldn't be—it was April. Though this *is* New England. As I left the building, I had the uncomfortable sensation of being watched—for the second time today. I jerked my head around, tracking Dr. Frazier's window shades. But saw nothing. I checked my watch and started down the block, hoping I hadn't gotten a ticket. A woman ran by me, snatching my purse from my shoulder.

Shocked and disoriented, I stumbled, then recovered my balance and my wits.

"Wait!" I shrieked.

I took off after her, chugging as fast as my legs could take me, my chest heaving. I'd run the fifty-yard dash once in junior high school PE—came in second to last. Intermittent yoga classes had not improved my wind and foot speed since then. Ahead of me, the woman flashed through the brick-paved courtyard next to Koffee on Orange Street.

"Help!" I called. "Stop, thief!" A homeless man slept on one of the benches, chin to reflective orange vest. His rheumy eyes flickered open, then shut.

I crashed around the corner into an alley and glimpsed the slender figure in jeans and sneakers. The purse strap broke loose and my stolen bag whipped over her shoulder, slammed into the wall of a building, and burst open on the pavement. The woman vaulted the wire fence at the end of the alley and disappeared. I leaned against the brick wall, huffing and cursing. The skies opened, releasing a torrent of cold rain.

Chapter 9

Legs trembling with fatigue and the shock of being robbed, I squatted down in the rain to gather up my sodden belongings—sunglasses, Palm Pilot, pens, lip gloss, wallet, Annabelle's day planner, tampons—littered amongst the junk that spilled over from the nearby Dumpster. My cell phone had skittered under a bag of rotting French fries. I jammed the stuff back into my busted bag, feeling myself slide from scared to angry. It's one thing to be a bleeding heart liberal and defend the desperation of the needy in the abstract, another to be robbed. I glanced at my watch. Damn. And now I was late. There was definitely no time to call the police and report the attempted theft. Or to dash home and change. Clutching the recovered pocketbook with its dangling strap, I hurried back to my car in time to collect a soggy parking ticket from the windshield. Double damn! What sadistic meter maid writes tickets in a cloudburst?

I blasted down Whitney Avenue and screeched into the

parking lot behind Dr. Phipps's office building at the corner of Edwards. I probed the recesses of the purse for my hairbrush. It was missing. Turning the heater up to max for a moment, I held my head in front of the hot air vent and finger-combed my hair. Then I blotted the worst of the mascara streaks off my cheeks and started for the building, cold, wet, and bedraggled. I hated to imagine how I'd appear to Annabelle's shrink friend: a slightly chubby thirtysomething with wrinkled clothes, scraggly hair, and smudged makeup. A not-so-young adult who seemed to have issues keeping herself up. And getting places on time. I tucked my hair behind my ears and marched up the stairs, on the defensive before even meeting this man.

He was waiting by the open door to his office, a tall man in a suit and tie, with thinning white hair and freckles that suggested his hair had once been red.

"I'm Dr. Rebecca Butterman," I said, thrusting my hand out and gripping his firmly. "I'm a friend of Annabelle Hart's. Thanks for fitting me in today. I'm so sorry to be late. My purse was snatched on the way over here." I held up the sodden square. "I'm lucky I got it back."

"Oh dear," he said, pushing his tortoiseshell eyeglasses up the bridge of his nose and ushering me into the room. "Please have a seat. How can I help?"

I settled into a soft chair, hoping my wet clothes wouldn't stain the buttery leather, and looked around, curious as always about the decorating choices of another therapist. I lean toward soft colors and generic artwork, featuring plants that don't require too much tending in the windows and sidewalk scenes from Paris over my desk. My theory is to make patients as comfortable as the situation allows and leave lots of psychological space for them to project their own fantasies. In other words, lay low in the personality department.

Dr. Phipps came from a different school. At the far end of the room he had two sand trays and a wall of figurines similar to Annabelle's. Closer to where I sat, African masks and an Italian mandolin with an ivory inset hung on the wall. A spear of some kind leaned into the corner behind his chair. The furniture was carved mahogany, and his carpet a deep blue Oriental. Either he was well traveled, sophisticated, and fearless, or eager to make that impression.

"I didn't actually come to talk about me," I said, shifting my gaze back to him. "It's Annabelle. The thing is, I'm not sure whether you're her therapist or her supervisor. But whatever the case, I need your help."

Dr. Phipps's expression remained kind but neutral. "Tell me more about what brings you in today."

My jaw quivered as I described what had happened to my friend.

"Oh my goodness," he said, finally dropping the phlegmatic mask. "I'm very sorry to hear that. Is she all right?"

"We're hopeful." I eased my feet out of my wet loafers and wiggled the toes, encased in damp stockings discolored by black shoe leather. "She's in a coma in the ICU so I'm taking care of her patients while she's out of commission. A few of them anyway." I shrugged sheepishly. "Most of them are either declining politely or just not showing."

"A coma!" he exclaimed. "Who in the world would have done something like that?"

I scrabbled through the contents of my ruined purse and pulled out the soggy papers with Annabelle's notes on the hated patient. "This was on her desk."

Dr. Phipps skimmed the notes and then looked up, cupping his square jaw.

"I was thinking this might have some connection to the person who attacked her," I said.

Dr. Phipps looked horrified. "The police think one of her patients hurt her? Does she have clients that troubled in her roster?" He seemed to be asking this more of himself than of me.

This is every therapist's worst nightmare—getting wounded by one of the people you're trying to help. "Not that I'm aware of. Not that I've seen so far."

Try another way in. "I feel awkward even mentioning this. There's some concern on the part of the police about someone she might have been dating." I ran my fingers through my damp hair. "I'll just ask you right out: Was she in an abusive relationship?"

Dr. Phipps pinched the bridge of his nose above his glasses, his expression worried. "We did not discuss this."

He wrinkled his forehead, removed his glasses, and twirled them in his fingers. "The police have asked you to consult?"

"Kind of." I told him how Meigs had insisted I meet him at Annabelle's house and asked me to interpret the sand tray. I sighed heavily. "I know enough to know when I'm in over my head. That's why I came to you. I understand that you can't tell me about Annabelle's therapy, if that's why she sees you. But if there's something in that tray that could help identify the killer . . ."

My lips were trembling again. I was freezing; his air-conditioning was blasting. "I know it's irregular. I've spent the last two days telling the detective I can't show him her day planner or let him into her office or see patient notes. But we're professionals, you and I. If there's something worth passing on to authorities, I would figure out a way to do that without violating her trust." I dropped my elbows to my knees and clasped my hands. "Please, won't you help me?"

"The tray at home," said Dr. Phipps. "Tell me about it."

I blew out a breath of relief, smiled, and sat up. "Thank you. I'm not much of an artist, but I made a little diagram of what I saw in the box." I handed over the scrap of paper. The blue ink had run into mostly indecipherable smudges.

"This doesn't look familiar," he said, slipping his glasses back onto his nose. "I don't recall that we worked on anything similar. Your theory is that she constructed this at home, for herself?"

I nodded. "That's what I'm thinking."

"So she wouldn't have been censoring. She would have put anything she wanted in the tray, assuming no one would see it or ask for an explanation." He smoothed the rumpled scrap on his thigh.

"Would you say she felt threatened?" I finally asked.

Dr. Phipps squinted at the paper and shook his head.

"I'm sorry about the scribbling." I leaned across the space between us and pointed at the lower quadrant. "There was a beautiful fairy perched on a leaf, right here. And some kind of horrible guy in a space suit holding an axe not too far behind her."

"The doom master," said Dr. Phipps, getting up to cross the room. He plucked a figurine off one of his shelves and brought it back to me.

"That's him!"

He nodded thoughtfully and sat down. "When you ask about her feeling threatened, do you mean on a conscious or unconscious level?"

"Either one I suppose," I said.

"That's what makes sandplay so difficult for lawyers and forensic types to understand. The meaning of the arrangements develops at many levels. And we learn a lot during the construction of the trays and the discussions with our clients afterward. We don't have any of that to go on with Annabelle."

"But if you simply had to guess?" I pleaded.

He sighed and shifted in his chair. "Death in the psyche isn't always bad news. The doom master threatening the fairy could mean the death of old ways, something child-like that she struggles with. She also might have been working with a patient's issues. Mulling them over."

"There was a baby buried in the sand," I said, remembering Meigs scolding me for reaching to pick it up. "That could mean she was feeling vulnerable, right?"

Dr. Phipps laced his fingers together. "I hold many possible interpretations and meanings in my mind as the client works in the tray, rather than making firm judgments. I note the order that she puts things into the tray and how her energy changes in the process. After the client finishes for the day, I sit with her, looking at what she's built. And then ask for her ideas about its meaning, where it came from, whether there are words to put with the pictures."

I sighed heavily. "This isn't going to be very helpful to the cops."

"Probably not," he said, his blue eyes soft and full of regret. "What would be most helpful to *you* right now?"

I sat back, gripping the leather armrests, exhausted and flooded with sadness. Wiping my face with my sleeve, I asked, "Can I do a tray?"

Chapter 10

On the way home to Guilford, I mulled over the sand tray I'd constructed in Dr. Phipps's office. Maybe the urge to build a tray came from the wish to help Annabelle and her patients. But it had felt more like a physical yearning to show something of myself—to me. Dr. Phipps had waited in silence while I walked back and forth between the tray and the shelves, choosing and placing figurines, at first feeling silly, then completely absorbed.

The unattended baby in the corner of my tray was definitely not breaking news: My mother's death when I was four might never be completely processed. And selecting the tiny plastic girl with yellow hair, a green dress, and a hobo-style stick over her shoulder for the center of the tray was no big revelation either. I'd left home, metaphorically speaking, when I was very young.

But the thick woods I'd chosen to lay along one end of the tray did surprise me. With Dr. Phipps watching, I'd advanced the little girl with her black sack toward the woods, then turned her around and marched her away. Once I sat back, seeming to be finished, Dr. Phipps dragged a chair up beside me.

"What do you think?" he asked.

I shrugged. "She's walking away from something." Duh. "Something not entirely conscious." Double duh.

"Once upon a time, at the edge of a deep woods," said Dr. Phipps in a singsong voice. I closed my eyes, imagined myself lying in bed, sinking into a bedtime story.

"That's how our fairy tales often begin," he said. "Any thoughts about what's in your forest?"

My eyes prickled and I covered my mouth with my hand. "It's a man," I said through the fingers.

"Are you working with someone in therapy?" he asked.

"Dr. Goldman," I said, heaving a sigh. "But I canceled my appointment today to see you." We exchanged rueful smiles. The timing couldn't be random—it meant something—it always does. "We've been needing to talk more about my father. I've been threatening to contact him."

Dr. Phipps raised his eyebrows. "Threatening?"

"We've been estranged for years. He left the family after my mother died and just never returned. I sent him an e-mail last Christmas saying I thought it was time we talked, but I received an auto-reply that he was on sabbatical in Thailand. The urge to reconnect seems to have slipped to the back burner this spring." I cleared my throat, feeling embarrassed. "I'm surprised that Goldman and I haven't dealt with this."

"Don't feel badly," he said with an encouraging smile. "Sometimes when words aren't enough to express a particular issue, the images in a sand tray can. Could be you've uncovered a deeper level of sadness and abandonment than what you already knew. It will be useful to take this back to Dr. Goldman."

Goldman would love hearing that I moved further psychologically with one sand tray than we'd managed to talk out in the past three months.

Dr. Phipps smiled and looked at the clock on the wall, a dark mask carved out of a piece of mahogany with the hours dancing around the edges of the face. I regretted thinking that his display of African art was designed to make him look worldly.

"It's been nice to meet you," he said. "If I think of any possibilities that might help with Annabelle, I'll certainly let you know. Will you kindly keep me posted about how she's doing?"

❦

Back in Guilford, I made a quick stop at Bishop's Orchards for stir-fry veggies and a carton of milk, fresh from a Connecticut dairy. The image of the small piece of flank steak marinating at home in soy sauce, sesame oil, and a little sugar had me salivating madly. Having skipped lunch and been through hell this afternoon, I wondered if I'd have the patience to wait thirty minutes for brown rice to cook. Though a meal without carbs is no meal at all.

Jackson attacked my ankles in his adorable kitten way as I came in with the groceries. I started the rice and called for Spencer, eventually tracking him down to a tight ball of gray fur tucked between my pillows. He pretended not to hear me come in. I rubbed his ears and ran my hand down the velvety length of his spine.

"Who's the most handsome cat in town?"

He yawned and stretched. I changed into my most comfortable sweats and Spencer followed me back into the kitchen, tail waving. He and I both lost our mothers too young—it's definitely affected my confidence, but not his. I fed the cats and dialed the nonemergency number for the New Haven police.

"I'd like to report an attempted purse snatching," I said, and described the incident outside Annabelle's office.

"What exactly was stolen?" the dispatcher asked.

"I recovered everything except a hairbrush," I said, adding a small chuckle. "No need to put a BOLO on that." She took down my information and a description of the girl, encouraged me to come into the station to make an official report, and scolded me for running the perpetrator down.

"This is exactly how civilians get injured," she said.

I hung up, too tired to argue. Switching on *All Things Considered* on National Public Radio, I began to julienne carrots and red peppers and cut an onion into bite-sized hunks. I swished a handful of minced garlic and ginger in a pan of hot oil, then added the sliced flank steak and stirred. My jittery nerves relaxed as the ingredients sizzled and their pungent aromas filled the kitchen.

Forty-five minutes later, Angie called as I was sopping up the last bit of sauce with a second helping of rice.

"I hear you chewing. What's for dinner?" she asked. I described the stir-fry. She moaned. "I'm stuck with takeout from Boston Chicken. How's Annabelle?"

"I still haven't seen her. It's been a day from Hades." I told her about the meeting with Meigs, chasing the girl in the rain, and the consultation with Annabelle's sandplay expert, whiting out the construction of my personal tray. That I wasn't ready to share. "I'll feel terrible if she got herself involved in an abusive relationship and I knew nothing about it."

"I don't know her as well as you do," said Angie, "but that doesn't ring true. Anyway, if the shrink thought Annabelle was being threatened, wouldn't he have taken some action?"

"Unless someone's life is in literal danger, there's not much to do," I said. "You can't make someone leave home if she isn't ready. In that case, building a therapeutic relationship so the woman can examine her feelings and her options *is* taking action."

"Have you met her boyfriend?"

"We were supposed to have dinner tomorrow. With Bob. That certainly isn't happening." My phone buzzed indicating another call coming in. I checked the screen: Meigs.

"I'll call you later," I yelped to Angie, and pressed the button to accept Meigs's call.

"Yes? It's Rebecca."

"They'll allow you to see her if I escort you. Can you be at the main entrance to the hospital in an hour?"

Chapter 11

Meigs met me outside the door to the ER at seven o'clock, as we'd planned. He nodded hello, then took a second look. "Did you do something different to your hair?"

Was he kidding? I hadn't touched a comb since this morning, unless you counted my fingers. "I've had a horrible day and got drenched in the rain. Give it a rest, okay?"

He looked like he'd been slapped, his face blotching red, almost in the shape of a hand. "Sorry." He pushed through the glass door, strode across the vestibule, and flashed his ID at the receptionist. I hurried behind him onto the elevator.

"Sorry to sound snappish," I said. "I appreciate you setting this up."

He punched the button for the sixth floor. "We're finished with your friend's house—it's no longer a crime scene. So you're free to go water the plants, feed the cat, knock yourself out."

He ducked his head, still staring down the lighted numbers above the door.

"If you're finished with Annabelle's place, that means what?"

"We have a guy in custody," he grunted. "A thug from New Haven. I told you—he hit a number of the houses in the neighborhood. And we found two of her rings at his crummy rat hole. He says he was set up—the house was supposed to be empty and she surprised him."

"How do you know they were her rings?"

"Can't discuss that," he said. "Take it from me, your friend was in the wrong place at the wrong time."

I squashed a fierce urge to lash out. He was doing me a favor. All I needed was for him to storm off the elevator and down the stairwell. I'd never see Annabelle. I pulled in some air and lowered my shoulders.

"She was in her own home, in a nightgown, beginning to get ready for work," I said, trying for a calm voice, something pleasant, conversational, and just a tiny bit curious. "How can that be the wrong place?"

He didn't say anything. Which brought on another burst of irritation.

"And you're closing her case even though this so-called thug says it was just an accident? In spite of those other theories you were so vigorously pursuing earlier?"

The elevator lurched to a stop and the doors swished open. Polson, the white-coated medical social worker, was waiting, cutting off any further discussion. Just as well, the way things were going.

"The head nurse told me you'd be coming." He smiled at me, but planted himself in the middle of the hallway. "I hope you understand that the staff hasn't singled you out for a hard time: Ms. Hart's condition is fragile and the family requested that outside stimulation be kept to a minimum. Her doctor agreed."

"You mean Victoria," I said. "Victoria is her family."

"Exactly," said Mr. Polson.

"Understood," said Meigs. He grabbed my wrist, circled around the social worker, and started toward the entrance to the unit. "Did the head of the department give us permission or did he not?"

Polson bobbed his chin, lips set in a thin line. He glowered at Meigs, then followed him over to the unit entrance, swiped his ID through the slot on the wall, and pushed open the door. "You just missed her sister," he said with another icy smile in my direction. "She's been here all day—Ms. Hart has experienced some additional cranial swelling."

Meigs stopped at the nurses' station and showed his badge to Nurse McHugh.

The nurse turned to me. She didn't look happy either. "As Mr. Polson no doubt told you, she's had a hard day. Believe it or not, it's not our job to make sure *you* get what *you* need here. The patients on our unit are gravely ill."

And the staff are grizzly bears, I thought. "Understood," I said.

"I'll be waiting here in the hall while Dr. Butterman visits her friend," Meigs told her. He started toward Annabelle's cubicle and signaled me forward.

"Thanks so very much for your support," I gushed, gesturing to include both the social worker and the nurse. I'd grovel if needed—they held the keys to Annabelle's cell.

I edged into my friend's room, dreading the sight of her so vulnerable and sick. At first glance, she looked worse than she had when I found her earlier in the week—if that was even possible. Most of her head had been shaved—not by a competent stylist—exposing a line of stitches around a flap just above her ear. Her top lip was swollen and split. I told myself that the rainbow of bruises around her lips, eyes, and cheeks meant healing in progress. The machines on the far side of the bed beeped softly as I watched the rise and fall of her chest. A clear plastic bag full of urine hung from the bottom of the bed.

I sank into the bedside chair and reached for her left hand, then pulled back, noticing the splint on her two smallest fingers. I folded my hands in my lap and searched for the right thing to say. Spring was the only thing that came to mind. Not that today had been a great example, but Annabelle wouldn't know that. This season is why New Englanders suffer through our miserable winters, gray and cold and overly long. We wait and wait and wait, until finally spring unfurls, bud by glorious bud. Annabelle loves it.

"Spring has sprung," I said, my voice coming out croaky and weak. "Those little baby pink and green leaves that you're nuts over, they're starting to show. And you should see the flowering pears in front of the Guilford Food Center. Gorgeous. Oh man, and the weeping cherry next to the April Rose bridal shop—absolutely stunning! But that forsythia bush on the triangle, just before the Madison Green? They must have pruned it when it was budding last year; it's just not that pretty. It's going to have too many leaves and not enough blossoms."

Her chest rose and fell, rose and fell, with no sign that she'd heard anything. I felt a surge of panic and blurted out: "For God's sake, Annabelle, wake up or you'll miss the whole damn thing." I covered my mouth with my hand—what an ass. You don't talk like that to someone in a coma. It's all supposed to be calm and positive. Some medical experts believe coma patients hear everything you say.

I took a deep breath and pushed myself to smile and radiate positive thoughts. Of all the equipment, Annabelle's breathing tube bothered me most. And the raw edges of skin exposed around it. I spotted a package of glycerin swabs on the nightstand, tore it open, and extracted one. After rolling it gently over her cracked lips, I threw it in the trash.

"You shouldn't worry about Jackson—I brought him home with me," I said after a few more desperate minutes listening to the hiss of her machines. "He's a doll. Well, Spencer doesn't think so, but they're getting used to each other. Jackson's following him around like a baby duckling. When you get back home, I suspect he'll really miss him. Oh, and I'll check on your plants tomorrow."

In the hallway outside, Nurse McHugh bustled by and flashed me the five minutes signal.

"I'm going to postpone the dinner with Russ," I told Annabelle, looking for a flinch or twitch—any negative reaction to his name. "First I wondered if we should go on without you, but that would be weird. He doesn't want to eat with strangers, right? You said he's a little shy."

She'd actually said "slightly awkward," but right now that sounded harsh.

"I'll tell him we'll take a rain check when you're feeling up to it. So I guess I'm cooking for Bob tomorrow night. What do you think I should make?" The machines beeped and gurgled. "Star Fish Market had some nice-looking salmon earlier this week. I could whip up a lemon caper butter sauce." I smoothed my hand over the stubble on her head, avoiding the tender-looking stitches that held together the gash above her ear.

"Yeah, I know, some men don't go for fish. It's not the most manly dish." I grunted like a cave dweller and then laughed. "I'll tell you a secret anyway: I'm not crazy about salmon. I make it for company because it never fails to impress and it's supposed to be so damn healthy. All those omega-3's or whatever." Annabelle's eyelids flickered and then settled. I sucked in a breath, waiting to see if this signaled a change in her condition. Nothing. Tears filled my eyes.

"I'm definitely not in the mood for grilling. I got soaked in the rainstorm this afternoon and I've felt chilled to the bone ever since."

I gazed around the room, fighting to keep my composure. The expensive arrangement of iris and daffodils I'd had sent over yesterday was sitting on the heat register. The water in the clear glass vase had evaporated down to its last inch and the flowers were drooping. I felt a spike of rage, imagining Victoria emptying out the water when she saw they were from me. Or deliberately placing them on the hot air vent. It had been a long, frustrating day: Maybe I was beginning to hallucinate. Annabelle's lips moved around the breathing tube, which probably meant nothing. I took another deep breath and continued, not wanting to waste my last precious minutes with her.

"I'm tempted to go right to comfort food, the hell with impressing Bob. I don't even care what his cholesterol level is. We haven't gotten that personal." I laughed sheepishly, thinking about my earlier conversation with Mark. "What about meat loaf and mashed potatoes? Or maybe spaghetti carbonara? With an antipasto to start?"

Nurse McHugh stuck her head into the room. "Time's up."

I collected my purse, stood, and touched my fingers to my lips, then to Annabelle's forehead. "You hang in there. I love you."

When I turned to leave, Meigs was leaning against the door, watching. How much had he overheard? What an idiot, he must have thought, babbling on about spices and menus with my friend unconscious.

"You were making me hungry," he said.

I pinched the inside of my arm and forced a smile. I was sick of sniveling in front of this guy. "Thanks for helping me see her."

He felt for his back pocket, then yanked out his cell phone and studied it, his forehead furrowed. "I have to go." He turned and banged out of the unit.

My phone rang as I walked down the hallway toward the exit—it was Bob. I perched on a chair in the waiting area, not wanting to lose our connection by getting on the elevator. And suddenly realizing I was exhausted.

"I've been trying to reach you," Bob said. "How are you doing? How's Annabelle?"

"Detective Meigs helped me get in to see her." I lowered my voice. "Frankly, she looks awful. And she's still unconscious. It's really scary."

"I can imagine," he said.

"What time are you arriving tomorrow?" One of his bear hugs would feel good.

"My plane gets in around three. If traffic's not too bad, I should get to your place by four thirty? Unless you want me to meet you at the hospital?"

"Home is fine," I said. "How do you like the sound of spaghetti carbon—"

The elevator doors slid open and a man came into the waiting room. I recognized him from a photo Annabelle had shown me of her renovation in progress. Russ Wheeler, the boyfriend/carpenter. My heart began to pound.

"Oh my God," I said under my breath.

"What's the matter?" asked Bob.

"I've got to go," I said. "Annabelle's boyfriend is here. I haven't had the chance to tell him much of anything about the attack." Or question his whereabouts that morning, or feel out any possible motivation or warning signs of an abusive history, I didn't say.

"There's no reason he shouldn't join us," said Bob. "Poor guy could probably use a home-cooked meal."

"But—" How did I explain that Russ might have been the one who put Annabelle in the hospital, when Russ himself was standing right in front of me?

"Go ahead and ask him," Bob said, blundering on in his cheerful way. "We'll have other chances to be together alone. It seems like the right thing to do."

"Fine. I'll call you back."

"I don't mind holding at all," he said, "unless you'd like me to talk with him."

I sighed, laid the phone on the chair next to my purse, and stood to introduce myself to Annabelle's friend, hoping he wouldn't notice the hair on the back of my knuckles and forearms bristling like dog hackles. It wouldn't hurt to have Bob listening in case things turned ugly.

Russ had a full head of spiky white-blond hair—no middle-aged thinning here—and a good tan for this early in the season. With eyes that blue, I wondered if he was at risk for skin cancer. Or was that an old wives' tale? He filled out a pair of pressed jeans and a white dress shirt in a solid way I couldn't help noticing. Different from Bob, who is tall and angular, except for the slight rounding of his belly.

"You must be Russ Wheeler," I said. "I'm Rebecca Butterman, Annabelle's friend." I managed a shaky smile but didn't offer my hand.

"How is she? I was hoping to see her," he said, holding my gaze long enough for me to notice the ring of darker blue around his pupils. His eyes were incredible.

"About the same," I told him. "But I literally needed a police escort to get in. The staff is brutal. How did you even get upstairs?"

"Sheer charm." He grinned. "In other words, sometimes it's better not to ask permission."

We exchanged shocked comments about the attack and I apologized for the spoiled dinner plans the next night, all while watching for any hint that he knew more than he should about her condition. "My friend Bob"—I gestured to the phone where Bob was patiently hanging—"was thinking you should come for supper anyway."

"Thanks, but I wouldn't want to intrude on your evening."

"Annabelle would want her friends to be together at a time like this."

Russ chuckled. "You can't give Annabelle *everything* she wants."

What did he mean by that?

Bob's tinny voice echoed from the cell phone, insisting that an extra diner would be no trouble. No trouble at all, and we'd love to meet him.

"No really, we insist," I echoed, and gave Russ directions to my condo, agreeing he could bring something to drink, his choice, since I obviously had no idea what I was serving.

"What project are you working on now?" I asked. "Annabelle said you've finished with her place. And by the way, it looks magnificent."

"I've got a job in Sachem's Head. We're gutting the inside and starting over. They had a new kitchen put in five years ago"—he shrugged, blue eyes twinkling—"but they write the checks and I do what I'm told."

"Must be long hours on a job like that," I said. "You guys start at the crack of dawn, right?"

"Not in that neighborhood," he said. "You fire up a saw or a nail gun before eight and the neighbors call the cops."

This information did nothing to reassure me. I tried to think of a casual way to ask him about the attraction between him and Annabelle, without coming right out and saying that on the surface they didn't seem to have too much in common. Other than that he was a hunk and she was a lonely single woman just waiting to be preyed on. But he looked restless and Bob was still yammering on the cell phone.

"I'll call you back," I told Bob and hung up.

"Are you headed out?" I asked Russ.

He shook his head. "I'm going to see if I can speak with her doctor."

"Don't hold your breath," I said. "Best I've been able to get is the social worker." I smiled quickly, wishing I hadn't sounded so snotty. Annabelle was a social worker after all, and a very good one. Polson just raised my hackles.

I dialed Bob again once I was out on the sidewalk. The afternoon's storm had cleared away, leaving a crisp, cold night—at least it smelled like spring, once you got past the cigarette smoke from the desperate patients and visitors toking up outside the entrance.

"What was all that about?" he asked.

"The cops were asking me about Russ just this morning," I said. "There was some question about whether he was the one who beat Annabelle up." I started into the pedestrian tunnel that led to the parking garage. "Now Detective Meigs says it was a random robbery that she interrupted, but I'm not so sure." Did Meigs *really* buy that version?

"Does he seem like that kind of man?" Bob sounded appalled.

"Not really," I said. "But this was the first time I met him so what do I know?"

"You're a psychologist. You have a nose for these things."

"You'd think," I said. "We'll both look him over tomorrow."

"I can't wait to see you!" said Bob. "My parents want to meet you too. Dad set up a golf date for us on Saturday. It'll be a low-stress introduction."

"But I don't play golf," I said, my teeth gritted. Nothing about golf is low-stress in my opinion. Not only am I an athletic zero, just stepping onto the golf course would bring back difficult memories of the golf psychologist who had been my dating "transitional object." That's shrink-speak for trying to rush things after a lousy divorce. Plus, Bob and I are nowhere near the stage of parental introductions. I didn't want to deal with this now, when I'd just come face-to-face with Annabelle's critical condition. And her possible assailant.

"Maybe another time," I added, trying not to sound whiny. "It's hard to concentrate on anything with Annabelle in the hospital."

"It'll get your mind off your problems," Bob said. "My mother doesn't play much either. We've got a tee time at the little public course in Old Saybrook—it's only nine holes. Katharine Hepburn's old house is right off the second hole. You won't believe it—water views from every tee box!"

I couldn't stop myself: I lost it.

"I. Don't. Play. Golf," I snarled, enunciating each word as I stalked out of the tunnel and into the parking garage. Maybe the person I didn't want to face in the deep forest of my unconscious was not my father: Maybe it was Bob.

"You're breaking up," he said. "Give me a buzz when you get home. I'm really looking forward to this weekend."

I snapped the phone shut. Elevator or stairs? I wasn't in the mood for hiking three dim flights, but elevators at night give me the willies even worse—you could get closed in with a creep and have your purse snatched at knifepoint before you got to the next floor. I hurried up the stairs to the fourth floor, breathing a sigh of relief as I pushed out into the garage, and started down the row of cars, keys in hand. This day couldn't end soon enough.

Seeing Russ in the hospital had been a shock. There was a lot I still didn't understand about him and Annabelle. I could certainly understand the *physical* attraction. But he hadn't been at all what I'd expected, actually more smooth than awkward. Could it be that Annabelle was uncomfortable about her friends meeting him, and not the other way around?

A large car, driving too fast for the garage, veered toward me, almost clipping my leg. I leaped away and it sped past.

"Asshole!" I yelled after him. "Don't be a drama queen," I muttered to myself, patting my heaving chest and trotting toward my parking space.

Then the same vehicle squealed around the corner again, headed right at me. Rigid with fear, I dashed between the closest parked cars, tripped, and skidded across the cold cement on my knees and elbows. The engine whined as the vehicle backed up, and then a car door slammed and I heard the echo of footsteps coming my way. I rolled under the SUV to my right and curled behind one of the tires. Blood rushed in my ears, I could smell gasoline, and my hands felt slippery with sweat and motor oil. I trembled like a frightened rodent, holding my breath and fighting the urge to scream and scream. With no one around to help, I'd only be giving myself away.

Seconds later, I heard another vehicle drive up and honk impatiently. The footsteps retreated, the door slammed, and both cars pulled off. I waited to be sure they weren't circling around the garage, then crawled out from under the truck. On hands and knees, I fumbled for the contents of my purse, which had scattered across the pavement for the second time today. The safety pin I'd used to fasten the strap had broken loose.

My hand closed over my cell phone and I crept along the edge of the garage until I had enough of a signal to call out. I speed-dialed Meigs's number.

"Meigs," he said.

"It's Rebecca," I whispered. "There was a hit-and-run in the parking garage. Well, not really a hit, but they tried."

"They tried? What do you mean? Are you all right?"

"I think so," I said in a trembling voice.

"What did the cops say?"

"I haven't called anyone. I called you."

"Listen to me. There's nothing I can do from here. Get off the phone, dial 911, and go to the emergency call box by the elevator—there's a blue light marking it. Go now— get some help," he barked, and hung up.

I held the phone at arm's length. Had this really happened? Yes, he'd hung up. I spotted the blue light against the wall, stumbled over, and stammered into the speakerphone.

"I've been involved in a hit-and-run," I said, and described my location. Only when I saw a patrol car nose up the ramp, lights flashing, did I sink to the curb and begin to weep.

Two uniformed hospital security people came running up the ramp behind the New Haven police cruiser.

"What happened?"

I stammered half sentences: "Car rushed me . . . rolled under . . ." I couldn't seem to catch my breath or stop crying. The policeman helped me into the backseat of the cruiser, where I heard the crackle of the dispatcher asking for information.

"The lady appears to be unhurt, just hysterical," the cop told her.

"We've had a problem with kids speeding in the garage lately," one of the security guards told the cop. "Sounds like another one of those."

Suck it up, Rebecca. I blew my nose, wiped my face with the sleeve of my raincoat, and got out of the car to stick up for my story. "It wasn't joyriding kids. They were heading right at me. They drove around"—I gestured to the right—"and came at me a second time."

"Could you identify the driver? Was there a passenger?"

"Probably not," I said. "It was too dark to see much more than shapes. A shape," I added. "I don't think there was a passenger. But the driver got out of the car and came looking for me. I rolled under this vehicle and crouched behind the tire." Not that they should have any trouble believing me—I'd torn the knees out of both pant legs and I was filthy and scraped up and smelled like motor oil. "If it hadn't been for the other guy who came up behind him and honked his horn, who knows what would have happened."

"Make and model of the vehicle?"

"Big and dark. Maybe an SUV." I glanced at the car where I'd hidden—a Suburban. "Not as large as this one. Sorry, I'm not too good with makes and models."

"License plate?" asked the younger security guard hopefully.

I shook my head, shoulders slumping.

"Any reason someone would be looking for you?"

I clutched my arms over my chest. My teeth had begun to chatter. "None that I know of. My friend's in the hospital. I was visiting."

"Are you going to be able to drive yourself home, or shall we call you a taxi?"

"I'll be fine," I said, tugging the raincoat around my waist.

"I'll follow you to the highway," said the cop. "Before you leave, let your husband know you're on the way."

"If only I had one," I said, wishing I could take it back before I even saw the pity on his face.

Chapter 12

I woke up the next morning at six feeling battered and tired. And spitting mad. Mad at all of them—cops, nurses, carpenters, Bob, Annabelle's sister—every single one. Meigs topped the list—I wanted to ream him out for blowing me off last night. Not that it was his job to follow me around, anticipating problems. But still, telling me to call security while I was being attacked by an SUV? Even if he was right, even if there was nothing he could have done, I wanted him to have tried. *Grow up, Rebecca*, another voice in my brain said.

Besides all that, I had strawberry bruises on both knees and elbows, and the knees had been ripped out of my favorite black pants—ruined beyond repair. It's not easy to find black pants that (a) disguise unwanted creases and bulges and (b) hold up neatly for multiple wearings without needing ironing or other time-consuming attention.

I brewed a pot of coffee, added steamed milk and a stick of cinnamon, and fed the cats. Spencer batted Jackson away from the food bowl, but it was a desultory swipe. He was well on his way to reconciling himself to Jackson's adoration, a graceful transition I didn't seem to be managing with Bob.

I settled back into bed with the cats and my coffee and called Angie. She was momentarily speechless after I described the parking garage disaster.

"He actually told you to call Security?"

"He is a busy man," I said. "And he was correct. The Yale security people are right there in the garage. Besides, there was probably some kind of emergency in Guilford," I couldn't help adding in a snotty voice.

"What, someone's cat on a roof? Too many teenagers congregating at the Jiffy Mart?"

I laughed. Angie reads the police blotter too.

"If it wasn't a juvenile delinquent on a learner's permit, who in the hell would try to run you down?"

I'd come right home, had a slug of cognac, and gone to bed—blocked that question right out. "Someone tried to kill Annabelle the other morning, that's what I think. I don't believe she came upon a robber. I think the beating was meant for her. And she's just lucky to be alive. If barely that." I sucked in a big breath. "You should have seen her. It's bad."

"What does her beating have to do with you getting mowed down?"

"Someone doesn't want me asking questions?" I set my coffee cup down on the bedside table. My fingers were trembling. No wonder I hadn't wanted to pursue this question last night.

"And that would be who?"

"Her boyfriend, her sister, one of her patients—that's who comes to mind for starters," I said.

"What are the cops saying?" Angie asked.

"Meigs said they're pinning the assault on a two-bit thug who was stupid enough to try to fence Annabelle's stuff. He's robbed some other homes in that neighborhood too."

"And you don't you believe this story because . . . ?"

"Even Meigs doesn't believe it. Why else was he still nosing around in Annabelle's business yesterday morning? Haven't you heard of false confessions? There was a story only yesterday on NPR—about a man who spent seventeen years in jail. His buddies said they heard him brag about the crime. He himself said he did it. Now the DNA evidence says he's innocent."

"You sound very dramatic," she said, using the conciliatory "there, there" voice she trots out when she thinks I'm about to lose it. "Why not just call your detective and ask what happened last night? While you're on the phone, maybe you can get him to tell you what he really thinks about Annabelle's case. Call me back after you've talked." And she hung up on me too.

I rolled out of bed and went back to the kitchen, considering the options over a bowl of oatmeal laced with raisins and honey and drenched with the rest of the steamed milk. Maybe I was acting dramatic. In that case, I wasn't going to call Meigs—I'd feel utterly pathetic. Last fall, I had befriended a woman who works in the records department after I'd made one too many visits to the police station. She might not have access to all the answers, but I thought she'd be willing to tell me what she did know.

While waiting for the records department to open, I read my e-mail and then showered, taking extra care with the blow-dryer. Not that you could ever erase the impression of a rat's-nest hairdo, once you'd worn one around town. I dressed in jeans, sneakers, and a sweater, then changed into corduroys and a heavy turtleneck. It did not feel like spring. At a couple of minutes past nine, I called the police department and asked for the records clerk.

"I'm Dr. Rebecca Butterman," I said when the woman answered in her unmistakable seal-bark voice. "You may not remember me but—"

"How could I forget?" she bellowed. "You were in here so often, I wondered if you were on the payroll."

I snickered weakly and asked if she'd heard anything new about Annabelle's case. "I'd call Detective Meigs, but I know how busy he is," I explained.

"He's not expected back for a couple of days anyway," she said. "Might even be the middle of next week."

"Was there an emergency in town last night?" I asked, fishing for his whereabouts but too chicken to come right out and ask.

"Not that I heard. All Quiet on the Guilford Front." She howled. She's a big fan of bad jokes. "But I can help you with the Hart case. It's definitely closed. The paperwork was here this morning when I arrived. Should I make you a copy?" A citizen can get copies of any closed cases she wants at a dollar a page.

"Why not?" I said. "I'll run by later to pick it up."

My landline rang as soon as I hung up. Caller unknown, the screen read.

"Hello?" I answered cautiously.

"Dr. Butterman," said a clipped male voice. "This is Dr. Craig Sebastian."

I couldn't have been more surprised. Sebastian is one of Mark's least favorite psychiatric colleagues, and he's even lower on my list. He'd prescribed medications for several of my therapy patients in the early days of my practice—oddly enough, most of them ended up quitting their work with me. Besides that, he and his wife had helped me escape from a possible stalker last fall—against his better judgment, of course. He'd made sure the entire psychiatry department heard a version in which I came off as a risk-craving nut job.

"I'm calling on behalf of our mutual patient, Laura Rose," he blustered. "She says you canceled her session for today. I'm fitting her in at noon as she appears to be in crisis."

"Dr. Sebastian," I said, pushing down a wash of bile that came with feeling embarrassed, angry, and most of all, scolded. "You know as well as I do that Laura Rose has a borderline personality disorder. She's very adept at splitting her caregivers. The worst thing we can do is take sides, one against the other."

"This is not about you or your practice," he replied. "The woman is in crisis."

Deep breaths, deep breaths. "Laura almost always presents in chaos—it's one of the issues we're working on. I spoke to her yesterday," I said, "and explained again that I was taking a few days off to go out of town and would see her next week."

"And yet here you are at home," he said.

"My plans changed," I stammered.

"The appointment will stand." He cleared his throat, a nauseating roll of phlegm against soft tissue. "I understand you are undergoing some emotional difficulties yourself. Should you need a consultation or a colleague to cover your cases while you reorganize your personal life, I recommend Dr. Frazier."

Unable to think of a response that didn't involve swearing like a crossed harpy, I hung up the phone, shaking with rage. What an imbecile. I couldn't believe he had the nerve to interfere with Laura. Even the most imperious medical

backup doc gives the benefit of the doubt when it comes to
this kind of patient. And where the hell did he come up
with Dr. Frazier as savior? Not only was it humiliating, it
was damn weird. Had she told him I was losing it? And if
so, why?

Chapter 13

Still steaming, I drove to the police department to pick up a copy of the case records, trying to shift my focus from ways to murder Sebastian to Annabelle's problems.

The records clerk handed me the papers she'd copied. "Doesn't it feel good when something terrible gets wrapped up so quickly?" she brayed.

Only it didn't feel good. The police had closed the case on Annabelle's attack, pinning the blame on a small-time doper from New Haven. This solution seemed way too simple.

I got back in the car and headed toward my friend's house. If I had been planning a crime, how would I approach this neighborhood? Of course it would depend on the job. A domestic spat involving an impulsive beating would require no planning at all. Russ's handsome face flashed to mind—I pushed it away. Nothing really pointed to him, aside from proximity and my own prejudices.

Many of the homes along the road leading to Mulberry

Point have small auxiliary pieces of property across the street that overlook a finger of the Sound. These parcels are designated as off-limits to outsiders, some claimed with rusty lawn chairs, others with unsubtle hand-lettered signs: *STAY OUT*. I pulled in on the one patch of unmarked grass. Someone could have parked here in the early morning or after dusk and then slipped up the hill to Annabelle's street. Would Meigs and his officers have considered this? Possibly not. Their investigation had been hasty.

I tucked a business card into my back pocket for "official" identification and crossed the road to talk to the neighbors nearby. No one responded to my knock at the first house. At the second, an elderly couple answered together, cracking the door and peering under their chain. The sweet smells of fresh coffee and cinnamon—sticky buns, I fantasized—wafted out. I pasted an earnest grin on my face and handed my card through the opening.

"You've probably heard about my friend Annabelle Hart who was attacked just up the hill?" I waved vaguely in the direction of her home. "I'm following up on a few loose ends for the police."

The old man nodded, glanced down at my card, and then rattled the chain off its peg and opened the door. "They're using psychologists for police work now, Mother. What next?"

I hurried on without correcting him. "We were just wondering"—the royal We, Meigs would be livid—"if you might have noticed any vehicles parked across the way last Tuesday morning? Over there." I pointed to my Honda.

The couple looked at each other. The woman thunked the floor with her cane. "I told you we should have called," she said.

"What did we know?" he shrugged, setting off a ripple of tremors in his neck and chin. "We get trespassers here all the time. People want to use our beach but it's all private property. That doesn't stop them, no, not at all. If we called the cops every time we saw a strange car, Mother, we'd never get off the phone."

"What did it look like?" I asked.

"Black, a luxury model like a Lexus or Mercedes," he said.

"That's why we didn't bother," said his wife apologetically. "Maybe dark green." She tapped her husband's leg with the cane. "He didn't have his glasses on. It was early."

"I can see fine," he said, shaking her off.

"Did you happen to notice the driver?" The old man bobbed his head yes; his wife shook hers no.

"He can't see that far," she insisted.

I left them squabbling, returned to my car, and drove up the hill. Had Meigs canvassed the neighbors around Annabelle's house thoroughly? My doubts snowballed—it seemed to me that they'd accepted the easiest possible answer and called it a wrap. I collected the mail from her box, slid the key out from under her pansies, and unlocked the door. The wind was whistling off the marsh, causing Annabelle's empty bird feeder to rattle. I could hear wind chimes clinking in the neighbor's tree across the road.

I locked the dead bolt behind me, turned on all the lights within reach, and set the mail on the kitchen counter. Annabelle had asked me to handle her professional affairs in case of emergency, not pay her bills. I reached for the pile and sorted through it quickly, dealing the junk mail to the right, bills and other real mail to the left. I was stepping over a line here, but who else would take care of this? Nothing appeared pressing. I considered the blinking light on the answering machine. Really, Victoria should be handling all this. Why hadn't she come by?

Next I went into the living room to tackle the mess the burglar had made. I swept the shattered pink clay vase into a

dustpan, debating whether or not to save the pieces. Before
dumping it into the trash, I fished out the two largest, which
spelled out "Mommy" when fit together. Swallowing the
lump in my throat, I collected the scattered pencils, pens,
and paper clips and stashed them in a ceramic mug that
read: "A house is not a home without a cat." The bare bones
of an advice column question that Annabelle could have answered well filled my brain, pushing the sadness away.

Dear Dr. Aster:
My divorce has finally come through. I couldn't wait to get my
own place—decorate it to suit my taste, spend time by myself, and
entertain my closest friends. Instead, nothing feels right and I'm
afraid of everything. Will my house ever feel like a home with just
me in it?
                              Sincerely, Sad in Susquehanna

Someone—Meigs?—had put the drawers back into
Annabelle's cherry wood desk. And some of the papers
had been gathered into a loose stack and replaced on the
desktop. I gathered up the stragglers and leafed through the
pile, looking for construction bills. *Or other clues*, I teased
myself. Dr. Rebecca Butterman, advice columnist and girl
sleuth.

Back in the kitchen, I sorted through the cleaning
products under the sink, found Annabelle's watering can,
and began to douse the houseplants. Returning for the
third refill, I noticed a packet of photos tucked behind the
phone on the counter. I set the can down and thumbed
through them quickly—a chronological documentation of
Annabelle's construction project. As the project unfolded,
the photos seemed to feature the carpenter more than the
building. Russ Wheeler was not only a hunk, he was a
clown. He mugged for Annabelle's camera in the process

of framing, carrying Sheetrock, and using a range of power tools.

There was no hint of tension between them—other than sexual, I had to admit. But my friend would hardly have been snapping cheery photos while they were fighting. And if they had been fighting, what over? Had she discovered a flaw in his workmanship and refused to pay his final bill? Or something much more personal?

Hearing a clattering from the front porch, I bolted across the room and peered out the window. Nothing was out of place. I was a sneak with a case of the creeps. My phone rang, nearly scaring the wits out of me.

Angie. "Hello?" I whispered.

"Why are you whispering?"

"I'm in Annabelle's house," I said in an almost normal voice. "I'm cleaning up but I feel like a criminal." My heart was thumping a million miles a minute. "What's up?"

"Did you call Meigs?" she asked.

"I called the records department. The clerk told me Annabelle's case is closed. But the neighbors down the street say they saw a luxury car parked in front of her home Tuesday morning. What are the chances of that belonging to a New Haven thug?"

"Drug dealers have some pretty fancy wheels," Angie said. "Or maybe it was an early riser out walking her golden retriever. They need a lot of exercise and if you don't have a big yard—"

"No one saw a damn dog." I shouldn't be snapping at Angie—she was trying to help. Besides, my detective work consisted of interviewing one old couple.

"If the case is closed, why are you still snooping?"

"I'm straightening up her place." She wouldn't know the layout of the neighborhood, though she did know me pretty well. I explained again about the one and only parking place in this exclusive neighborhood and the elderly couple's perfect view. "I don't buy the official version. If you could see Annabelle"—I sniffed—"this is no simple robbery."

"It doesn't sound right to me either," she conceded. "So I made some calls for you. No news about a false robbery confession, but I reached my lawyer friend in Greenwich. Victoria White cleaned out both of her ex-husbands in the process of divorcing them. If I was number three, I'd definitely be concerned. And there have been money problems between the sisters—something to do with the disposition of a trust. I couldn't pry out any details. Attorney-client privilege and all that good stuff."

"Hmmm." I rubbed my chin against my shoulder. "What if the fancy car belonged to Victoria?"

"You think she swooped in early, beat her own sister up, then went back to Greenwich to a party?"

"It does sound far-fetched," I admitted.

"What's your plan from here?"

"Finish watering the plants and tidying up." I replaced the green plastic can under the sink and closed the door with my hip. "After that I'm going to talk to her neighbor across the way and then call Mark."

Angie's voice went on full alert. "Call Mark for what?"

I told her how Dr. Freaking Craig Sebastian had phoned to inform me he was taking over one of my patients because Dr. Freaking Frantic had tattled I wasn't in any shape to take care of her. Or that was my working hypothesis anyway.

"Mark's the only one in the psychiatry department who will poke around for me without asking too many questions first."

"But isn't Bob arriving tonight?"

"I'm not asking Mark on a date. Give me a little credit," I said. Angie had been the one who introduced me to Bob, her old college buddy, back in December—and she's a little more invested in the outcome than I'd like. *Distract her with a feint and parry*, I thought.

"Bob insisted that Russ come to dinner too."

"Without Annabelle? Won't that be weird?"

"Bob insisted," I said flatly. "Why don't you come along too? We can both check him out."

"I'm there," she said, sounding a lot more cheerful. "I'll bring the wine, a bottle of white and one of red."

No arguments from me. With the week I'd had, this was shaping up to be a more-than-one-glass evening. "Seven o'clock. But call me if you hear anything new about the case."

I hung up and headed off to do the job I'd been avoiding: cleaning up Annabelle's bedroom. She shouldn't have to come home to a mess that reminded her of the trauma. I stripped the sheets from the bed, gathered up the rag rug and two towels that had been splattered with Annabelle's blood, and dropped the bundle by the front door. Better to work on the stains at home. I remade the bed with sheets I found in the closet—100 percent organic Egyptian cotton and sprinkled with cheerful yellow roses—they smelled like they'd been dried on the clothesline.

Sweeping the house one last time for anything out of place, I squatted down beside Annabelle's sand tray, studying the fairy, the monster, the baby. What troubles was my friend trying to work out? She hadn't told me anything. Not that I blamed her for being private: Each of us manages heartache in our own way. Some of us air our grief publicly, earning sympathy, support, and "there but for the grace of God" reactions—most of those behind our backs. The rest of us keep our sadness locked away in a dark space until one day it grows too big to be contained. Since the visit to Dr. Phipps's sand tray, my secrets had started to rustle again.

I returned to the kitchen to collect my phone and keys,

and at the last minute, punched *play* to listen to the messages on Annabelle's answering machine. Who else would do it? I assured my guilty self. Victoria sure didn't seem interested.

"Annabelle," said a languid voice. "Can't wait to see you again. Unless you'd rather go out alone—I'd make it well worth your while." A sexy laugh. "Shall I pick you up on Friday? What time?" Definitely Russ. "I promise we won't discuss sick families or dead babies, okay?"

What the hell was that about?

Next came a message from the Guilford Free Library. The books she'd requested—*Killer View* and *Mad House*— were in, and would be found at the circulation desk. Because *Killer View* was written by a popular new author from Guilford, it would only be held a week.

And finally, a courtesy call from the Toyota dealer spooled out of the machine, a woman following up on Annabelle's satisfaction with a service visit last week. As I made notes about the calls, I saw an envelope that had been tucked under the phone, hand-lettered on heavy cream stock. I slid the contents out.

Annabelle: Your plan is not acceptable. I will fight it legally and otherwise. You should expect a document to be served shortly. V.

Victoria. Had to be her sister, the ruthless bitch. I slipped the note back under the phone and left the house.

After stuffing the dirty linens in my trunk, I marched across the street to bang on the neighbor's door. No answer, other than a chorus of hoarse yapping from inside the house. But the pansies in the bathtub had been freshly watered and the hood of the rusting Dodge in the drive was warm to the touch. I circled around back and tapped on a glass pane in the kitchen door. A heavyset woman in pink terrycloth slippers and a University of Connecticut Huskies women's basketball T-shirt shuffled over, looking mistrustful. As soon as she cracked the door, one enormous black pug and two off-white ones wearing pink and green harnesses pushed out and flung themselves at my knees.

"I'm Rebecca Butterman, a friend of Annabelle Hart's?"

The woman's eyes narrowed even smaller as I passed her a business card and babbled about how I was trying to help the police. This story had gone over just fine with the old couple down by the water but this woman wasn't swallowing it. She studied me from the sneakers up to my tired eyes and blow-dried hair. I wished I hadn't said anything about the cops. What would win over a Huskies/pug fan with a bathtub in the yard?

"Annabelle's in the hospital—I'm sure you've heard." I decided to throw myself on her mercy. "The police investigation has tied this incident to the robberies that happened around here over the winter," I explained. "I'm not so sure they're right. Detective Meigs said you weren't home when the police canvassed the neighbors"—here I smiled conspiratorially—"so I wondered if you might have anything to add. Did you notice any unfamiliar cars or pedestrians that morning?" The black pug scrabbled for purchase on my leg.

"Get down, Finnegan," the woman scolded. The pug sat and stared, eyes bulging, looking from his owner to me, and back. "I didn't see anything," she said.

"What about the carpenter who's been working on her home, was his truck here at all?"

"Not this week," she said, wagging her head and sipping from a large foam Dunkin' Donuts cup. "He finished the job—came back for a few repairs, but I haven't seen him around this week at all."

I hated to tell her Annabelle's private business, but knowing the truth felt more important than confidentiality right now. Besides, this woman probably knew more about their relationship than I did just from watching out her window. "Turns out they've been dating," I said. "Was it possible he stayed over that night and left very early?"

"Nope," she said, sinking into a kitchen chair and loosening the folds of her shirt out from under her breasts. "I haven't seen his truck. The menopause has me, so I don't sleep much nights." She plucked at her collar and patted her belly. "It's a good night if I fall asleep by three a.m. But Finnegan here"—she pointed to the black pug—"he always knows if someone's out there who doesn't belong. If it's a man, that is," she said thoughtfully. "He never barks at the neighbor."

"Please call me if you think of anything else?" I touched the business card that she'd dropped on the table.

"How is she doing?" the woman asked. "Nobody deserves to be knocked around like that. I don't care what the man said she did." Her lower lip quivered and the smallest white pug jumped onto her lap and swiped her chin with his tongue.

"What man?" I asked.

The woman just stroked the dog and shook her head. "I'm just saying . . ."

"Are you saying someone hit Annabelle before the other day?"

She pressed her lips together and shook her head. "How is she?" she asked again.

"She's holding steady," I said with a sigh.

I got back in my car, wishing I'd been able to squeeze more details out of the taciturn neighbor. My watch read almost ten. Just enough time for a quick stop at the hospital before I went grocery shopping. Maybe the nurse who'd seen me visit last night would take pity and let me stop in—or at least give an unofficial update on Annabelle's condition. I dialed Mark's cell phone on the drive to New Haven.

"What's up?" he asked brusquely. "I'm about to go into a meeting."

"I'll be quick," I said, already regretting the call. I explained how Dr. Sebastian had interfered with my patient and how I suspected this had been set in motion by Annabelle's suite-mate. "I have the feeling she resents my friendship with Annabelle. She implied that she should be the one handling Annabelle's caseload, not me. Not that many of her patients are choosing to come in anyway," I finished.

"I don't know Dr. Frazier well," Mark said. "But I'll ask around and see what I can find out. Have a good weekend with what's-his-name," he added stiffly.

Would I ever figure Mark out? We hadn't been happy together; now he didn't seem happy apart. But I sincerely doubted that a reunion was the answer to either of our problems, at least in the long run.

Chapter 14

I circled around the streets radiating from the hospital until I found a parking spot several blocks away. I felt like a psychology lab rat who'd been shocked hard the last time he reached for the food lever: I could not make myself go back into that garage. Nor was I willing to pay the inflated bandit prices of the valet parking service.

I marched into the main entrance through the revolving doors and approached the desk, trying to radiate confidence and goodwill. And wishing I'd worn something more professional than corduroy jeans and sneakers.

"I'm here to visit Annabelle Hart, room six fourteen," I told the clerk.

She tapped the number into her computer. "Sorry, no visitors except immediate family."

"But they let me in last night. Has she taken a turn for the worse?"

The woman shrugged.

"Can you tell me her condition?"

She returned to her screen. "Serious."

Which meant nothing major had changed—worse than fair, not as bad as critical. "Why? Why can't she have visitors?"

The clerk turned away. "I don't make the rules, ma'am."

Feeling furious and helpless, I stomped toward the atrium, skirting the security guard without making eye contact and trying to think what to do. I wasn't calling Meigs, that much was sure. I have plenty of connections with the psychiatry department, but not with doctors in other medical branches. Would my gynecologist help me get in to see her?

I groaned and sank down onto a tiled ledge near the fountain to watch the people wandering through the space. There were patients in hospital pajamas pushing IV poles, some alone, some accompanied by relatives and friends. A frazzled mother breast-fed an infant while attempting to corral two noisy toddlers. And hordes of medical professionals in a rainbow of scrubs inhaled their caffeine fixes. What was going on with Annabelle that her would-be visitors weren't even allowed as far as the sixth-floor waiting room?

In the distance, I recognized the now-familiar, overly entitled figure of Annabelle's sister bustling toward the café. I sprang up, sprinted after her, and gripped her arm before she could get in line for coffee.

"Ouch!" she yelped, trying to brush me off. "Get away from me!" I let go. Then she recognized me and reverted to her usual unfriendly snarl. "What do you want?"

"We need to talk," I said. "It can be here"—I gestured toward the chairs and tables in the atrium—"or with the police. Your choice."

The bluff worked.

"You don't need to be so rough. Let me get a damn cup of coffee. We can talk while I drink it. That's all the time I can give you." She sniffed and called back over her shoulder. "You may be aware that my sister is ill."

I nearly knocked her down on the spot, but fell into line behind her for hospital sludge instead. *Stay cool, be calm*, I told myself. The oily film on my coffee trembled in its foam cup. We paid and settled into plastic chairs across the table from each other.

She crossed her legs and stretched them out. Her ankles were a little thick relative to the size of her calves, I couldn't help noticing cattily.

"Now what is your problem?" she asked.

"It's not me with the problem," I said through clenched teeth. "You're the one whose vehicle was seen parked several blocks away from your sister's home the morning she was beaten."

"What are you talking about? Are you crazy?" She took a small sip of coffee and wrinkled her nose. "I haven't been anywhere near Annabelle's home in months," she said. "I came directly here as soon as you called me and I have remained here ever since, except for the few hours a night I try to sleep. I understand that you're upset about Annabelle's condition, but really"—she tapped my hand—"there's nothing you can do for her right now. Maybe you need to take a closer look at your friendship with my sister. I understand that you might be feeling jealous, but truly, harassing me is not helping the situation."

I couldn't remember the last time I'd had such a strong urge to snap someone's neck. "You don't call trying to run me down in the parking garage last night harassment?"

Her eyes widened. "What is wrong with you?" She stood up, stroking a strand of highlighted hair into place with two manicured fingers. "Honestly, I think you need professional help."

"I saw the nasty note you wrote to Annabelle," I hissed.

"It was lying out in plain sight on her kitchen counter." A bit of a stretch, but she'd never know the difference.

The color drained from the skin around Victoria's lips, accenting a set of fine wrinkles that surely would be Botoxed into submission once she noticed them. She sank back into her chair.

"You can talk to me," I said quietly. "We're on the same side—Annabelle's. I know you love her too, whatever your differences might be."

"I never tried to run you down," she said, twisting the gold bracelet on her wrist. She glanced up. "You're attacking the wrong sister."

I sat back in surprise. "The wrong sister?"

She leaned across the table and squeezed my fingers, pale lips quivering. "I know the police are saying this incident resulted from a robbery," she said, "but I'm terribly afraid our younger sister did it."

"I didn't know you had another sister," I said, unable to keep from feeling a twinge of betrayal.

"We certainly do." She slumped back into her seat and pushed the cup of coffee away.

"Why in the world would she hurt Annabelle?" I wondered aloud.

"Long story." Victoria sighed, then leaned forward to whisper, "She's unstable. Has been for years. Bipolar disorder."

"Bipolar?" I said, then remembered Dr. Frazier's comments about fish oil capsules. Annabelle must have been desperate about her sister to even consider them. Why hadn't she said something?

"Heather's been in and out of treatment facilities for years," Victoria said. "My mother babied her. Why should she take responsibility when there was someone to bail her out every time she screwed up? Hence, the note," she said in a sheepish voice. "I simply couldn't bear to see Annabelle repeat the same mistakes that our parents did." She smoothed her hair behind her ears again. "You can't imagine how badly I feel about that note now that all this has happened."

"But why would she hurt Annabelle?" I asked again, not quite ready to forgive Victoria's coldness—either to my friend or me.

"I wish I knew." She sighed again. "If Annabelle said she'd help her and then didn't come through in a big enough way, it's possible that Heather might lose her temper. If she's off her medication and back on the sauce, anything can happen."

"Does she drive a Mercedes?"

Victoria just laughed. "Not likely." Her expression darkened. "Though she's often mixed up with creeps who'd love to get their hands on our family money."

"Why did you tell the staff I wasn't allowed to visit this morning? They wouldn't even give me a pass to get up to the waiting area."

"You shouldn't take everything so personally," Victoria said.

This from a woman whose job is gossiping in public, who had alienated half of Greenwich, Connecticut, not to mention at least two husbands.

She dropped her voice to a whisper. "Shock Daddy is on the floor."

I must have looked puzzled.

"You know, the gangsta rap star? He's very well known and very controversial. Apparently he was in a skateboarding accident." She made air quotes with her fingers when she said those last two words. "They're only allowing immediate family onto Annabelle's unit."

"Shock Daddy? No one at the desk mentioned that."

"They aren't going to tell random people he's there. What kind of security would that be? One of the nurses told me they expect to transfer him to a hospital in New York by tomorrow morning—so he can be close to his fans, I suppose. Or his dealers." She laughed, a mirthless tinkle.

"Will you help me get in to see her tomorrow?"

"I'll try." She stood up and gathered her purse.

"Have you met Annabelle's new boyfriend?" I asked, changing tactics.

"I haven't had that pleasure," she said, rolling her eyes. "Though he does sound better than the last one—a psychiatrist. Dating a shrink is so dreary. Who needs reruns of your family foibles during foreplay?" She chuckled, then got serious again. "Did you really get run down in the parking garage?" I nodded, rolling up my pant leg to show her the scrape on my knee. "The security guys think it was joyriding kids."

"There are all kinds of unsavory characters around this hospital and that spooky garage," she said. "I heard there was a robbery at knifepoint last month. If you insist on using it, stick to the parking spaces near the tunnel and the Security office. I won't go in there at all." She patted my hand again and swept out of the room, leaving her coffee cup and napkin for me to bus.

Chapter 15

I drove across town to Romeo and Cesare's, a small Italian market that stocks authentic pancetta and imported cheeses. I added baby artichokes and pencil-thin asparagus to my basket, along with a hunk of parmigiano-reggiano, a smaller piece of pecorino romano, and a loaf of crusty Italian bread. At the deli counter, I ordered two kinds of olives, a quarter pound of *sopressata,* pancetta, and a small container of mini-balls of fresh mozzarella.

"Spaghetti à la carbonara? Antipasto?" the round man at the cash register asked. He grinned when I nodded and looked pointedly at my empty ring finger. "This is the way to the man's stomach," he said, patting his own ample, apron-swathed belly. "My wife made it for me before we were married—that's all it took." He winked and fitted my deli packages and vegetables into a brown bag.

On the drive home to Guilford, I thought more about Annabelle's sister. In the end, I had a hard time believing everything she said. There might very well be a celebrity on Annabelle's ward, but that didn't explain Victoria's ice-cold reception the first day we met. As I mulled over her news about a third sister with chronic mental illness and a sleazy boyfriend, I remembered the graduation photograph I'd seen on Annabelle's bookshelf. And then flashed on the woman who'd asked about Annabelle's condition outside her office. I was suddenly quite sure this was the same woman who'd watched me leave the office the other day, and then fled in the rain. The skin on my neck crawled: I had a bad feeling my purse snatcher had been Annabelle's younger sister.

But why rob me? Drug money. Of course.

Once home, I unloaded the groceries, scarfed down a peanut-butter-and-raspberry-jam sandwich on wheat bread, and started to cook. If I had everything ready when my guests arrived, I could focus on making sure the chatter flowed comfortably. Not that Bob would have any trouble holding up his end of a conversation. Or Angie either, for that matter. I was most worried about Russ.

I diced the pancetta and scraped it into the frying pan, then began to mince an onion, the first Vidalia of the season. The hot oil would bring out the sweetness—a luscious contrast to the salty Italian bacon and cheese.

Mental illness in a family member can definitely split the family apart. I've seen it with my own patients, as families tried desperately to find a treatment that might normalize their loved one. And then struggled with the fallout when nothing worked—or not to their satisfaction. They almost always end up asking, "How much is enough?" Between the two sisters, I could picture Annabelle as the softie, even with all her experience with and training in mental health issues. It's much easier to set clear limits outside your own family.

I rustled six carrots out of the vegetable bin, peeled

them, and cut them into sticks. While they steamed along with the artichokes and the asparagus, I whisked together a mustard-balsamic vinaigrette. I doused the vegetables in the marinade and started on dessert, a three-layer red velvet cake with whipped cream, mascarpone, and cream cheese icing that never fails to impress. Even if the guests didn't gel tonight, the dinner would.

Once the chocolate cake batter was in the oven, I opened my advice column files, searching for sibling troubles. Maybe I could channel my worries about Annabelle into something useful.

Dear Dr. Aster:
At the risk of sounding harsh, my older brother is sucking my parents dry—both emotionally and financially. He's forty-four years old and has yet to hold a job for more than six months at a time. Each time he gets canned for using drugs or booze, he bounces back home to mooch off my folks. They aren't in good health themselves, and I resent the way his antics stress them out. Guess who's left to pick up the pieces? I also resent the steady drain on their assets—and my future. How can I turn things around?
Sincerely, Peeved in Portsmouth

Dear Peeved:
Is it possible that your brother is not the only one sucking your parents dry? Excuse Dr. Aster's high horse, but unless your parents are mentally incapacitated and you are named power of attorney, how they distribute their life savings is not your decision. That said, you certainly can talk with them about the difficult pattern you see the family falling into. Maybe they'd be willing to attend a session with an experienced family therapist? You don't say this, but it's possible that your brother suffers from a mental illness along with

addiction. A good therapist might help you and your parents assess the collateral damage to your family, think through possible treatment options, and offer support.

I saved the file and headed off to get ready for the party. I'd read it again tomorrow to see whether I'd been too hard on Peeved in Portsmouth. Funny how most of my advice ended up with the same refrain: find a shrink, see a therapist, talk it over with a professional. Probably not what most people wanted to hear.

The doorbell rang as I stepped out of the shower. I threw on my bathrobe and went to answer. Bob handed me a huge bouquet of spring flowers and swept me into a hug.

"I'm so happy to see you! Something smells amazing."

I squeezed back, feeling a little quivery and definitely grateful to have a boyfriend with good manners. "Same here. And the flowers are lovely. Do you mind taking them into the kitchen and making yourself a drink while I get dressed?"

He reached for the bag of groceries that sat on the stoop. "Bloody Marys okay? I brought the ingredients for my family's secret recipe."

"Wonderful. I'll be out in a flash."

I swiped on mascara and blush, and then sorted through my closet for the right outfit. My best-fitting black pants had been trashed in the parking garage incident. I pulled on my second favorite pair, slightly snug after the daily winter assault of extra calories and a reluctance to exercise if the temperature dropped under fifty. Pretty much a given in a New England winter. Leaving the top button undone, I layered on a pink silk baby doll blouse that Angie had talked me into— I still wasn't sure it was me, but it did have the double advantages of maximizing the average girl's cleavage while drifting low enough on the hips to disguise visible panty lines. I studied myself in the full-length mirror: A pair of pearl earrings and this would have to do.

"I used a stalk of your celery and a couple of olives," Bob said when I returned to the kitchen. "Hope you didn't have designs on them for dinner." He handed me a glass of red liquid topped with a green olive and a pepperoncini that I'd probably purchased last time I was single. "To the prettiest girl in Connecticut. And Georgia too." He clinked my glass and watched me gasp as the alcohol, Tabasco, and horseradish blasted my lips and throat.

We moved to the living room, where I lit the faux log from Stop and Shop in the fireplace and settled on the couch next to Bob. "You won't believe what's happened since I talked to you last night."

I told him about the parking garage, confronting Annabelle's sister, and my sweep of the Mulberry Point neighborhood. "Her neighbor doesn't think Russ was there the morning of the attack. I don't know if Annabelle and her boyfriend"—I cleared my throat delicately—"have been intimate. But she did allude to the possibility that he'd been violent."

"Annabelle said that?" Bob squawked. "How would this guy have the balls to accept a dinner invitation from her friends if he'd behaved that badly?"

"Annabelle didn't say it—the neighbor did. But some of these guys don't even recognize they're abusive," I said. "The power of denial is amazing."

"We'll size him up tonight," said Bob, his fists clenched in a boxer's stance. "I'll take care of him." He squeezed my knee, hard.

I yelped and nearly dumped the drink down my top.

"Sorry," Bob said, and leaned in for a soft kiss on the lips. "I'm awfully worried about you getting run down in the garage. Why didn't you call me?"

"There was nothing you could have done," I said, taking another swig of the Bloody Mary. After the first fierce fire down my gullet, the drink was spreading a pleasant glow. Lucky most of the cooking was finished.

Bob took the glass out of my hand, set it on the coffee table, and kissed me harder. I felt a *zing* that ran right down to my belly. The doorbell rang.

"Is it hot in here or what?" I popped up, fanning my face with my hand and grinning like a monkey.

Both Angie and Russ were waiting on the front stoop, Angie carrying two bottles of wine, Russ, a six-pack of Budweiser. Decked out in a swirling flowered skirt and her blond curls clipped up into a messy bun, Angie managed to look youthful but very, very elegant. Russ wore another white dress shirt and pressed jeans, and a look of supreme unease. He seemed bigger than he had in the hospital, not quite as tall as Bob, but more solid. Bob appeared at my elbow, kissed Angie's cheek, pumped Russ's hand, and drew them both into the living room.

"What would you like to drink?" he asked. "I'm plying the hostess with Bloody Marys, unless you'd rather have wine?"

Angie raised her eyebrows and smiled. "I'll stick with wine."

"Beer sounds good," said Russ. Bob returned with the drinks and began to pelt Russ with polite questions about carpentry, finding competent help, and the high cost of waterfront housing.

Over a second drink, I served the antipasto: brightly steamed asparagus, marinated carrots and artichokes, piles of olives, little blocks of sharp cheese, and miniature rolls of Italian salami. The conversation between the men toured through the surprise upsets in college basketball and Tiger Woods's prospects in the new season.

"This is one gorgeous dish," Bob said, winking at me.

I rolled my eyes. "Mind opening the Australian red?"

Russ drained the last of his beer.

"Another beer for you?" Bob asked him.

"I'll get it," I said, thinking Annabelle had reeled in a first-class oaf. As I got up to fetch the drink and start the carbonara, my knees buckled under me.

"Ahoy there, matie," said Bob, grabbing for my hand.

Angie followed me into the kitchen.

"I don't like him," I whispered, setting a pot of water to boil for the pasta and turning up the heat under the onion/pancetta mixture.

"I think he's just out of his league," she said, kneading my shoulders. "He doesn't know how to talk to smart women. I'll take him the beer—let me know if you need a hand."

I added wine to the frying pan, grated a mound of cheese, and whisked three eggs together. Annabelle was definitely a smart woman—what had they discussed? Did they have *anything* in common? With the salad dressed and carbonara steaming, I called my guests to the table.

"Did you ever get to see Annabelle last night?" I asked Russ, as we sat down to dinner.

"They wouldn't let me in," he said, splashing a bit of sauce on the tablecloth in the process of mounding his plate with pasta. "I called again this morning and the clerk said not even to bother."

"Apparently there was a punk rock star on the unit," I said.

"Gangsta rap," he corrected me. "Shock Daddy. He hit the top ten last week with "Assume I'm Right, Bitch." It's interesting stuff." Having twirled a wad of spaghetti onto his fork, he shoveled it into his mouth, chewed, and swallowed. "Don't give me no lip because I earn the check," he grunted, swaying his upper body like an overdeveloped snake charmer and tapping my grandmother's sterling silver knife on my Christian Dior china. It would take a hundred and fifty bucks on an eBay auction to replace that one plate. "Don't give me no lip, bitch, assume I'm correct—"

"You can't be serious," I said. "That's undisguised misogyny! That's the kind of bullshit music that gives young men a license to abuse."

"Whatever," said Russ, laughing. "Don't take it so seriously. It's just music. When you're working with your hands all day, you need tunes with a good strong beat. Rap does it for me. Could you pass the cheese down this way please?"

Bob stood and walked around the table to top off my wineglass. He patted my shoulder and smiled at Russ. "Another Bud for you?"

Russ raised a finger and Bob trotted into the kitchen to get the drink.

"Tell us about the renovation at Annabelle's house," he suggested when he returned. "Rebecca says it's beautiful." He sat back down at his place. "She says Annabelle loves it."

Russ grinned. "Lucky for me, that woman is easy to please."

"Oh for God's sake," I snapped. "Have some respect— the woman's in a coma."

"I meant it as a compliment," Russ said, frowning.

"What do you say we clear the dishes and play a game before dessert?" Bob asked and shot me a pleading look that said a decent hostess would throw her drowning party a life jacket.

"You have Boggle, don't you, Rebecca?" Angie asked. "We played it here last winter. Okay with you, Russ?"

He shrugged his massive shoulders. "Whatever you ladies want. I'm not much for games."

Steaming with annoyance, I went to find the Boggle box

while Angie and Bob stacked and rinsed the plates. Mr. "Don't Give Me No Lip" took up a comfortable lounging position on the couch.

"It goes like this," Angie explained when we were gathered around the coffee table. "We each take a turn shaking the cubes in the box. Then you have three minutes to make words out of the letters—diagonally, across, it doesn't matter."

"But the letters have to touch and you can only use them once," I added. "Shall we have a practice round?"

"Not on my account," said Bob.

"I'm fine," said Russ.

I handed out pens and paper, picked up the plastic box of letter cubes, and shook it hard. "Get the timer," I told Angie. "Ready?"

We scribbled words on our sheets while a stream of sand drifted through the blue plastic timer.

"Time!" Angie yelled.

"Would you like to begin?" I asked Bob sweetly. "Cross off any words that he calls out that appear on your list," I explained to Russ.

"*Rote, rest, these, hoe, get, grate,* 'to go,' " Bob said.

"Got all those," I said, "except for *to go.*"

"*To go?*" Angie said. "No way, pal, that's two words. You've been bageled, buddy. Russ, you're up."

"*Get, pog, hoe, rats, toy,*" he read.

I'd been hoping to use Russ's answers as a kind of Rorschach test—he'd project his psychological issues into the words so I could interpret them. But there's not a whole lot you can read into *pog.* I grimaced. "Pog?"

"It's a kid's game," he said, "using little colored disks."

"That's a proper noun," I said.

"You didn't warn him that proper nouns were illegal. Let him have it," said Bob. "But I already said *hoe* and *get,*" he added apologetically, then grinned. "Russ takes the lead with three words."

"*Trope, grope, these, tease, ogre, treats, treat, teaser, grates, raped, ropes, heats,*" I said, unable to suppress the note of triumph in my voice.

"I've got none of those and nothing to add," said Angie.

I grinned. "You get one point for three-letter words, two for four and five, three for six, and—"

"I vote we skip the scoring and move on to the magnificent chocolate cake," said Bob.

"But half the fun is scoring the results. Wasn't this your idea?" I asked.

"That was before I realized you were a Boggle piranha," he said, laughing.

"Fine." I stood up, whirled into the kitchen, and carried the cake to the dining room table. "Dessert is served."

The others moved to the table and I carved out four big pieces of red velvet cake layered with whipped cream. "You must have gotten to know Annabelle's neighborhood pretty well while you were working there," I said to Russ. "Did you notice many strangers? I still can't believe they think Annabelle was a robbery victim. Wouldn't a person like that stick out?"

"I stay pretty focused when I'm on a job," he said.

"So your current project is in Sachem's Head," I said. "That's what, ten minutes from Annabelle's place?"

He nodded and tucked into his cake.

"What kind of educational background do you need to be a contractor?" I asked. "Do you do an apprenticeship? I swear, the repairmen I've hired lately don't seem to have a clue."

"It varies," he said. "I happen to have a degree in accounting. Most of the hands-on stuff I learned on the job, working for a master carpenter."

"A bachelor's degree?"

"Associate." He put his fork down and stared at me. "If you have a problem with me being too dumb for your friend the fancy doctor, why don't you have the balls to just come out and say it?"

"She's not a doctor, she's a social worker," I said through gritted teeth. "Do you even know what sandplay therapy is?"

"I'll tell you what we had in common, because that's obviously what you've been wondering all night. Why did your smart friend go for a big dumb dope like me? She was depressed," he said, jabbing his right pointer finger at me. It was missing the tip. "We laughed all the time. Which is more than she could say about the rest of her friends."

"Everybody settle down," Bob said, patting the air with his hands.

"I think I'll call it a night." Russ stood up and bowed stiffly. "Thanks for the grub."

"I'll see you out," said Bob. The murmur of their voices drifted in from the hallway. "She's under a lot of pressure . . . shouldn't have mixed the second drink . . . hope we can all get together again when Annabelle's feeling better."

The blood pounded so hard in my temples I wondered if my head would explode. Angie carried the cake into the kitchen.

"You don't need to make excuses for me," I hissed when Bob returned. My lips seemed to have sprouted a mind of their own. "Everything in life doesn't always work out to be pretty. You should know that from your first marriage."

Bob looked stricken and so did Angie as she rounded the corner back into the dining room. "It's okay," Bob said, in the pained voice relatives use for a child in a tantrum. "Rebecca's had a rough week."

"Dammit, she knows what kind of week I had."

Bob reached out to hug me, but I pulled away. "Our tee time's at noon tomorrow," he said, game face not slipping. "Shall I meet you at Fenwick or would you like me to swing by and pick you up?"

"I won't set one toe on a golf course," I said, the words slurring drunkenly.

"Maybe we should call it a night," Bob said. Angie wrinkled her nose and nodded.

"I'm sorry. You're right. It *has* been an awful week," I said. "I'll call you tomorrow, okay?"

"This was a lovely dinner," he said brightly. "You're a marvelous cook." He kissed me on the top of the head and followed Angie to the door.

"Wow, you drove two of them out in the space of fifteen minutes—that has to be a record," Angie said when she returned from seeing him out. "What a way to ruin a perfectly good cake."

We both laughed. "I'm a drunken ass," I said, sinking into my chair and forking in a big bite of red chocolate. "What did go wrong in his marriage?"

"His sister Ruthie told me his ex said he was just too nice. I took that to mean she was a bitch. The nicer he acted, the meaner she got."

I groaned, scraping the last of the whipped cream off my plate. "Doesn't say much for me either."

"Want me to help you clean up?"

"I'll do it tomorrow," I said. "Penance. I can see apologizing to Bob but I'm not calling Shock Daddy."

"I didn't like him much either," Angie admitted. "But I'm not convinced he put Annabelle in the hospital."

Chapter 16

I woke up hungover and supremely mortified. The Boggle was bad, my behavior with Russ, worse. And floating to the surface, most hideous of all, came the unpleasant memory of attacking poor Bob. Instead of a sweet morning spent snuggling with a nice man who treats me like a princess, I was left with the dinner party mess and a soggy brain swirling with regrets.

I struggled out of bed, started some coffee, and curled up on the couch with Spencer and Annabelle's kitten. Was the relationship with Bob a case of Humpty Dumpty? All the king's horses, etcetera, etcetera . . . Even if I could repair the damage, did I want to, especially if it required golf with his relatives? The phone rang and I let the answering machine pick up.

"Rebecca, it's Mark. I know you're busy today, but call when you can. It's about Dr. Frazier. I heard something a little worrisome—"

I grabbed the receiver. "Mark? I'm here."

"I didn't expect to hear your voice this morning," he said.

"Things didn't work out exactly as planned," I muttered. "Does the offer for breakfast still stand?"

He let hang a moment of dead silence where I thought I'd die of embarrassment, praying he wouldn't insist on the gory details of my date night failure. "Sure. Hidden Kitchen at eight thirty?"

I took a quick shower, ran a comb through my hair, and threw on jeans and a long-sleeved white henley. I refused to play the what-should-I-wear game again, this time for Mark. He knows what I look like, from best face to worst; and besides, I wasn't supposed to care what he thought. Stuffing Annabelle's article on the hated and hateful patient into my purse, I dashed out the door.

Mark was seated at a table by the window with two cups of coffee waiting, along with a little silver pitcher of milk. Either this meant he no longer took his coffee black or he'd miraculously remembered that I despise those little fake creamers. Maybe there was something to be said for ex-husbands—maybe they try harder. He stood up and kissed my cheek.

"Hope you don't mind that I ordered for you. A rush of folks came in right after me and I was afraid the kitchen would back up. If you're not up for a cheese and bacon omelet, I'll swap for the blueberry pancakes."

I glanced at the open window behind the counter where the cooks sweated, pouring pancakes, whisking eggs, and calling out to the waitresses to pick up their food. A line of paper orders was pinned to a string at the top of the window.

"Perfect. You're an angel," I said, adding milk to the steaming coffee cup and taking a sip. Mark looked good in his flannel shirt and jeans—relaxed in a tousled, little-boy way that I hadn't seen often when we were married. We'd both been too busy jacking up our careers.

"Occasionally," he said with a lopsided grin. "What happened to the boyfriend?"

"Bump in the road," I said, wiggling two fingers in a breezy wave and moving on by. "Tell me about Dr. Frazier."

"All confidential?"

"Of course." I looked around the restaurant. "Me and thirty breakfast regulars, that is."

Mark lowered his voice and leaned in over the table. "This is from a psychiatric attending at the clinic, who shall remain nameless. Let's call her Dr. X." Mark smiled. "In the third year of her residency, Dr. Frazier developed what she called an 'unhealthy attachment' to Dr. X. After Dr. X refused her request for extra sessions, she noticed that she was often running into Dr. Frazier in unusual parts of the hospital, places where she wouldn't have expected her to be. Places where she had no clinical business."

A tall waitress with a stubby black ponytail delivered our breakfast. I had a home fry in my mouth before the plate even hit the table.

"Can I get you anything else?" she asked.

"A tall glass of water and another of OJ please," I said, swallowing the crunchy bite of potato.

"A little dehydrated, are we?" Mark asked, grinning.

"Finish the story," I said.

"Eventually Dr. X felt she had to raise this in one of their sessions—for her own peace of mind. And even worse, she was worried that similar patterns might crop up with Dr. Frazier's patients. Frazier was furious—she denied that the meetings were anything but coincidental. There wasn't enough to go on to lodge a formal complaint—and her clinical work seemed otherwise quite capable."

"So she was stalking the supervisor?"

"Something like that—a mild version anyway. The

story definitely raised my antennae, given what's happened to Annabelle."

I dug the article out of my purse. "I found this buried on Annabelle's desk. What are the chances she was reading this to deal with Dr. Frazier?"

He skimmed the first paragraph and shrugged. "I'm not seeing the connection. If it was an article about repelling creepy stalkers, maybe." He scratched his chin. "You said you've met her a few times. What was that like?"

"A bit of a pissing contest, really—who knew Annabelle better and who should be taking care of her patients, that kind of thing. It doesn't surprise me at all that she would complain about me to Sebastian. Watching me go down in departmental flames would be her way of winning." I shuddered with irritation. "Those two deserve each other."

"Watch it with Sebastian. He could make a lot of trouble for you. He's a mean little man who takes his grudges seriously. He already doesn't like you."

"Damn." I carved off a bite of my omelet, scraped the escaping melted cheese back onto my fork, and added a piece of bacon.

"Did Annabelle ever specifically mention trouble with Frazier?"

I swallowed hard, wishing I'd listened more carefully between the lines of our conversations. "We joked about it a little. She referred to her as 'Dr. Frantic.' Annabelle was starting to set some limits with her—things like not chatting in between each of her patients. She actually changed her schedule on Tuesdays to get some relief."

"So Frazier attacked her because she changed her schedule? Sounds far-fetched. Besides, I've seen her in grand rounds: She's not a very big person. Isn't she about your height, only thinner?"

I set my fork down on the plate and picked up a piece of toast, annoyed with the chubby implication. The girl he'd slept with, the marriage breaker, had been a stick. Let him take her to breakfast next time. He could order her a nonfat yogurt and watch her nibble at a couple of teaspoonfuls before declaring she was full. I tried to redirect my churning mind but my voice came out mad anyway.

"Mark, whoever did this used a hammer." One of my brother-in-law's incessant sports facts leaped to mind. "It's like a baseball swing: As long as you get the wrist and elbow levers working properly, the avoirdupois behind them doesn't matter."

He reached over his plate and squeezed my wrist. "I didn't mean anything by it, Rebecca. Honest. I think you look terrific. Women should have curves."

I pulled my hand away, finished off the toast, and returned to the home fries.

"Anyone else on your list of suspects?" he asked.

I could pout and ruin the rest of the meal and get nothing useful from him. Not to mention eat more than I really wanted, just to prove a point. Or I could try to let it go.

"Annabelle's new boyfriend came over to dinner last night. They're a horrible match—he's a beer-swilling boor—not a subtle bone in his body." I felt my cheeks flushing and the heat leaching down my neck, as I remembered the excruciating details of last night's botched party. "He could have beaten her to death if he wanted, but why would he? From what Annabelle told me, she loved his work, enjoyed his company while he was there, and they had just decided to try dating. They were in those early, rosy days of a relationship where everything looks good. I can't see a motive."

"You never know what's really going on between two people," he said.

"You got that right," I said.

"What about her caseload?" he asked, tapping the article. "Any problems there?"

"I've met with a couple of her patients so far and read through some notes, looking for transference issues." I sighed. This is the hardest part of a therapist's job, but also the most important—recognizing and interpreting what feelings and issues the patient is bringing to the sessions from her past, projecting them into the therapy. "But those sand trays are another world. I even went to see her sand-play shrink and I still can't make heads or tails of it."

Mark's eyes widened. "You went to see her shrink? Spill."

I made the quick decision not to mention the tray I'd asked to build. "Nothing much to tell, really. I guess I should go back to Annabelle's office and spend a little more time reading her notes."

Now his eyes narrowed. "Come on, Annabelle's shrink told you nothing?"

I sighed. "He said the meaning of a tray comes through on many levels. He feels it's not accurate to interpret a tray without watching the patient put it together and then discussing their reactions."

Mark pushed aside the remains of his pancakes and took my hand. "I could drive you over."

I flashed on the incident in the hospital garage and felt my upper lip break into a sweat. I hadn't mentioned it and wasn't about to. I squeezed his hand and then dropped it. "I'll be fine."

"And you'll be careful?"

I nodded. "I'm thinking of calling my father," I said. Which sounded like a non sequitur, but it wasn't.

"It's time," he said. "Good luck."

Chapter 17

I sat in the car for ten minutes after we left the restaurant, listening to Click and Clack on *Car Talk* and feeling at loose ends. Even their zany humor couldn't make me laugh today. Finally, I phoned Dr. Goldman and left him a message apologizing for canceling the session on Thursday and wondering if he had any openings Monday. Much as I dreaded the prospect, it would be a mistake not to process all the personal angst I was busy stirring up. The uninformed layperson could make the case that getting trashed and humiliating your dinner guests was a fluke, but I knew better.

I drummed my fingers on the steering wheel and listened to the auto mechanics dish out advice on cars and love affairs to a national radio audience. An odd combination, but sometimes their opinions sounded better than mine. Hours to go before Bob's tee time and I still wasn't sure I had the nerve to show up. What would he have told his parents in the meantime? What would Click and Clack advise?

I started up the car, got on the highway, and headed west to New Haven. The chat with Mark had left me feeling as though I'd missed something in Annabelle's office. The parking lot outside her building was mercifully empty: Most therapists draw the line at giving up Saturday mornings for their patients' convenience. We need time to recharge—and to have a life. I trudged around the building to the front stoop and noticed a small white paper tacked onto the bulletin board to the left of the doorbell. *A.H.* was penciled on the bottom. I unfastened it and went into the privacy of the vestibule to read.

"Annabelle, please call me. Are you okay?" A local phone number had been added, but no signature. The note was written with a pencil that needed sharpening. I stuffed it into my pocket to be dealt with later.

My heart beating hard, I slunk upstairs and unlocked Annabelle's office, dreading the possibility of running into her neighbor. Wouldn't it be just my luck that she'd be on the job this weekend and in between patients? I closed the double doors behind me and leaned against them, surveying Annabelle's space.

Then I paced the perimeter of the room. Everything looked the same—the sun angling in and glinting off her shelves of figurines, the neatly raked trays of white sand, the piles of professional journals and correspondence on her desk, the dark computer screen. I opened the closet door again, this time noticing a small file cabinet pushed to the back wall, partly covered by a black raincoat hanging from the clothes bar. I tugged on the handles of the drawers. Locked.

Backing out of the closet, I wondered where she would keep the keys. I crossed the room and opened the desk drawers, one by one. Nothing. I returned to the shelves of figurines and began to pick up anything with a possible

cavity—a mummy in a sarcophagus, a teepee, a dugout ca-
noe, a hideout cave embedded under a set of steps. Feeling
frustrated, I sank into her rocking chair. Hiding a key in
those objects didn't make sense anyway—the keys would
distract any patient who picked it up. Not to mention re-
vealing the secret to her confidential material.

I went back to the desk and searched again. One folder in
the bottom drawer had dropped down lower than the others.
The label said *Rebecca*. Inside the folder was a small key
taped to a note card—the key to my office—along with a
smaller key I didn't recognize. The key opened the file cabinet in the closet. I slid the top drawer open and found folders
of closed cases, marked with the dates of the patients' termi-
nation from therapy. I riffled through several of them, finding notes in Annabelle's crabbed handwriting along with
computer disks. It would take weeks to go through all of this.
And to what purpose?

I pulled the lower drawer out. The folders inside were
marked only with initials, M on one, Amm on the second,
RT on the last. I carried them over to the rocking chair and
began to skim the contents. A sheet in M's folder read: *42-
year-old, married. Hx of mar diff. 2 children. Neg psych hx.
Prefers sandplay.* There were four colored printouts of sand
tray arrangements, three of them sparse, all featuring a female figure that looked like Snow White. In the fourth photocopy, Snow White had been placed on one side of the
tray, with Robin Hood on a white horse on the other. A
deep line had been drawn in the sand between them. *Line
in the Sand!!!*, Annabelle had scrawled in the margin.

Inside the second folder, I found the following notes:
married 12 years. LGD how many? One photocopy of a
sand tray was included, divided into two sections by a
picket fence. One side contained a small wooden box with
prisoner's bars, with a young girl peering out. A gladiator

had been placed in the far corner of the other half of the tray, facing away from the girl in her cage.

The third folder contained the following notes: *24 y.o. swf. YUmss. Ptsd? Supv har? CS????* A blurry photo showed a tray peopled by a baby and a medical doctor.

After studying all three folders again, I knew very little more than I had when I'd begun. If Annabelle had meant to conceal identities, issues, and all possible meaning from the casual file cabinet burglar, she'd done one hell of a job. Who were these patients who needed special protection?

The clock on Annabelle's desk chimed eleven times. If I had any hope of salvaging things with Bob, I had to leave now. I returned the folders to the file cabinet, locked everything up, and hurried out to my car. The sun had warmed the air up to a comfortable temperature, and I began to feel the tiniest bit cheerful about spending a couple of hours outdoors along the water—even if it did involve golf clubs. Why not just walk alongside Bob and his parents and admire their shots? Not everyone has to be an athlete.

I made it to the Old Saybrook exit off I-95 in under half an hour and wound my way through town to the spit of land hosting the Fenwick Golf Club. The marsh on one side of the road glowed with the pale greens of spring. On the other, the sunlight glinted off the choppy waves of the Sound.

I drove past the entrance to the small weathered pro shop on the left side of the road, trying to work up the courage to pull in and apologize to Bob. He would be polite in front of his parents, definitely. Would he have told them about last night's dreadful dinner? Maybe I wouldn't even mention the unpleasantness, just act breezy and sorry for being late. From my brief experience as girlfriend to a golf psychologist, I know that golfers are fanatics about starting on time and then keeping up a forced march pace over the course of their rounds. I turned my car around in the driveway of a gray beach house, not yet occupied for the season, and went back to face the music—a dirge this morning.

Bob and his folks were the only people in the lot. Not that I would have had any trouble locating him in a crowd, wearing pink and blue plaid Bermuda shorts, his flamingo ankles and knees pale pink and bony. But his face lit up when he saw me. He tapped his mother and pointed to my car. Then he trotted over to open my door.

"I'm so glad to see you," he said without a trace of sarcasm. "I wasn't sure you'd come."

"I'm so sorry about last night." I swung my legs out of the car. "It was simply unacceptable behavior. I have no excuse—"

He touched his fingers to my lips. "I'm just glad you're here. Come, meet my parents." He took my hand and led me to the pair of older folks who stood nearby, their golf bags perched on pull carts with enormous wheels.

"You must be Rebecca," said the small, round woman with dark curly hair and blue eyes. "Bob's told us all about you. I understand you're a little nervous about playing golf. Not to worry, I hardly ever break seventy—that's for nine holes!" She laughed merrily and pressed both of my hands between hers. "We'll have so much fun. We can't help it on a beautiful day like today!"

"This is my mother, Susan," said Bob, squeezing her shoulder. "She's not quite as dreadful a golfer as she claims."

"I'm terrible," she whispered, giggling.

"I'm Bob Senior," said her husband, enveloping my hand in a steel grip. "Welcome to Fenwick." He was Bob's height—tall; all hips, knees, and elbows; in a pair of lime green slacks and a yellow sweater. "Let's get going, people.

We're due on the tee. Bob, why don't you get Rebecca's clubs out of her trunk and I'll get her a cart."

"I don't have clubs," I said, thinking I'd sooner rot in hell than spend hard-earned money on golf equipment. "I thought I'd just watch today."

"She can play out of my bag," said Bob's mother. "Don't get your knickers in a knot."

We straggled across the road to the starter's hut, where Bob and his father argued over who would pay the greens fees.

"Aren't they dear?" Susan asked. "Bob told me you fixed spaghetti carbonara last night. I'm crazy for that dish. Now did you make it with cream or just the cheese and eggs?"

"No cream," I said. "But the cheese must be very good quality. The pancetta too." I filed a note away to ask Angie, and Annabelle, when she was able to really pay attention: Do you continue to date a guy because you've fallen in love with his mother?

We rolled the carts over to the first tee, my hands sweating profusely. I hate making an ass of myself—physically, that is—and I hoped I could hold the line as a spectator only.

"Katharine Hepburn's former home is on the second hole," said Bob's mother. "I understand she was quite an athlete. Why do you think it is that some people have multiple talents and others of us are just plain ordinary?"

"There's nothing ordinary about you, Mom," said Bob. He kissed the top of her head and mussed her permanent-wave curls.

Bob's father strutted onto the tee box, pressed the ball and tee into the earth, and took a fast cut with his driver, losing his balance slightly in the follow-through. His ball sailed out and began to bend in a huge arc to the right.

"Dammit," he said. "A slice! We'll never find that ball. That's why I hate rushing onto the first tee. It carries through the whole damn round."

"Sorry, that was my fault," I said.

Just then my cell phone beeped, notifying me of a text message.

Bob's father turned and glared.

"First deadly sin of a golfer," his mother chuckled. She clapped her hand over her mouth. "Oh dear, are you on call today?" she whispered through her fingers.

I shook my head and pulled the phone out of my back pocket. "AB's worse, V," the message read.

"I've got to go," I yelled over my shoulder as I sprinted down the path to the parking lot. "Annabelle's in crisis. I'll call you later, okay?"

Chapter 18

I dialed Victoria's number as I roared back onto I-95. No answer. In New Haven, I hurtled off the highway onto the connector leading to the hospital. No time to search for a parking spot on the street, so I pealed into the garage, suppressing my nerves. *Annabelle needs you now*, I told myself firmly. Once parked, I sent off a text message telling Victoria I was on the way up to the ICU.

The receptionist on duty in the vestibule gave me a visitor's pass without any hassle. Shock Daddy must have moved on, as Victoria predicted. I burst out of the elevator and bolted down the hall to the lounge. Behind a fake ficus tree in the far corner, two young boys colored at a child-sized table. Victoria was pacing along the back wall decorated with Impressionist-style pictures of boating, water, beaches, and summer. What if your loved one had hit his head on a diving board or become paralyzed in a boating accident? The watery prints wouldn't be so soothing.

"Victoria," I yelped, rushing into the room. "What's

happened to Annabelle?" Victoria was crying too hard to answer, but she grabbed my elbow and dragged me toward the unit.

"They're still working on her," she managed to croak out. "Someone put something toxic into her IV. I think I overheard someone say insulin."

"Is Annabelle diabetic?" I asked. One more thing I hadn't known about my friend.

"She never used to be," she said as she tapped a code into the box on the wall, and then pushed me past the empty reception desk to Annabelle's cubicle. We stopped to watch through the window. A doctor held a stethoscope to her chest. Two nurses in flowered scrubs stood by. A clear oxygen mask pressed Annabelle's bruised cheeks flat. That had to hurt. If she was feeling anything.

Mr. Polson, the medical social worker, touched Victoria's shoulder from behind. She jumped and so did I.

"Sorry to startle you. Ladies, I'm going to have to ask you to move to the lounge. Your sister's doctor will come out and speak to you as soon as he's finished here."

He put a hand on each of our backs and steered us back into the hallway. After insisting that Victoria take a seat on the blue tweed couch, he went to fetch a glass of water. I paced around the table where the boys had been coloring earlier, too upset to think of any platitudes that might help Victoria.

Polson returned and handed her a Dixie cup. "Don't worry, we'll get to the bottom of this," he said with a well-oiled heartiness. "Excellent, here's Dr. Jensen now."

The doctor we'd seen in Annabelle's cubicle swept into the lounge. "Ms. White? I'm Dr. Jensen. Your sister will be fine."

"What happened to her? Something was injected into

her IV?" Victoria's lower lip began to quiver and she tightened it into a fierce frown.

"Insulin," said Dr. Jensen. "She appeared to suffer from a bit of shock, but we've administered glucose intravenously, and the effects appear to be completely reversed." He smiled and started to turn toward the door.

"Wait just a minute," I said. "How did this happen? We were not even aware she was diabetic."

"And you would be . . . ?" asked the doctor.

"Dr. Rebecca Butterman. I'm a clinical psychologist with an adjunct appointment in the psychiatry department. And I'm Annabelle's friend. I found her after the attack in Guilford earlier this week." Which felt more like weeks ago than days. I sank into the chair next to Victoria. "How did this happen?" I said again. "Did someone make a mistake?"

Dr. Jensen sidestepped the question. "Fortunately," he said, "our head nurse noticed the patient was having some breathing difficulties and we were able to administer glucose. There should be a complete recovery." His beeper chirped. He waved at Mr. Polson to take over and headed down the hall to the elevators. "Excuse me, folks. I'll check in on her later."

"This wasn't a mistake," Victoria said. "It was an attempt on my sister's life." She crumpled into sobs. I patted her knee and glared up at the social worker.

"How could this happen?" I asked for the third time. "Usually, this unit is guarded like a penitentiary."

He placed his hand on Victoria's shoulder and shrugged apologetically. "We had several major patient crises this morning. Everyone's stretched thin. It's been an utter zoo." He smiled. "And speaking of animals, Shock Daddy was transferred out, so hospital security dropped back to normal levels."

"But what do you think happened?" I asked, my voice growing a little shrill. I understood that he had to parrot the hospital line—with all the cutting edge surgery and medical treatment Yale performs and the miracles people expect, they must always be poised on the edge of a lawsuit. They'd have to jump all over damage control. He'd probably already said more than he should have—but it explained nothing about how Annabelle had careened into a medical crisis.

"There's a procedure for investigating these kinds of events," Polson said. "We're very thorough. I can assure you this incident won't be ignored."

"It could have been anyone," Victoria whispered, fresh tears taking a mascara luge run down her cheeks.

"But who?" I asked, letting go of her hand and slumping back into the chair. "Someone had to have the medical know-how to get into the unit without drawing attention and then inject the insulin into her IV. That rules out a lot of casual bad guys. It had to be either a visitor or someone who works here at the hospital." I drummed my fingers on the arm of the chair. "Are the police involved with this?"

The color leached from Victoria's face. "My sister Heather was here earlier with a really scummy-looking guy. He had the worst-looking teeth. I saw them across the cafeteria, but she took off when she spotted me. Right after that, the unit secretary phoned me to say Annabelle had taken a turn for the worse."

"Terrible-looking teeth?" asked Mr. Polson. He leaned forward and tented his fingers.

"Even from a distance, they looked brown, almost rotten." Victoria curled her lip in disgust.

"That can be a sign of a methamphetamine abuser," said Polson.

"I'm not following this," I said. "Why would your sister's boyfriend want to hurt Annabelle?"

"A meth addict doesn't need a normal reason," Polson said. "It's all about the next fix. Coming down from a high is extremely uncomfortable—the user feels dysphoric, irritable, and desperate. Quite capable of lashing out at anyone."

Polson's beeper went off and he glanced at it, clipped to his belt. "Will you be able to stay a bit with Ms. White? She's had quite a shock." Standing behind Victoria, he widened his eyes and bugged them out. The universal man-signal for *Help! This woman's a basket case.*

I waved him away.

"We'll get to the bottom of it. Not to worry. I'll check back in with you later," he told Victoria. "Let the desk clerk know if you need me." He strode back into the unit.

I squeezed Victoria's hand and she shook her head sadly. "Why would she bring someone in here to hurt Annabelle?"

"As Mr. Polson said, drug users don't tend to have sophisticated reasons for doing what they do," I said. "But we don't actually know that your sister was involved." It sounded to me like a crazy theory.

Victoria stared. "She had nurses' aide training. That program was one of my family's many attempts to get her to stand on her own two feet. Apparently she met her new addict boyfriend in the last treatment facility she attended—he was one of the staff."

Then she folded her upper body onto her lap, shoulders shuddering. I patted her back until the shaking stopped and fished in my purse for a Kleenex.

"That's what Annabelle and I had been arguing about," she said through her sniffles.

"Sounds like there's been a lot of stress in the family recently," I said. "Will you tell me a little more about Heather?"

"It's not just recent." She sat up, took the tissue, and blew her nose. "Please try not to judge." She met my gaze and I nodded. "You have to understand that over the course of our lives, we've seen money, time, and energy go to this girl for every kind of treatment. We've been dragged to family therapy, paid for inpatient hospitalizations and drug rehab programs, made runs to jails and police stations. Have you ever been in family therapy?" she asked.

"I've seen my share of families in treatment, of course, but never actually experienced it myself." I shook my head, trying to imagine hashing things out in front of a professional with Janice. And maybe my absent father. And maybe my old-school, stiff-upper-lip, don't-air-your-dirty-laundry-in-public grandparents, may they rest in peace. The thought was both ludicrous and painful.

"It's the worst," she said. "Watching my mother cry and Daddy withdraw farther and farther away from all of us. And Annabelle, of course—the social worker even as a kid—trying to get everyone to settle down and see how much we all loved each other and if we only reached out to Heather one more time, it would work. When my folks died three years ago, I told Annabelle it was time to settle this for good. If we gave Heather the money directly, I knew she'd run through it. And then be back knocking on our door with the next sob story." She clenched her fists. "Or send some horrible creature like Mr. Methamphetamine to try to squeeze it out of us."

"It's terribly hard to have a family member who's mentally ill," I said. "My mother was depressed to the point of suicide," I was surprised to hear myself tell her. "It skews the family dynamics because everything ends up revolving around the needs of the person who's sick."

She nodded and focused her reddened eyes on me. "I'm sorry about how rude I've been. I can see how much you care about my sister. It must feel really good to have a friend like you." She wiped her face with the tissue I'd given her and tucked it into the cuff of her silk blouse. Then she shrugged and smiled ruefully. "It's not so easy to keep friends when you're in the gossip business."

A small light flickered in the back of my brain. "Are you thinking the assaults on your sister might be connected to you?"

Another elegant shrug of her shoulders set her silk blouse rippling. "No one hates me enough to kill my family," she said after a long pause.

"But like all of us, you've made some enemies," I said. "Just for now, let's not rule any possibilities out."

"Both my ex-husbands despise me," she said with a strained chuckle. "When the first marriage went sour, you can believe I hired the best divorce lawyer I could afford— in fact, I couldn't afford her—and she negotiated a very favorable settlement. Very favorable." A wistful smile. "With the second marriage, I knew enough to go into it with a watertight prenuptial agreement. It's not romantic," she said, shaking her finger, "but neither is an ugly divorce. Or postnuptial poverty."

"Of course I don't know your ex-husbands, but isn't it difficult to imagine one of them trying to beat your sister to death? And then creeping in here to finish her off?" Interesting that Victoria hadn't said a word about her current husband.

"Larry is a world-renowned orthopedic surgeon. Specializes in spines," she said with a huff. "Though he never developed one himself when it came to his mother. She's still egging him on to dispute the settlement. He consults all over the country. Including Yale New Haven Hospital."

"It should be easy enough to find out where he's been the last couple of days," I said, "and hopefully rule him out as a possibility."

"I saw him in the cafeteria yesterday," she spat out.

"Young interns and residents hanging all over him. Why is it that men don't seem disgusting until they're really old, but one small wrinkle and we women are set out with the trash?"

"He's still angry about the divorce?" I asked. "How long ago was that?"

A cat-who-ate-the-canary smile edged onto her lips. "He's mad that I leaked the news about his second wife cheating in my column. They hadn't been hitched for three months when she popped in the sack with one of his partners."

I didn't know what to say to that. Pretty much struck dumb. "Anyone else?" I asked, just to get a breath from the venom.

"I get death threats through the website all the time," she said. "You're probably familiar with that too, Dr. Aster." She smiled again when I acted surprised. "I googled you last night."

I gave a small smile and shrugged. "Sometimes people don't like my advice, but they don't get that worked up over it," I said. "They can ignore it easily enough. Tell me more about the threats."

She sighed. "I'm under a lot of pressure to produce new material every week. The juicier the better. So if something falls into my lap, like seeing Larry's wife's green Mercedes in the Hi-Ho Hotel parking lot, you can be damn sure I use it."

Which might make someone want to kill Victoria, I thought, but did not say; hard to see why they'd hurt Annabelle instead though.

Just then Mr. Polson returned to collect Victoria. "You can see your sister now." He smiled apologetically at me. "I'm sorry, but with the scene we've had on the unit today, it's immediate family only."

"I'll call you later and give you the full report," said Victoria. I hugged her and started to the elevator. "Please tell her that I love her," I called back over my shoulder, voice choked up.

I speed-dialed Angie on the way home.

"Are you just getting up? That was one hell of a dinner party you threw!" She laughed.

"No, I'm not just getting up." I summarized the latest incident with Annabelle and my conversation with her sister.

"Good God," said Angie. "It must have been a staff error, don't you think? Wouldn't the police be there if it was foul play? Were there any cops on the scene?"

"Not while I was there. But think about it. The hospital wants to cover their backs—I'm betting they'd make a concerted effort to find out what actually happened before they called the police."

"So you don't believe it was a simple mistake?" she asked.

"No," I said. "Think of it this way: Someone tried to kill Annabelle, tried to beat her to death. But instead of dying, she's hanging in there, threatening to come back to life and ID her attacker. That's reason enough to risk slipping into that hospital unit and doing her in for good. Luckily, someone caught on and saved her life."

"Sounds like it would be hard to pin this on Russ," said Angie, "even if he is a dweeb with no manners. Have you spoken to Bob today?"

I sighed. "I went over to Fenwick to grovel. I started to follow him and his parents around on the golf course. Unfortunately, Victoria texted me on the first tee so I had to bolt. Bob was very kind about everything, but I'm sure he's annoyed."

"Did you call him to let him know it was a real emergency?"

"Not yet. I need to eat something first. I'll let you know

how it goes. You're breaking up." Which she wasn't, but I wasn't up for even the slightest hint of scolding.

I took the Guilford exit off the highway, feeling some of the stress melt away as I got closer to the water. Once inside my place, I played with the cats, warmed up some of the leftover pasta, and polished off a large piece of cake, reasoning that stress burns a lot of calories. Then I sucked in a deep, deep breath and called Bob.

"I'm desperately sorry about ruining the golf game," I said as soon as he answered, exposing my figurative neck and belly before he had the chance to blast me.

"Is Annabelle all right?" he asked.

Did his voice sound a little stiff or was it my paranoia? I told him about the insulin overdose. "They wouldn't let me see her. Maybe tomorrow," I added. "Her sister's with her right now."

"I'm so glad she's okay. We had a beautiful day at Fenwick," he said cheerfully. "My mother thought you were adorable."

"That's sweet." I felt my shoulders relax. "Would you have any interest in grabbing a drink? I could meet you at Café Routier in Westbrook. I'm beat, but maybe one glass of wine would be just what the doctor ordered."

Dead silence. "Listen, Rebecca. I like you a lot. But it seems to me that you might need a little more time as a single person before you start dating. Or maybe it's me." He chuckled sadly. "Maybe I'm not the guy for you. But if you get it all figured out, I'd love you to call me."

We exchanged a few meaningless pleasantries and I hung up, entirely deflated. I pulled on a jacket and started down the path to the town dock, willing myself not to think about anything. Not Annabelle, not Dr. Sebastian, not Victoria, not Russ, not Mark, and most of all, not Bob.

I sank onto the picnic bench by the water and stared

across the channel. In the gathering dusk, I trained my eyes on the abandoned red shack perched on the far beach, the scene that never fails to help me feel peaceful.

I gasped. Graphic curse words had been spray-painted in white on the faded wood. My romantic chances felt a lot like that right now—a beautiful thing gone sour.

Chapter 19

The next morning, I made it to church just as the last bells were ringing. Sliding into a back pew, I scanned the Sunday bulletin. Our new minister was preaching. Sigh. Not that the Reverend's a bad speaker, or even all that new, but in church terms, anyone who's been in the pulpit less than seven years is new and therefore subject to the churchgoers' lament: "That's not how Reverend (fill in the blank with the former preacher) did it." Besides, both of our recent pastors left under murky circumstances that made the adjustment that much trickier. And worst of all, we'd also had to hire a new sexton after Mr. McCabe resigned just before Christmas. He moved to his daughter's trailer in the Ozark Mountains and the bathrooms haven't smelled quite clean since.

Why is change so damn hard? I realized this was part of my negative reaction to Annabelle's boyfriend. I'd gotten used to her being single and doing single girl things with me. Russ threatened to change all that. Never mind that I was searching for a long-term relationship too: Jealousy by definition isn't fair and welcoming.

As the minister stood and approached the pulpit to read the call to worship, my cell phone trilled. I scrambled in my purse to find it and glanced at the screen—unknown caller. I pushed the *off* button. Then I settled into the service, which turned out better than expected—more soothing lullaby than fire and brimstone. After hearing a gorgeous tenor solo, we sang "Come and Find the Quiet Center" and listened to a sermon based on the scripture that said if God's eye was on the sparrow, surely He was watching over the rest of us too. The voices in my head settled down to a manageable din.

After the service, I wandered over to coffee hour in the fellowship hall for a quick cup of tea and some church chatter. On the way out to my car, I remembered the missed call, switched the phone back on, and played the voicemail.

"Dr. Butterman, Fred Polson here, from Yale New Haven Hospital. Could you call me when you get this message? I'm trying to reach Annabelle Hart's younger sister and hoped you might have some current information."

I slid into my car and punched *redial*, uneasy at the strain I thought I detected underneath his polite words.

"Polson," he answered.

"Mr. Polson, it's Rebecca Butterman."

He cleared his throat. "Um, yes, thank you for returning my call. Unfortunately, I have some bad news. Victoria White is dead. I need to contact her next of kin and we have no relatives on record, other than Ms. Hart, of course. I understand there's another sister and I was hoping you could help me locate her."

My mouth went so dry I was unable to speak. "Victoria is dead?" I finally stammered. "My God, what happened?"

"She was shot," he said in a flat voice. "Police are inves-tigating. Meanwhile, I need to find her sister."

"She was shot?" I moaned. The news bobbed on my brain, not sinking in. "Where? By whom?" My stomach churned with tea and chocolate donut holes.

"They found her behind a Dumpster off Temple Street," he said. "They believe she was on her way to the Omni Ho-tel. I can't imagine why she'd walk there alone at night," he added. "I warned her against it. New Haven is much safer than it used to be, mind you. But still—"

"She was afraid of the parking garage," I said. "That's why she was walking. And you know how hard it is to get a cab in New Haven. We're a city lacking city amenities and we won't ever get on the map for real until—" I was bab-bling way off point. "Who do they think shot her?"

"The cops aren't saying anything. At least, I'm not in the loop," he said. "Can you help me with her sister?"

"Annabelle never mentioned her at all. I can check her day planner, but I've studied it pretty carefully in order to prepare myself for handling her caseload and I don't re-member anything about another sister. I'll keep looking, okay?" Then I begged him to smooth the way for me to visit Annabelle again.

"She doesn't have anyone else there for her now," I said, snapping on my seat belt.

"Definitely, I'll see what I can do," he said. "Will you call me if you think of a way to get in touch with the sister?"

"Of course," I assured him. "This is just awful." He hung up.

I started the car, squealed out of the church parking lot, and drove back to New Haven. Poor Annabelle. She had no relatives left, aside from one crazy sister. If you believed Victoria's version of the family history. Oh God, what had happened to that poor woman? Could it possibly be random bad luck? I couldn't believe she was dead.

I found a parking space on Temple Street, just blocks from where Polson said they'd found Victoria. But it was broad daylight now, the streets peppered with hospital employees headed to their shifts or out to grab lunch. Still, I trotted briskly from my car to the hospital entrance and heaved a sigh of relief once inside. I procured a visitor's pass and headed upstairs.

Nurse Lyn McHugh buzzed me into Annabelle's unit, then murmured to the security guard who sat beside the nurses' station. He remained seated.

"So sorry to hear about your friend's sister," she said as I walked in.

"What a horrible shock," I agreed. "Have you heard anything new?"

"Not a thing. You can go ahead and talk to her for a couple of minutes. Keep it light. Don't mention her sister, okay?"

"Of course."

Nurse McHugh gathered her hair back into a ponytail, then let it go and touched the photo of the dog on her badge. "I thought about bringing Simba in to visit—she's a certified therapy dog. But having a good friend here is even better."

"How's Annabelle doing?" I asked, relieved that the nurse was beginning to thaw.

"Holding steady." Her gaze dropped back to the computer screen in front of her.

My mouth felt like it'd been stuffed with gauze pads: If she had good news, she definitely would have told me. People don't look away from good news.

I slipped into Annabelle's room and stood by the bed

for a moment, watching her sleep. The bruises on her face and arms had faded from that first angry purple to a mottling of egg-yolk yellow and maroon. Marbled, a decorator might call it, if she was describing wallpaper, not my good friend's skin. I took the chair beside the bed and touched her hand. Here, the wash of red and yellow spread from the back of her hand and bled up the fingers, underneath the taped splint that held the pinkie and fourth finger together.

"It's Rebecca," I said softly. "I'm so glad to see you. You look better." My eyes filled. I needed to change the subject to something that wasn't personal. "You should have heard the soloist in church today. A gorgeous tenor. The voice, not the man." I chuckled. "Our Steinway piano is finally back—completely refurbished. Did I tell you about that? Our new music director discovered that the battered piano in the fellowship hall is a valuable antique. He just about died when he saw us putting our cups and purses on it during coffee hour." I forced out another laugh. "It's lovely now, both inside and out."

Underneath the tape that held her breathing tube in place, Annabelle's lips smacked. And her eyes fluttered briefly.

Did that mean she'd heard me? What else to say? Victoria's murder was the elephant charging through the room.

"I think your caseload is under control," I said. "Most of them are opting to wait for you to come back, rather than talk to a stranger. I'm afraid I'm doing a better job with the kitten than the patients. Spencer's gotten over the shock of having him around and now he seems to enjoy Jackson's company. I caught them both hanging from the drapes this morning. Hard to be mad at a ball of fluff. And that little devil knows it too."

The nurse tapped on the door. "There's a police detective here who would like to speak with you," she said in a low voice. "He said he'd meet you out in the lounge."

My heart leaped. Meigs must have heard the news. "I love you," I told Annabelle. "I'll come back to see you tomorrow, okay?" I kissed her forehead and hurried out to the hall. Meigs was not in the lounge, nor across the hall in the small sleeping area designated for families on watch for their damaged loved ones. I started back to the unit.

"Dr. Butterman?"

I whirled around to see a large swarthy man in a blue blazer with thick black eyebrows that merged over the bridge of his nose. "I'm Detective Petrocelli from the New Haven police." He held up his badge.

I pressed my hand to my chest, hardly able to contain my disappointment. "Oh sorry. I was expecting someone else."

"I'd like to speak to you for a moment."

He directed me back into the lounge. "I'm investigating the murder of Victoria White. You're a friend of the family?"

"A friend of Annabelle Hart. I only just met her sister. Is there news about the shooting?"

His eyebrows tightened. "I have a couple of questions, starting with where were you Saturday night between ten p.m. and midnight?"

Stunned to silence, at first I just stared. "I was home in bed. In Guilford."

"Alone?"

"I do have two cats. They're not likely to be able to vouch for me though. I've warned them not to talk to strangers."

The detective didn't appear to find that funny.

"Victoria called me yesterday after the incident with the insulin," I said, forgetting how Meigs had warned me in the past to answer the question asked during an interrogation and not one word more. But he wasn't here so I'd have to handle this my way. "I'm sure you've heard about the insulin? Of course it could have been an error, but the medical people on this unit are absolutely top-notch. I've been very impressed with the nurses."

The detective broke in. "You believe the incident with Ms. Hart yesterday is related to the shooting?"

I nodded. "It's certainly possible. Victoria told me there were any number of people who might have been unhappy with her because of the column she wrote. She worried that someone wanted to get back at her by hurting her sister."

"Go on," he said.

"I assume you know about the third sister and her low-life boyfriend. Mr. Polson, the social worker, wondered if he was a methamphetamine user."

He tipped his chin for me to continue.

"Victoria had ex-husband problems too. Though I didn't get the idea they were the kind that would lead to a street shooting." I began to sniffle, beginning to feel the true weight of that death—how devastated Annabelle would be when she finally woke up. It wouldn't matter how rocky the sibling relationship had been. I pinched the skin on my arm to pull myself together. "She was a gossip columnist, and rather vicious. Though you'd never guess it when you met her." I flashed a pale smile. "Are the police working on any leads that you might be able to share?"

He ignored the question and finished scribbling notes on everything I knew about Victoria White—not all that much in the end. Then he pulled a card from his inside jacket pocket and held it out between two fingers.

"Call if you think of anything else. We'll be in touch."

Chapter 20

Only when I reached my own home, car parked safely in the garage, dead bolts locked, cats in lap, did I allow myself to feel how close I was to unraveling. I punched in Meigs's cell number. No answer. *What's the matter with you? Why won't you answer your goddamn phone?* I took a deep breath and called the Guilford police station, the non-emergency line.

"I need to speak with Detective Meigs," I said, my voice wobbling in an embarrassing way.

"He's not expected back until the end of the week at the earliest," said the woman on the other end of the line.

"There's been a murder," I said, "possibly related to one of his cases. Annabelle Hart's sister was shot and killed in New Haven last night."

"Then you need to call the New Haven Police Department," she said firmly and rattled off their number. "That would be their jurisdiction. I'll certainly leave a message for Detective Meigs. He'll get it when he's back in the office."

I hung up and slammed my fist onto the arm of the couch, startling the cats. Bang, bang, bang—goddammit, he was no help at all. And the New Haven cops were about as likely to be interested in more of my theories as Condoleezza Rice was to consult with Hillary Clinton. I could tell that from the dead eyes of the detective who interviewed me at the hospital.

I took a deep breath and instructed my inner child to grow up. Fast. Meigs wasn't my personal bodyguard after all. And his wife had a chronic illness. Maybe he'd taken her on a long-awaited and well-deserved vacation. I needed a different kind of help than he could offer.

So I called the smartest two people I knew, Angie and Mark, and filled them in about Victoria. "Won't you please come to dinner?" I asked Angie. "Full disclosure—I'm inviting Mark too. I need your support—badly. If Annabelle's coma wasn't hideous enough, now her sister has been murdered, and I'm close to losing my mind. Could you play nice just this once?"

It was asking a lot—once a good friend has taken sides against an ex-husband, it's hard to go back.

"I'm making chicken chili, cilantro coleslaw, and cornbread. Plus, we hardly made a dent in the red velvet cake on Friday. It's perfectly good. Otherwise I'll have to throw it out."

The cake bait did it for Angie, the chili for Mark. We settled on dinner at six. I pulled shredded chicken out of the freezer, and chopped onions and peppers. If the food was good enough, maybe they'd overlook their mutual dislike. An hour and a half later, the chili bubbled on the stove, the cornbread browned in the oven, and my guests waited at the door, barely speaking.

Mark thrust out a bottle of red wine and pecked me on the cheek, avoiding eye contact with Angie. He had a CD in his other hand. "I thought you might enjoy this. It's Kenny Thompson's latest. I already downloaded it to my iPod."

I kissed him back. "That's sweet."

They followed me into the kitchen, Angie radiating disapproval. I distributed glasses of wine, settled them at the kitchen table, and resumed chopping cabbage. Then I outlined what little I knew about the shooting, including the conversation I'd had with Victoria the day before.

"She was worried that someone tried to hurt Annabelle to get back at her. And she was sick about the possibility that their own sister was involved in the insulin caper."

"Why don't you just call the New Haven cops back and tell them what you know?" Mark said, frowning at Angie.

"Like they would listen to her," Angie sniffed. "She already said they were only interested in her alibi for Saturday night. And being that she's a single woman, she was A-L-O-N-E." She spelled the letters out and glared harder at Mark.

"There's no point in being nasty," said Mark.

"Maybe there is," she replied. "Maybe the guy who cheats on my best friend deserves whatever he gets."

Mark shot off his stool. "I guess I'm not needed after all."

I pressed on his shoulder. "Please sit down. Look, he's apologized several times," I said to Angie. "And besides, that bimbo I found him with has already dumped him."

Angie snickered as Mark's face reddened.

"Let's call a truce and eat dinner," I said. "I really need both of you." I spooned chili into three bowls, sprinkled them with cheddar cheese and chopped scallions, and beckoned my warring guests to the kitchen table. Soon mellowed by the meal and the wine, the cloud of antagonism between the two of them lifted slightly.

"Let's go over the whole case, starting with when you found Annabelle," Mark suggested.

I summarized every detail I could remember, from the point I found Annabelle in her bedroom to this afternoon's unsatisfying conversation with the New Haven cop.

"I keep thinking there might be a clue to the attack buried in the sand tray at Annabelle's home," I said. "If only I understood how to recognize and make sense of it."

"But then you're assuming that Annabelle arranged the tray," said Angie. "Isn't it possible that she saw patients at her home and one of them produced it? In that case, it might help identify her attacker—or have nothing to do with any of this."

"She didn't see patients at home," I explained. "And don't worry, I checked her day planner again to be absolutely certain. She and I agree about setting boundaries and keeping space that belongs only to us. Otherwise, it's too easy to let the job leak into your life and gradually take over."

"I once watched a *CSI* episode," Mark broke in, "in which the serial killer left behind a complete diorama of the murder scene after each kill. Could it have been something like that?"

Angie snorted. "We're solving a crime using plot devices from network TV? Could we possibly get any more simpleminded?"

"The attack on Annabelle didn't look premeditated," I said, glowering at Angie. "It looked like the work of someone in a rage. Maybe the hated and hateful patient," I said, remembering the article I'd found on Annabelle's desk. I explained the concept of countertransference again to Angie, as Mark nodded in approval.

"Sometimes an unpleasant or angry or miserable patient raises a lot of uncomfortable reactions in the therapist. But we professionals"—I pointed to me and Mark—"are obligated to try to understand our feelings as part of the patient's life experience. Which is not that easy. So why was

Annabelle reading this article? Either she was merely interested in the phenomenon as an intellectual exercise, or she was having trouble tolerating one of her patients. So far, of the ones I've met—a small sample, mind you—none fit the bill."

"If it wasn't one of Annabelle's angry patients," said Mark, "let's think of other possibilities. If you really believe someone injected the insulin into her IV on purpose, they'd have to have the medical skill to do that and access to the drug."

"That pretty much rules out Russ the builder," said Angie, laughing. "Unless he completed medical school, then decided he really wanted to do something with his hands." She was laughing harder now.

"Why not take up surgery then?" I giggled. "After all that training . . ."

"Not so funny," said Mark. "If someone tried to kill Annabelle—twice—and then Victoria figured it out, she would become a target."

"Or she was the target all along," I said, feeling the playfulness evaporate and the frustration mount.

"Where's your computer? Let's pull up Victoria's column," Angie said. "And why isn't Meigs doing this?"

"Why would he? It's not his jurisdiction. He works in Guilford, not New Haven." I opened the laptop, and typed "Victoria White Southwestern Connecticut Town Talk" into the Google search bar. Her column loaded and we took turns skimming the material.

"She was ruthless," Mark said after reading the description of a socialite drinking one too many glasses of high-end champagne and getting caught by a local policeman in the backseat of her neighbor's car, her skirt up around her waist.

"Listen to this," Angie said. "What prestigious Manhattan orthopedic surgeon's new wife was caught with another man—much younger—in a Greenwich Village nightclub?"

"That sounds like her divorced second husband," I said. "The one who's in town for a special consultation at the Yale University Medical School symposium," I added. Angie and I both looked at Mark. Everyone knows that physicians answer phone calls from other physicians first.

"Fine," he said glumly. "I'll try to reach him tomorrow."

After my dinner guests left, I cleaned up the kitchen, wiping down the counters, sweeping and swabbing the floor. Our theories bounced around my head like boats loose from their moorings. I had to concentrate. I had to find Annabelle's remaining sister. She would understand the family in a way that no one else could. As I scraped the few remaining crumbs of the red velvet cake into the trash, memories of the drunken dinner party resurfaced. Russ had informed me haughtily that Annabelle was depressed and that he was the only one who made her laugh. He might know more than I gave him credit for. I dialed his number.

"It's Rebecca Butterman," I said when he answered. "I wanted to apologize for my behavior on Friday night. It's no excuse, but I've been so stressed about Annabelle and I'm afraid I took it out on you."

"Forget about it," he said, projecting over the TV that blared in the background.

"Her sister was murdered last night." My voice caught raggedly. "I thought you might be able to help me contact the younger sister, the one with the manic-depressive illness?"

"I really don't know anything about her," he said after a long pause during which I could hear a pitch for Budweiser on his TV. "And you know what? This is all getting way too weird. Annabelle is a great gal and I wish her the best. But please don't call me again." He hung up.

Now I felt my spirits sinking lower, lonely and restless, afraid of what I'd find in my dreams if I went right to bed. I paged through the phone book until I reached the Guilford *M*'s: Meigs, J and A. 78 Broad Street. Without any more thought, I pulled on my jacket and got into the car, inserting Mark's CD into the player. The voice of a heartbroken man singing the country blues swelled to fill the small space: His old love still thought he still cared.

I drove to the town green and turned onto Broad Street, cruising slowly enough to read the house numbers. This was an old-fashioned neighborhood, just blocks from the river in one direction and an easy walk to the green in the other. Number 78 was a sweet white saltbox with wooden shingles rippling down the roof. A white picket fence lined the sidewalk. There would certainly be roses in summer.

Meigs's minivan was parked in the driveway, pulled up tight to the garage. Another car had nosed in behind the van, and several others lined the street outside the house. The lights were on in the living room, with the blinds half-turned so I could see shapes but no detail. My friend hovered on the edge of life in the ICU, her sister murdered behind a trash bin, and Meigs and his wife were having a party.

I peeled down the street and went home to bed.

Chapter 21

I checked my voicemail in the morning. Dr. Goldman had left a message saying he could see me at noon. No more time to think about Annabelle or Mark or Detective Meigs— I had four patients of my own this morning. I dressed, ate a quick bowl of oatmeal, and headed into my office. The traffic on the highway was worse than usual for a Monday morning and I was fifteen minutes late. My first patient, Tom, waited on the back stoop, fuming.

As I unlocked the door, I apologized and described the pileup over the Saltonstall Bridge. Then I started up the stairs.

"Don't you always say nothing is an accident?" he snipped from two steps below me.

"I'm sorry," I said again, biting back the urge to say more. A lot more. Tom is the poster child for a bad attitude that he often blames on my incompetence or the boneheaded mistakes of anyone close to him. Today I felt tired and crabby— not eager to absorb his negative energy. I managed to make it through the session without lashing out, then cruised through hours with my graduate student, Wendy (almost ready to end her treatment); a new mother coming out of her postpartum depression; and Miranda, an unpleasant, chubby woman with an intractable case of bulimia.

With no time for a real lunch, I grabbed a package of peanut butter crackers from my bottom desk drawer and hurried out to Goldman's office. He greeted me at the door and we settled into our customary chairs. His eyebrows peaked with what looked like more than his standard professional curiosity.

I flashed on the tray I'd built in the sand with Dr. Phipps. Ridiculous as it sounded, I felt like I'd cheated on him with Phipps and his figurines. I had the urge to skip over it. But then I'd waste the hour covering my tracks, not talking about what was really on my mind. Better to confess and try to understand the parallel, as totally mortifying as that might feel.

"My friend Annabelle was beaten in her own home last Wednesday," I began, feeling the tears burn my eyes. "I found her." I squinted to squeeze them back and took a couple of deep breaths before continuing. "You know I was supposed to go to Boston this week with Janice and Brittany? Instead I ended up seeing some of Annabelle's patients and trying to spend as much time with her as I was allowed. Which wasn't much."

"She's in the hospital?" Goldman asked.

"ICU. A coma," I said, gripping the armrests of my chair. "And then her sister was murdered yesterday—actually Saturday night. Right here in New Haven."

Goldman looked shocked. "Are the incidents connected?"

I leaned forward, sweaty palms on my knees. "That's the big question. Wouldn't you think someone would be asking that—someone like a detective, for example?" I said fiercely, thinking of Meigs. "Meanwhile, I was having a devil of a time understanding Annabelle's sandplay patients so I went to see her supervisor/therapist, Dr. Phipps. That's actually why I had to cancel last week."

Dr. Goldman pursed his lips, smelling blood I supposed. "Her supervisor/therapist?"

"I believe he does a little of each. At any rate, I ended up making a tray with him myself."

Goldman spread his hands out. "And?"

I shrugged and laughed weakly. "Turns out I'm a little girl lost in the woods of my own psyche. Ha-ha." But it didn't feel funny, and Goldman wasn't going to let me get away with a joke at my own expense.

"Explain."

So I told him about placing the girl with her hobo stick into the tray, and then marching her up to the woods, and walking her away when she got too close.

"It probably has to do with my father, don't you think?" I asked. "Anyway, Mark agrees it's time to really pursue getting in touch with him."

"Mark agrees?" he asked, eyes bulging slightly. "Have I missed something here?"

"Not really," I said, then: "Sort of. We had breakfast on Saturday, then last night he and Angie came over for supper. It wasn't a social get-together. We were talking about Annabelle and the murder case. The New Haven cops aren't all that interested and Detective Meigs seems to have dropped off the earth." The last words wobbled out.

"New Haven is not his jurisdiction?" Goldman suggested gently.

I nodded and sighed. "I guess I figured he'd be interested anyway. That's what's in my deep forest—men who don't care. Men who say they do, but don't follow through."

"And Mark?" he asked. "What's the meaning of picking things up with him?"

Goldman had to be thinking about the months we'd spent hashing over the disappointment of Mark's infidelity and the effort it had taken to decide to end the marriage. I hate it when patients backslide and wipe out hours and hours of work during the weakness of one lonely moment. Did I want to start over again with Mark?

"I'm not certain," I said. "I'd like to say that I just want a shot at a better ending, but I don't know that for sure." I told him about the dreadful dinner party on Friday and how I'd bolted from Bob and his parents on the first tee.

"You're not quite ready for a man who does care," said Goldman, "a man whose intentions are straightforward."

"Maybe Bob's not the right guy," I argued. "Maybe I need support from someone who knows me well. Mark understands exactly what it would mean to contact my father. I could spend the next thirty years trying to explain that to Bob."

"You're still afraid to let people really know you," Goldman said. "You still feel like the little girl whose family was destroyed by depression. You're afraid a normal guy will find your history repulsive. Mark already knows it, so nothing would surprise him."

"Maybe," I said.

"If you protect your secrets, they keep you separate," he said.

"I know that," I said. "Exposing the jugular is not as easy as you make it sound."

"Let's talk more about your father," said Goldman.

"He's supposed to be coming back from his semester in Thailand this weekend," I said. "I think it's time that I called and had a few words with him."

Goldman looked at the clock on the table next to the couch. "Our time's up for today. We'll continue on Thursday?"

⁓

I left the session feeling drained and sad. Goldman hadn't had that much to say in the entire last half year. The sand tray must have hit a nerve with him too. I stuffed my hands into my pockets and noticed the small square of paper I'd removed from Dr. Frazier and Annabelle's bulletin board, jammed into the bottom seam.

Annabelle, please call me. Are you okay?

I didn't feel much like comforting someone else, but I dialed the number anyway and left a message saying I was covering for Annabelle and would be happy to talk. The phone rang as soon as I'd finished.

"It's Mark. Dr. White agreed to meet in the cafeteria for a coffee. I told him it was about a research study."

"I'll be there in a few." Amazing how a sense of purpose could dispel the gloom.

Chapter 22

I zipped over the six blocks from my office to the hospital and found a metered spot near the Yale Physicians' Building. Sooner or later, I would work up the courage to reenter the parking garage. But not today.

Mark was seated at a table in the atrium, near the bronze statue of a woman with a sleeping child sprawled on her lap. He was deep in conversation with another dark-haired man in a white coat. I paused behind the fronds of a tall plant, mired in the doubts generated by the session with Goldman. What *had* I been doing with Mark over the last week? In most ways, it was hard to picture going backward. First of all, the entire Yale community knew he'd stepped out on me. Which technically should reflect on him, not me. The truth was, I felt deeply shamed by his treason. Second, was I willing to live with the back of my brain tracking his actions, looking for signs of dissatisfaction that might lead to another betrayal, more upheaval? Still, my stomach lurched at the sight of him, wearing the tweed jacket I'd given him the first Christmas we were married.

Mark spotted me, smiled, and waved. I ignored him, strode over to the table, and offered my hand to Victoria's ex. He looked up and frowned.

"Dr. White? I'm Dr. Butterman, a friend of Annabelle Hart's. I'm deeply sorry for your loss."

"Thank you." His eyes were veiled behind a pair of tinted glasses. But his shoulders had tensed and his voice was wary.

I dragged a chair over from the next table and sat down. "I was hoping we could talk a bit about Victoria. I assume you know that her sister, Annabelle, is upstairs in the ICU?"

He nodded, then frowned and turned to glare at Mark. "I thought *you* and *I* were having coffee to discuss a possible research collaboration. Psychiatric predictors of successful spinal fusion in postcombat troops. I believe that's what you said."

"Rebecca insisted on meeting you," said Mark apologetically. "You know how aggressive an ex-wife can be."

Now we were both glaring at Mark.

"I honestly didn't think you'd agree to meet me if I told you the subject of discussion would be your former wife," he said.

"You were correct," Dr. White said sharply, but his mouth drooped, looking sad. "I can't believe this happened to her."

"We're terribly sorry," I said again. "This must be so hard."

"Her current husband is in South America and couldn't be bothered to get a flight out until the end of the week," he said, "so I had to make the ID."

"That sounds just awful," I said, watching for signs of suspicious behavior mixed in with the sadness. It would be hard to fake the gray skin color and the slight tremor of his hands. He looked like a man in mourning.

"Victoria mentioned that your divorce was somewhat rancorous," Mark said.

Dr. White jerked his chin back and drew his spine up straight. "The police already interviewed me on that topic," he said. "I have nothing else to say. And when did *you* talk to Victoria?"

Mark flushed.

I jumped in. "Actually, I had that conversation with her," I said gently. "We're not trying to accuse you of anything. It's just that Annabelle's life could be in danger too. She's a dear friend," I added. "If Victoria's murder was related to what happened to Annabelle, she's still in grave danger."

The doctor looked at Mark's face and then mine. "You're quite a tag team. You two aren't married now?"

Mark's face turned purple and he began to stammer.

"Just friends," I answered with a breezy wave. "Would you mind awfully telling us about your conversation with the police? Any little detail might help."

He reached for his wedding band and began to rotate it around his finger. "Mostly they were interested in where I was Saturday night. Fortunately for me, I was at dinner with colleagues. It was past ten when they dropped me off at the hotel and I went right to bed."

"Where are you staying in New Haven?" I asked. "For a town as busy as this, our accommodations are a little dated."

"The Omni," he said, glaring again. "I'm well aware that Victoria was checked in there. And murdered just blocks away. I've already reviewed that with the cops."

"Were you close to Annabelle?" I asked.

"I liked—like her just fine," he said. "But the sisters weren't close so we didn't have that many opportunities to relate. Honestly, Victoria described her as something of a goody-goody. And you may or may not be aware that they were in conflict over their other sister, Heather, and the distribution of the family trust."

"Would you be willing to tell us a little more about that?" Mark asked in his kindliest bedside manner.

Dr. White drew his palm across his forehead and tugged on his ear. "I tried not to get involved when we were married. It's too easy to end up as the bad guy yourself once you come down on the wrong side of an old family drama. Next thing you know, the wind's shifted and your sails are flapping.

"This girl had had problems her entire life. Her parents tried everything—understandably, you don't want to allow your child to sink. But Victoria wanted to draw a line in the sand once and for all. I tried to suggest that it was only money and there was plenty to go around, but she squawked so fiercely I kept my other opinions to myself."

"Do you think it's possible that Heather murdered your ex-wife?" Mark asked.

I thought Dr. White might cry, but he shook his head and fell silent for a moment. "I wouldn't like to think so. But if there were drugs involved, we all know anything's possible."

"And what about her gossip column?" I asked, tensing for his reaction. "Any chance the shooting was related to something Victoria wrote? Someone she slandered?"

He scowled and knocked his fist on the table. "Victoria was a rat—truly ruthless when it came to that stupid column. I'm sure you know that she broke the story about my present wife's so-called infidelity."

"That must have been difficult," I said, patting his hand. If Mark and I still carted postmarital baggage, it was carry-on compared to the trunks this man dragged around from his marriage to Victoria. How in the world had he managed to meet another woman so quickly and marry again? My eyes narrowed: Maybe he too had had someone on the side.

He tugged at the knot of his tie. "It took me some time to realize that nothing was sacred with that woman. She did not understand the concept of privacy. Her reputation as the social diva of southwestern Connecticut was more important than anything else." He removed his glasses and pressed his face into his hands. "She was so desperate for attention." He slid his glasses back on.

"In the end, her neediness simply overwhelmed our marriage. She was jealous of my work, jealous of my students, jealous of the time I spent traveling. Most astonishing of all, she didn't understand why I wasn't willing to tell her everything. I'm still stunned about what she printed about me and Dora."

I snuck a glance at Mark to see if he noticed it too. This man may have divorced Victoria and gone on to marry another woman, but he remained deeply conflicted by the loss. And her betrayal.

"I hate to be blunt," said Mark, "but any chance Dora could have shot her?"

"Not a chance in hell," the doctor said firmly. "It was all lies. Dora forgave her. Listen, even Annabelle's caseload wasn't off-limits," he added.

"She included information about her sister's patients in the column?" Mark asked.

"So Annabelle said."

"Surely Annabelle would have the sense not to speak with her sister about her patients," I said.

"One would think." Dr. White shrugged. "I need to be on my way," he said, pushing his chair back and standing abruptly.

"Will you be handling the funeral arrangements?" I asked.

"I've spoken with Jorge—the current husband—by phone. Victoria will be cremated. We'll hold the ashes until her sister is out of the woods. Then perhaps he'll deign to reenter the country for her funeral." He bared his teeth in a humorless grin and hurried off toward the elevators.

"I'd like to hear Victoria's side of that story," I said.

"Too late for that," Mark said. "Regardless of what he might have done to deserve it, she screwed him good."

"In spite of everything, he still loved her," I replied. "Did you see? He had tears in his eyes. He loved her in spite of all the damage she did. In spite of how he might have betrayed her first."

"You don't know what he did," Mark started.

"My point exactly," I snapped.

Mark cracked a grin. "You can love someone and hate her at the same time," he said. "Didn't they teach that class in your psychology program?"

I slapped his wrist and he stood up and bowed. Just then, a slender young woman approached our table. A blond braid hung nearly to her waist and she clutched a notebook and a water bottle.

"Dr. Sanders, will you be holding office hours later this afternoon? I'm Tara Darling. I so enjoyed your talk at grand rounds this morning but I have a few questions."

He glanced at his watch. "I have some time now if you're free. Oh, this is Dr. Butterman. Rebecca, Tara Darling. She's one of our top interns."

I shook her hand—weak grip, moist palm. A nervous groupie.

"Now would be perfect!" she almost squealed.

"Thanks for setting this meeting up," I said to Mark.

"You're welcome. Call me later with any news." He

faded into a crowd of chattering medical workers, Tara
shadowing close behind. I pushed away an uncomfortable
mix of jealousy and annoyance.

As long as I was here, I decided to shoot up to the sixth
floor to visit Annabelle. Upstairs, I pushed the buzzer on
the wall outside the ICU and announced my name and purpose. The double doors swung open. Nurse McHugh hurried out from behind the desk.

"Good news," she whispered. "They extubated her this
morning. She's breathing on her own!"

"Thank God," I said, feeling a surge of joy and hugging
the nurse. "Is she conscious?"

"Not yet," said the nurse. "But the signs are good. She's
withdrawing from painful stimuli and her eyes are roving.
Go ahead in and see her." She looped an arm around my
shoulders. "We feel so awful about her sister."

I nodded in agreement and headed into Annabelle's cubicle. She definitely looked better without the tube taped to
her face. A fine burr of hair was beginning to darken her
scalp and the repaired trauma flap was no longer inflamed.
She appeared to be sleeping but sighed and turned her head
toward the window.

"Annabelle," I breathed, leaning over the bed rail to
touch her shoulder. Her eyelids flickered, but there was no
sign of obvious recognition. "You're looking so much better. I just met Larry White, your ex-brother-in-law? He's
terribly sorry about your accident and sends his best re-
gards." Not that anybody could describe it as an accident,
but I was still baffled about what to say and how much she
understood. "He seems like a nice fellow."

I perched on the chair beside the bed. "Not that he and
Victoria seem like they were a great match. But you never
know why two people can't make a marriage work, do
you? Most of us have no idea what's involved when we

promise to commit ourselves to someone for life." I sighed and rested my chin on the guardrail. "Mark's been really sweet this past week. Dr. Goldman wonders if I'm regretting the divorce. In some ways, I know I am. Goldman thinks I'm willing to settle because I'm afraid to let someone else in." I felt a flash of anger, thinking of Mark heading off with the fawning student.

"But you don't want to hear that old garbage again." I searched my mind for something cheery to report and ended up summarizing the plot of a romance I'd finished the night before. "Of course she lived happily ever after—with the right hunk." I snickered. "Think that ever happens in real life?" I patted her arm, careful to avoid the IV lines and the bruises. "I'll see you tomorrow. I love you."

Chapter 23

I switched my phone back on as I walked to the car and played back the two messages that had been recorded during my time in the hospital.

"Ummm. Hello. This is Annabelle's sister, Heather." The quavering voice paused and I could hear shallow breathing. "I wish I could talk to you. I'm so worried about Annabelle. But Victoria won't let me see her. She told the nurses—" She burst into tears and a man in the background yelled for her to get off the goddamn phone. "Is there any way I could meet with you? You're Annabelle's best friend, right? Maybe I'll come by her office later, see if you're there." The connection ended abruptly. I tried pressing *redial*, but no number came up.

I listened to the second message, thinking it couldn't possibly be worse.

"Dr. Butterman? We met the other day. Last week, I mean. I'm sorry for running out on you like that. It's three o'clock now. If you possibly could call me back in the next hour?" She read off a phone number. "Please don't call after that." No name, but it sure sounded like the patient with the abusive husband.

I slid into my car, turned on the engine, then turned up the heat. The day was cooling off quickly and it looked like rain again. I called Annabelle's patient back.

"Thank you so much for phoning," she said before I even had the chance to identify myself. "Could I possibly come in for my regular time at six tonight?"

"Absolutely." I started to rattle off directions to my office on Orange Street.

I could hear her hyperventilating on the phone.

"Do you have a sand tray there?" the woman whispered.

"No." If I insisted on having her come to my building, she probably wouldn't show up. "Never mind, I'll see you at Ms. Hart's office at six. That will be fine. I'm glad you called."

I hung up and sighed, thinking how much more comfortable I would have felt on my own turf. The weight of the last week's stressful events was taking its toll. But Annabelle's patient needed to feel safe more than I did. And this way, I'd be available in case Annabelle's sister actually showed.

I was very curious to meet this sister. Victoria and Annabelle seemed to have so little in common. And from all reports, Heather was another 180 degrees from either of them. Or however you'd figure the math. How could one set of parents produce three such different results? Annabelle would want me to be kind to her sister—within reason. It sounded as though Heather hadn't even heard about Victoria's murder—unless that was a smoke screen for her own part in the death. Which I didn't quite believe. What blood relative shoots a sibling and pretends it didn't happen? Just to be on the safe side, I left messages for both Angie and Mark about my plans for the rest of the day.

The peanut butter crackers I'd eaten on the way to my therapy session were definitely not going to hold me through this afternoon. I called Thali, an Indian restaurant at the end of Orange Street, and ordered takeout—My Mother's Andhra Chicken, hot and spicy enough to singe the skin off the roof of my mouth. And an order of fried cauliflower in hot cilantro garlic sauce. My mouth was already watering.

I swung by the restaurant, located exactly across the street from where the New Haven Coliseum had once stood—first reduced to a pile of rubble, now just a vacant lot. I grinned: Didn't therapy feel just like that sometimes? The psychological structure is so flawed you have the urge to tear the whole thing down and start over.

I nipped into the restaurant, grabbed my fragrant bag, and drove to Annabelle's office. Before parking, I circled the block once, just anxious enough to want to check for anything out of place. Noticing nothing worrisome, I dashed through the fine mist that had started to fall and bolted up the stairs.

After locking the door, I settled behind Annabelle's desk and began to eat, the tension easing as the hot food hit my stomach. Halfway through the cauliflower, I was hit with a wave of exhaustion. I folded Annabelle's afghan into a pillow and stretched out on the carpet, hoping to doze off for a few minutes. But sleep refused to come as the madness of the last few days spun through my mind.

I got back up and went over to the computer, thinking that giving advice might feel more soothing than hashing out my own questions. At least I'd be in control of the answers.

I opened up the file of letters from *Bloom!* readers and began to scroll through. The first one I opened sent me whirling all over again:

Dear Dr. Aster:
I finally told my best friend since high school about a problem I was having with my husband sleeping around. I've never talked to any-one about this—and never will again. Several days later I heard my story repeated back to me by another friend. The names weren't in-cluded of course, but I feel so betrayed and angry. I'm very tempted to do something that will hurt her back—like spill the beans on an affair she had. I can't emphasize how angry I am . . .

Was this why Victoria died? Did she learn a secret that made her a murder target? Was her death related to Annabelle's attacker? I simply couldn't believe that Annabelle would have told her sister anything about her caseload. She would have known better than to trust her with patient information. Although Victoria had probably been expert at filling in gaps and making educated guesses.

I typed in the web address for Victoria's gossip column. A small black box had been added to the page, lamenting the death of the column's writer. Details about a memorial service would be posted as they became available. Hard to imagine this website would garner a lot of mourners.

I scrolled through the last few months of columns, look-ing for a secret so big that someone would kill because it was leaked. Or was in danger of leaking. And juicy enough to make sizzling gossip. Most of the names seemed to be connected to the Fairfield County area, some from as far south as Manhattan. But one paragraph caught my eye:

"Which Yale professor has been dipping his wick into his own student population? Will he be brought up on charges of sexual harassment? Check back next week for the gory details . . ."

There would be no next week for Victoria's column. And there wasn't enough information here to draw any conclusions about whether this entry had a connection to Annabelle, beyond her proximity to Yale. Rather than give in to feeling discouraged, I forced myself to search a second time through Annabelle's files. Maybe I could come at the problem from the other direction.

Starting with her top desk drawer, I opened each patient folder, paged through the sand tray photos, and read—tried to read—my friend's scribbles describing standard stories of wobbly relationships, bruised feelings, life's roadblocks. Nothing jumped out so I moved to the file cabinet in the closet—the one filled with notes so cryptic I wondered if Annabelle herself would understand them.

Only one looked promising: *24 y.o. swf. YUmss. Ptsd? Supv har? CS????* Could this be the file for the Yale medical student I'd seen here last week? She'd come in complaining of feeling harried and exhausted, then left almost immediately. PTSD had to mean post-traumatic stress disorder. *Supv har*? Hard to decipher. I studied the sand tray photo with the naked baby and the medical doctor. It was a leap, but supposing she'd come in to discuss sexual harassment by a supervisor? *Supv har? CS?* I crossed the room and pulled the Yale directory out of the top drawer. Dr. Craig Sebastian was one of three male faculty members whose initials fit the bill.

I knew Sebastian supervised students in their psychiatry rotation at the medical school, in addition to overseeing interns and residents. While serving as my medical backup, he'd proven that his professional boundaries could be porous. Would he feel terribly threatened if someone planned to expose his sleazy practices? Definitely. Was he capable of shooting a woman in cold blood or beating my friend in her home? That seemed like a stretch.

I set that folder aside and continued through the others. At the back of the drawer I found a sand tray printout that looked as though it had been misfiled. With a jolt, I recognized the arrangement as very similar to the tray I'd seen in Annabelle's home, though the spacing looked slightly different: a fairy on a leaf threatened by the doom master, the half-buried baby, a knight. The knight had not been present in the tray I described to Dr. Phipps. Or was I losing my mind and my memory?

I leaned back in Annabelle's chair and ran my fingers through my hair. If Annabelle didn't discuss her patients with her sister (and I knew she wouldn't), was there someone else she might have discussed them with? And would that someone have leaked privileged information to Victoria? Only two names came to mind: Annabelle's office mate, Dr. Connie Frazier, and her therapist, Dr. Howdy Phipps. I decided to start with the one I was positive wasn't involved. I punched in Dr. Phipps's office number.

"Dr. Phipps, it's me again. Rebecca Butterman, with a follow-up question?"

"Of course. How's Annabelle?" he asked.

"She's improving. They took the breathing tube out. That's a very good sign. But there's bad news—her sister was murdered."

"Good Lord," he said. "What a dreadful coincidence."

"Or not," I said. "It happened just blocks from the hospital. In fact, I'm wondering whether some information about one of Annabelle's patients might have been leaked to her sister? Supposing you had a really ugly secret—something you'd told only to your therapist. And then it showed up in her sister's gossip column. You might be mad enough to kill someone."

"You very well might," said Dr. Phipps.

I waited a moment. "If you had any ideas, I could take them to the police. Or you could."

"Annabelle never discussed a problem like that," he said.

I wished I could see his face, just to be certain, though his voice was appropriately incredulous.

"You remember the sand tray that I sketched when I was in your office? I found a photograph of that same arrangement in her file cabinet. It appears that one of the figurines was missing: a knight in full armor. He was placed in the far corner of the tray near the buried baby, but looking away from the scene inside the tray."

"Fascinating," he said. And then, "I've been thinking about this ever since you left the other day. There was so much sadness in that tray. Along with a certain sense of inevitability. The figure you say was missing is a strong male— at least on the outside, the armor. Inside? Who knows? And you say he was turned away from the rest of the tray?"

"That's right."

"Could it have fallen onto the floor? Does she have a cleaning service that might have been careless?"

I hadn't thought of something that simple. I hung up after telling him I'd keep in touch, feeling certain Phipps hadn't been involved in this or any other crime. What had Annabelle been so sad about? Her family? Was Russ the builder her knight in shining armor? I sat up straight. Sometimes a therapist's spouse hears bits and pieces about the lives of her patients in the process of normal unwinding. Supposing they had drinks, or dinner, and she revealed more than she should have, and then he called Victoria and fed her the dirt?

Ridiculous. What would that possibly gain him? Besides, Annabelle barely knew Russ—he wasn't a longtime trusted confidant. And what were the chances he'd even been introduced to Victoria? Practically nil.

Annabelle's clock rang out five strokes. There was no sign of Heather, still an hour to wait for the battered woman, and I was drooping. I grabbed my purse and headed out for a latte at Willoughby's coffee. If caffeine and pure sugar didn't get me through the next few hours, nothing would.

Chapter 24

Feeling perkier and more cheerful after a latte and a sugar cookie, I took a power walk down Whitney Avenue and then Trumbull before heading back to Annabelle's office. Not far from the building housing Goldman's office, I noticed a small brass sign that hadn't registered over the many times I'd walked this route before: a short list of lawyers, followed by *Dr. Craig Sebastian, Diplomat in Psychiatry*. With my bravery fortified by the busyness of rush hour, I made the quick decision to stop in and try to see him. If I caught him by surprise, maybe he'd slip and say something incriminating. Something specific I could turn over to the cops. For as much as I disliked the man, I wasn't going to point a finger without some concrete and believable facts.

The dark wood paneling in the lobby of Sebastian's brownstone was brightened by crystal wall sconces and a pair of paisley love seats. An attractive woman with eyebrows plucked too thin and a mole just to the left of her top lip manned the desk facing the door. She had earphones on and was typing furiously into a computer.

"Can I help you?" she asked, pulling the headset off her ears and balancing it on her shoulders.

"I'd like to see Dr. Sebastian," I said. "I don't have an appointment but I'm a colleague. I took the chance that he might be free." I pushed my card across the polished wood surface of her desk and flashed a megawatt smile.

"I haven't seen anyone go up in the past hour," she said, and punched some buttons on the phone. "A Dr. Butterman to see you?" She held the phone away from her ear and winced. "He's coming down," she told me once she hung up. She righted the headset and resumed typing.

Heavy footsteps echoed from a stairway at the end of the hall and Sebastian emerged. He was physically reminiscent of a punching bag, but dressed in an expensive-looking dark suit. "Yes?"

"Perhaps we should speak privately," I said.

"I only have a minute," he huffed impatiently. "I'm booked right through to eight o'clock."

"Fine." I smoothed my hair behind my ears. "Does the name Victoria White mean anything to you?"

He shrugged and frowned. "Not really."

"How about the 'Southern Connecticut Town Talk'?"

He tapped the watch hanging from his belt loop. "Could you get to the point?"

"Sexual harassment," I said firmly.

He drew his chin back, skin doubling under his partial beard. "You're accusing me of harassing you?" He chuckled and waved a dismissive hand. "I don't even find you remotely attractive."

"I'm talking about your student," I said, working to keep the shake out of my voice. Reminding myself this man was an idiot and that under no circumstances should I bow to his humiliating tactics. "A young medical student who does not appreciate or deserve the lascivious and inappropriate attention from a professor, a woman who expects and deserves respect—"

"This is ridiculous," he said. "What is this all about? Do you have a vendetta against me?" He took a step away and tightened the knot of his tie. "I don't generally condone interpreting the issues of other professionals, but I will make an exception in this case because I'm concerned about your competence. And I've seen you crashing around enough to feel a warning is warranted. I believe you have some father issues that are being translated into these desperate cries for attention. I strongly recommend that you bring these up in your own treatment. Excuse me." He turned and waddled back down the hall and up the stairs, the kind of man who would have taken an elevator had it been available.

I started past the secretary.

"Nasty little toad, isn't he?" she muttered as I went by.

I flashed her a grateful smile and headed back to Annabelle's office, having succeeded in nothing more than aggravating a man who was quite capable of making trouble for me in the future. It was close to five thirty—the streets clogged with impatient commuters, the headlights of the cars cutting through the gathering dusk. I hurried down Whitney Avenue and cut over to the row of brownstones behind Ninth Square, then came to a screeching halt. A green Mercedes was parked in the lot, the same make and model as the car reported by the sweet older couple in Annabelle's neighborhood.

I glanced up: The lights in Dr. Frazier's office were on. I could panic again and assume the worst of her. Or I could go in, do the job I'd promised to do, and get home.

I dashed up the stairs and collapsed into Annabelle's rocker, the door locked firmly behind me. Then I reviewed

Dr. Loathsome Sebastian's parting sally: My father issues were being translated into desperate cries for attention. For five minutes I wallowed in pure outrage. Then the memories of the woods I'd constructed with Dr. Phipps and my conversation with Mark pushed away some of the fury.

If you believe in this kind of thing, which I generally don't, it seemed as though the universe was speaking this week: "Call your father."

So I booted up the computer, determined to face the confrontation I'd been avoiding for years. My father's office phone number was listed on the Michigan State University Department of Agriculture website. I took a deep breath and dialed.

"Arthur Butterman." His words sounded harried and curt.

"Dr. Butterman . . . Arthur . . . this is Dr. Rebecca Butterman. I'm sure you're quite busy—"

"I did get your e-mail message," he said, his voice softening. "I'm just back in the country. I was planning to call."

"Not a problem," I said. But it was a problem. What kind of man waits four months to respond to his estranged daughter's e-mail? My place on his list of priorities had been a problem all along. "I know I said in my e-mail last December"—I emphasized *December*—"that I had some questions about family medical history."

"I'm so sorry I didn't call sooner," he said. "Is something wrong?"

"I wasn't completely honest," I said. "I have some things I need to get off my chest." I felt myself mentally gathering speed.

"Maybe we could set up a time to talk," he started.

"I'd like to say this now," I said. "I've been waiting to ask for years and I'd just as soon get it over with. How could you have left us alone to deal with our mother's death? We were children."

Dead silence.

"Your grandparents were there to take care of you," he finally said. "Your grandmother was determined to handle it her way. They refused to let you girls leave Guilford. We were all overwhelmed with guilt and grief. I simply couldn't stay."

"And so you let us go, just like that?"

"The job came up in Michigan and I intended to come back for you once I was settled in—"

"But you didn't. Two girls under the age of ten and you just never showed."

"Your grandparents—"

I rolled on before he could offer more lame explanations. "A father isn't a place saver, you know. Psychology 101—a little girl learns about relationships by watching her parents. And by what she experiences with her *father*. Did you ever think of that? Did you stop to consider what it meant to lose both parents at once?"

He stayed quiet this time. A moment of silence as the bell tolled for our relationship, I thought. A death knell for all the possibilities.

"I'm sorry," he said softly. "You can't imagine the regrets I've lived with. Are you married?" he asked.

I wouldn't have answered if I hadn't been so surprised. "I was until I found him with another woman," I said.

"Rat bastard," said my father.

I burst out laughing. "He's not a bad guy. We had breakfast on Saturday. And he's been a big support lately. He has regrets too. I seem to specialize in men who let me down and feel just awful about it later. Or so they say."

Annabelle's buzzer sounded, announcing the arrival of her six o'clock patient. I crossed the room with the phone in my hand and pushed the button to release the latch for the downstairs door.

"I have to go," I said.

"How's Janice?"

"She's fine," I said. "She has a husband and an adorable daughter. If anything, you'll find her to be a tougher nut than I am."

"May I call you another time? I'd be very grateful if we could continue to talk," he said. "And listen: You shouldn't have to settle for any man. You deserve a man who will be there for you fully. Regardless of any mistakes I made."

I read off my home and cell phone numbers and hung up, thinking of Mark blowing hot and cold, and Meigs, the same thing on a different level. What was that all about anyway? And then there was Good Old Bob. Did faithful and attentive have to equal the excitement of drying paint? That wasn't fair, and I knew it.

I had about thirty seconds to get my head together before Annabelle's patient hit the room with her own set of problems—a lot more current and pressing than mine.

Chapter 25

Loud footsteps clattered up the stairs and someone began banging violently on the office door. I crossed the room again, opened the inside door, and peered through Annabelle's peephole. It wasn't Annabelle's patient; it was her sister, Heather. Had to be. Up close, the resemblance to Victoria was striking. She was hysterical, leaning against the door, sobbing and howling. She dropped out of view, fingernails scraping the wood, and began to pound rhythmically on the bottom of the door.

I cracked it open, pushing against the weight of her, and peered out. Too late, I wondered if I should have dialed 911 first. "Can I help you?"

She scrambled into the office on hands and knees and staggered to her feet, clutching her arms and shivering. She was dressed in a long skirt, sneakers, and a filthy white sweatshirt. I shifted into hyperalert: This *was* the same woman who had snatched my purse.

"Victoria's dead. Victoria's dead. Annabelle's dying," she moaned. "He did it, he did it. He killed her!"

"Who did it?" I asked gently.

She swayed and keened. "He wasn't supposed to hurt her."

Sounded more and more like Victoria had been right—this girl was involved in some kind of scam gone bad. "Where is he?" I asked, thinking I could send the police after the boyfriend while I tried to calm her down.

Heather threw back her head and howled.

Leaving the door ajar so neither one of us would feel trapped, I took her hand and tried to lead her to Annabelle's rocker. She shrugged me off, her eyes widening. I heard the sound of rushing liquid and watched in disbelief as her skirt darkened and a pool of urine spread around her sneakers. She had to be high as a kite. The downstairs buzzer door rang at the same time that someone else knocked on my door. Could things get any worse?

Dr. Frazier poked her head into the office, absorbing the sight of the disturbed girl and the puddle of urine that had beaded on the wood floor and threatened to seep into the carpet. Heather stumbled across the room and, with one sweep of her arm, smashed an entire shelf of figurines to the ground. The buzzer rasped a second time.

"Are you expecting one of Ms. Hart's patients?" Dr. Frazier asked.

I nodded. "I hope that's who it is." I lowered my voice to almost nothing and gestured at the keening girl. "This is Heather, Annabelle's younger sister. I'm afraid her boyfriend killed their older sister. This is the same girl who snatched my purse the other day too."

"Good Lord! May I take a run at calming her down?" she asked. "Then we can figure out what to do with her."

"Be my guest. I'm out of ideas."

Frazier smoothed her hands over the plaid pleats on her

hips and took a step toward Heather. "I'll take her to my office to do a quick evaluation, and then we can put our heads together after you've handled the other patient."

Never in my life had I felt so confused about what was happening and whom to trust. Heather crouched down to the level of the lower shelf and began to grab figurines and hurl them across the room. A goblin whizzed by my head. Dr. Frazier eased across the office, clucking her tongue as though the girl was a feral cat.

"Heather," she crooned, "look at me." The girl shifted her gaze to meet Dr. Frazier's eyes. "Heather, won't you come with me and I'll get you a drink? Would you like something to drink?"

Heather swallowed and nodded.

"Would you rather have a cold soda or something hot? I have some lovely herbal tea. And crackers too. Come now, come now." Once she reached the girl, she bent down and began to rub her back in slow circles.

Heather's sobs quieted into hiccups and Dr. Frazier drew her out of the office and down the hall. The psychotic patient whisperer, I thought with admiration. I hustled across the hallway to grab a handful of towels to blot the urine leaching from the floor to the Oriental rug. Both women had tracked through the puddle on the way out.

Annabelle's patient appeared in the doorway, looking worried and pale. She scanned the mess in the room and me on my knees. "Do I have the time wrong?"

"No, please come in," I said. "We had a small crisis but it's all under control."

I pasted on my most reassuring smile and scrambled to my feet. She crept over to the rocking chair and sank down, clutching her purse to her stomach. I dropped the paper towels in the trash, shut the doors, and then squeezed a dollop of Purell from the bottle on Annabelle's coffee table and rubbed my hands briskly. Lowering into the chair opposite, I filled my lungs with air and let the breath out slowly. I had to focus on what was happening here now, not what might be blowing up in the office next door. And not on how badly I wanted to scrub my hands with soap and hot water.

"I'm glad to see you," I said. "I don't believe I ever caught your name."

"M-M-Mary," she said, her hands twisting.

"You mentioned that you might wish to use the sand tray this evening?"

She glanced at the chaos on Annabelle's shelves and shook her head. "I'm so confused about my marriage," she said.

"Tell me about it." I leaned forward, balancing my elbows on my knees.

"He can be so kind," she said, dabbing a bit of moisture from the corner of her eye with the back of one hand. "We have an elderly cat. Orange tiger. Charlie." She looked up. "Eighteen years old."

"That's a good long life," I said smiling. "I love those big tabbies."

"He's become diabetic," she said, her eyes filling again. "I'm phobic about needles. So my husband gives him injections twice a day. He doesn't even like animals. He does it for me."

She began to cry, unlatched her pocketbook, and drew out a newspaper clipping. Her hand trembled as she handed it over. It had been neatly snipped from page three of the weekend edition of the *Shore Line Times*.

GUILFORD—Annabelle Hart, a social worker in New Haven, was found severely beaten in her Guilford home on Tuesday night. A spokesman for the

Guilford police department stated that Ms. Hart had apparently interrupted a burglary in progress. A suspect in the assault is under arrest.

"It's terribly upsetting when something bad happens to someone you care about deeply," I said, starting to brush my hair back with my fingers and stopping as I remembered the urine-soaked towels. I was also remembering the insulin overdose in the hospital, every nerve ending in my body now vibrating danger.

Mary was crying harder now, shuddering sobs that racked her shoulders.

"That isn't what happened," she said.

A sharp knock rapped on the office door. Mary's face tightened and she clenched her purse with one hand, poised to bolt.

"Don't worry," I said, "it's the therapist in the office next to ours. We have a patient in some distress. I'll need to speak with her for just a minute."

"No," she whispered in a panicky voice. "Please don't answer. They'll go away."

I stood up, placing the article on the table between us. She was obviously in worse shape psychologically than I'd even imagined—paranoid and quite possibly psychotic. And probably in some real danger at home too. But I couldn't leave Dr. Frazier hanging with Heather.

"I do have to attend to this. I'll be right back."

"He'll kill me," she whispered again. "He said he'd kill me if I came back." She sprang up, darted across the room, and disappeared into Annabelle's closet, pulling the door closed behind her.

I crossed the room, opened the inner door, and peered through the peephole. A man in a doctor's white coat stood outside, his hands in his pockets, facing the stairs. I felt a surge of relief: Thank God, Frazier had called for backup.

"Thanks for coming," I said, cracking open the outside door. "The young lady is next door with Dr. Frazier. Is there an ambulance on the way? Hopefully, they'll come without sirens. She's quite hysterical and that would really spook her. If you haven't already, please call the police too. The woman thinks her boyfriend might have been involved with a murder," I whispered. "I'm with someone right now, but I'll come over as soon as I can, okay?"

The man turned and smiled, a puzzled look on his face. The hospital social worker, Fred Polson. Pieces were falling into place faster than I could process them. The diabetic cat. The secrecy about Mary's name. She had tried to tell me that her abusive husband was in a health-related profession. But I'd been too busy thinking about my own marriage to listen. Another more terrible truth settled: I had to get him out of here before he realized what I knew.

He walked around me into the room. "There must be some confusion. I have a couples' session scheduled with my wife."

"Your wife?" I stammered.

He reached behind me to close both of the office doors. "Do you mind? When you go into this business, you never really think that you might be dealing with mental illness in your own family. It still pains me to admit it, even though I know it's no reflection on her. Or me."

I nodded and waited, trying to work up enough spittle to swallow. I pictured the matching broken fingers on Annabelle and Mary. What was my *plan*?

"I'm terribly concerned about Mary," Polson said, lowering his voice. "She seems to be getting more paranoid by the hour. I hate to think another psychiatric hospitalization is in our future. She was in Silver Hills down in Fairfield County for a month just last fall."

"I'm so sorry to hear that," I croaked.

His face, beaded with sweat, hovered just inches from mine. He tipped his head toward the closet. "She's in there, isn't she? She did that last time too." He clucked his tongue, crossed the room, and opened the closet door before I could protest. His wife gave a little cry of despair.

"Darling, please come out and we'll have a nice talk with Dr. Butterman. We're here to help you, aren't we, Doctor?"

"Everything will be okay," I declared with a heartiness I didn't feel.

Mary crept out of the closet.

"I misplaced my raincoat last time I came for a session," she said, looking tight enough to shatter into pieces.

"We don't have to talk today, Mary," he said. "I'll drive you straight home if you'd rather."

"Let's all sit down," I said, pulling a third chair over from Annabelle's desk, stunned by the idea that Polson was married to Mary. My image of Mary's spouse had been a universe away from this man. I scrambled to make the mental adjustment. This poor woman had been so frightened every time she mentioned her husband, I couldn't possibly let them leave. On the other hand, how could I force them to stay? Would that even help? And who was crazy here?

Mary shook her head and sat down, gathering herself into the smallest imaginable packet. She was shaking so violently that I carried the afghan over to her and tucked it around her shoulders. Polson lowered himself into the other chair and sighed, cocking one foot over the opposite knee. He straightened his white coat and then glanced at the end table, his gaze lighting on the article about Annabelle. He picked it up and read it over. Twice.

Looking up, he caught me staring at his wife's bruised

face, then her bent fingers. The same two fingers that were splinted on Annabelle's hand in the hospital. Polson placed the clipping back on the table. He uncrossed his legs and leaned forward, so earnest. My stomach clenched with fear: He knew.

"Why did you go to her home?" I asked sternly.

"You must understand that I didn't go with the intention of hurting her. Ms. Hart was trying to talk Mary— my *wife*—into leaving me." He reached over and took his wife's hand, squeezing the fingers until she squeaked. "That morning, I stopped in to tell her we were finished with therapy. That she was not to either contact my wife or agree to see her again. Ever. But she was absolutely fine when I left her."

One tear drifted from Mary's eye, liquefying the makeup meant to conceal her fading bruises.

"Of course, Mr. Polson." I scrambled to my feet, keeping my arms pinned to my chest so he wouldn't see the spreading sweat stains or smell the stink of fear. "I'm sure you meant no harm. But I think it would be best if you leave. Your wife is terrified. She doesn't want to go with you right now. Can't you see that?"

"This is our marriage," he said, his voice cold and steady. "Not yours. Not Annabelle Hart's. You have no business interfering. You're making this very difficult." He thumbed the cleft in his chin and frowned. Then he rose from the chair and pointed across the room. "Ladies, you'll need to step into the closet while I go to the car. Where is your cell phone please, Dr. Butterman?"

"That's none of your busi—" I stopped when he pulled a gun from his pocket.

"In my purse, on the desk." Voice shaking, I tried again. "Think of your future. This will cause you unimaginable

trouble. Why don't you leave us alone? Go ahead now. It will
save you some ugliness and, quite possibly, your career."

He ignored me and glared at his wife. "Mary," he said
fiercely, "get in the closet. Now."

"Dr. Butterman, please, please come with me." As Mary
wobbled to her feet, the blanket dropped to the floor and
she clasped her hands in prayer position. I looked at Polson, at the sheer bulk of him and the red face and the furious
expression and the pointed gun, and knew I had no choice.
If I tried to run, even if I got out, she would be at his mercy.
Whatever small mercy he might have.

I took her hand and we walked into the closet. The door
banged behind us and we heard the lock turn. "I'll be back
shortly," his muffled voice said.

"Mary, listen to me," I said. "Do you have a phone in
your purse?"

"N-n-n-no," she said, beginning to snuffle. "Only a car
phone. He's going to kill us."

"He's not. I won't allow it." I found her shoulders in the
darkness, gripped hard, and gave her a shake. "You have to
calm down. You have to be ready for anything. Tell me
everything you know about this."

"I was so worried when Ms. Hart didn't show up last
week. But I wouldn't let myself believe he would hurt her.
Then when I saw the article about the beating in the newspaper, I knew he'd done it. He'd gotten so angry when I
told him I was thinking of leaving."

A soft murmuring of voices wafted through the closet
wall that backed up on Dr. Frazier's office. I yelled her
name and banged on the wall, then began to tap what might
or might not be the Morse code: tap-tap-tap, three long,
tap-tap-tap, three short, tap-tap-tap, three long. And then I
reversed the sequence, just in case I'd messed up the order.

"Shhh," said Mary. "He's back."

Polson threw open the closet door and we huddled together, blinking in the sudden light. He was still holding the gun, along with a roll of silver duct tape. He motioned us into the office.

"Mary, put your hands behind your back. Dr. Butterman, kindly take the tape and fasten them tight. Don't try anything funny." He pointed the gun at his wife's head. Her eyes shimmered with unshed tears.

I took the tape, unrolled a section, and began to wind it loosely around her wrists.

"Tighter," he growled.

I pulled the tape taut, desperate with fear. When I finished, he taped mine behind my back, my skin crawling at his touch.

He disappeared into the closet. Returning with Annabelle's raincoat, he draped it around his wife's trembling shoulders and zipped it closed. Then he buttoned my coat around me, chucking my chin as he fastened the top button.

"Now, ladies," he said. "We're all going out to the car. I will tape your mouths if I need to. I'd rather not, but you can let me know if this is necessary."

"No," sobbed Mary, "please."

"Dammit," I spit out. "You'll never get away—"

He ripped off another length of tape and slapped it across my mouth, obstructing the left nostril too. I pushed back a tide of panic. *Little yoga sips of breath*, I told myself. *Little yoga sips.*

"Let's go." He jabbed his wife in the back with the pistol, opened the door, and gave her a push. I followed her into the hallway, shivering as the cool metal of the gun touched my neck, and started to the stairs. Dr. Frazier's office door swung open. Polson leaped ahead, gripped my arm, and shoved me behind him. He slung his arm across Mary's shoulders and pulled her close. A sociopath's do-si-do.

"Good evening," he said pleasantly to Dr. Frazier. "Feels like spring has finally sprung."

I peered around Polson's left shoulder, and widened my eyes, bulging them over the duct tape. Surely Frazier would notice. Just then Heather stuck her head out of the office, spotted Polson, and let loose an earsplitting scream.

Dr. Frazier winced, covered her ears, and prodded Heather back into her office. "Excuse us, so sorry," she called over her shoulder, her glossy black hair swinging as she followed the girl.

I didn't have time to read her face. Had she understood the situation? Had she heard my tapping from the closet? Surely she'd noticed the tape; if she hadn't, we were dead. Even if she had, Polson would have a big jump on the cops, enough time to dispose of us. And then bolt.

Filled with rage and terror, I inhaled through my free nostril, pushed Mary aside, and head-butted Polson in the back with every ounce of strength I had. He stumbled, clawing for the banister, and crashed down the stairs.

Dr. Frazier's door opened again and Heather's howls echoed into the hall.

"Mmmmph!" I shouted, sort of. I nudged Mary into the office, motioned to Dr. Frazier to close the door, and slammed the inside door shut with my butt.

Chapter 26

Dr. Frazier ripped the duct tape off my face. "What's going on?"

"OWWWW," I yelped. "That really hurt! Get the cops here right away!"

She picked up the phone and pressed 911. "What do I tell them?"

"That was Mary's husband." I glanced at the quivering woman. No point in trying to soft-pedal the facts when she already knew them. "Fred Polson. He attacked Annabelle," I yelped. "He has a gun and he'll kill us if he gets in here.

"There is a police and medical emergency here on Court Street," Dr. Frazier announced when a dispatcher answered her call. "We have a dangerous armed man in the stairwell who may be injured, and three women upstairs who need ambulances." She hung up the phone. "They say they'll be right over."

Both Heather and Mary began to sob.

"Cut the tape off our hands," I shouted over the bedlam.

Dr. Frazier found a pair of scissors in her desk drawer and sawed at the tape binding my wrists. Just then the doorknob rattled.

"Don't answer it! That's him!" I squeaked.

A gunshot echoed loudly outside the room. Heather wailed.

"Get behind the desk," I hissed to the whimpering women, and scanned the office for something we could use as a weapon. Nothing. A mental health professional's arsenal is all in her mind. The doorknob rattled again.

"Goddammit, Mary, open the door! I swear I'll kill you if you don't get out here right now," Polson yelled.

She began to shuffle toward the door. I lunged forward, throwing my weight behind her knees and knocking her to the ground.

We heard pounding footsteps, scuffling, then: "Drop the weapon!"

Someone banged on the door. "Police! Open up!"

"Is that him?" I asked Mary, my face pressed close to hers.

"No."

I rolled off her.

She curled into a ball, still weeping. "Oh my gosh, what has my poor baby gone and done now?"

Dr. Frazier crawled out from under her desk, trotted across the office, and opened the door.

The police and paramedics swarmed into the room. I insisted that Mary and Heather be attended to first and assured everyone I was quite capable of driving myself to the hospital. Besides a good scare, the only injury I'd suffered was the patch of skin ripped off my upper lip from the duct tape incident. Dr. Frazier disappeared into the ambulance with the others, the door slammed shut, and the taillights faded into the dusk.

"What happened to Polson?" I asked the policemen who'd been assigned to document the crime scene.

"He's lucky," he said. "Looks like the worst he suffered was a twisted ankle in the tumble. Usually a man waving a gun like that, we shoot to kill. But he was a damn coward, dropped it before we even ordered him to."

"He shot at us through the door," I said.

"A detective will take your statement at the ER," the second cop said. Which stirred up a small pang of regret—it certainly wouldn't be Meigs.

The policeman escorted me back upstairs to lock both offices. I paused on the stoop outside the building as I left, breathing in the night air, and offering a quick prayer of thanks. I started to my car. The SUV that had tried to run me down in the hospital garage was parked next to my Honda. Polson. Poor Mary. Bad enough to have an abusive husband, never mind a murderer. I'd have a few choice words if I ever saw him again.

I called Angie on the short ride over to the hospital and described what had unfolded.

"I'll be there in twenty minutes," she said.

"There's no need—"

"You need a friend," she said. And I did. After hanging up the phone, I tuned in the NPR news and turned up the volume, determined not to think. I parked in the garage near the security guards, and hurried through the tunnel and into the triage area for the ER. Dr. Frazier was waiting in the lobby.

"I'll show you where they are," she said, and led me to the cubicles in the back where both women dozed. A line of drool ran from Heather's lips to her chin.

"You seem to have a gift for working with difficult

patients," I said, with a warm smile, feeling guilty for all the negative thoughts I'd had about her this week.

"Don't be too impressed," said Dr. Frazier. "This time it's a heavy dose of benzodiazepines." She smiled briefly, and then pulled me down the hall, out of range of the two women and the staff bustling nearby. "Heather told me on the way over in the ambulance that she saw Polson shoot Victoria."

"She saw him do it?" I asked, stunned.

Dr. Frazier nodded. "She was following her sister, keeping an eye on her," she said. "Polson stepped out from behind a Dumpster, shot her, and ran."

"She didn't tell the cops?"

"No. She's off her meds and quite psychotic. No way she was taking a trip to the police station. We're looking to transfer her upstairs to the inpatient psych unit."

"That poor girl," I said. "What a mess."

❧

Angie sat with me through the police debriefing and then insisted on accompanying me to the sixth floor to see Annabelle.

Nurse McHugh, tapping at the nurses' station computer, buzzed us in immediately. She hurried around the counter and enveloped me in a hug. "Oh my God, we just heard about Fred Polson. I feel so awful—if only I had been paying more attention. But we've had such a zoo here lately, with Shock Daddy and all . . ."

"How would you have known?" I asked. "He seemed quite polished and professional the times I met him."

"He was hanging around the unit more than usual—and that's a little strange. He mostly works with patients about insurance and placement issues and doesn't get involved in the actual counseling. We call the psychiatry department when we think we need more of that." She cupped her face with both hands. "So I just assumed that he was horrified about this nice woman being attacked in her own home in such a safe neighborhood. I didn't think it through."

She leaned forward and whispered, "Most of us think Polson must've injected her with the insulin earlier this week too. I imagine he was desperate to finish the job so she wouldn't tell on him when she regained consciousness."

"The Polsons have a diabetic cat," I said. One small confidence I felt comfortable breaking. "It would have been easy for him to bring in the needle and the insulin."

"Does Annabelle know about her sisters?" Angie asked.

The nurse nodded. "That's the good news—she's awake. Bad news—Dr. Jensen had to tell her Victoria was murdered. He was afraid someone else would get to her first and he wanted to monitor her when she heard. She's very sad. Obviously. So go easy."

Annabelle's bed was canted at a high enough angle that she spotted us coming down the hall. Her face lit up.

"Where have you been?"

I kissed her cheek and stood by the bed, holding the rail. "Doesn't matter, we're here now. I'm so sorry about Victoria."

She blinked away her tears. "How's Heather?"

"Resting comfortably," I said, taking her hand. "Once they get her meds back on track, she'll be fine. Probably more than ready to agree to long-term treatment."

Annabelle nodded slowly. "And Mary Polson?"

"Physically fine," I said.

"She's going to need another therapist," said Annabelle, pulling her hand from mine. "I don't see how we'd work through this."

I patted her knee. "No need to worry about that today. You can sort all that out when the time comes."

The nurse stopped in the doorway. "Better wrap things up," she said, smiling. "We need our patient rested. She's being transferred to Gaylord Rehabilitation Hospital tomorrow."

Chapter 27

After seeing my patients the next day, I drove over to Janice's house in Madison. I'd slept poorly, the night filled with horrible memories of Polson's attempted kidnapping. I needed to see my family in person.

"What's wrong with your lip?" Janice asked after I hugged her and Brittany twice and heard my niece's report about her school art project and the Boston Children's Museum. I raised my eyebrows. "Can we talk in private a minute?"

"Honey, will you run the dog out to the backyard?" Janice asked her daughter. "I'll pay you two dollars for each time you run around the garden." Brittany scampered off.

"Wow, bribery prices have skyrocketed," I said.

Janice fingered her pearls and frowned. "What's wrong?"

"I had some trouble last night," I said, and told her a whitewashed version of what had happened in Annabelle's office. Her eyes widened and her perfectly painted lips trembled. To escape her worried stare, I glanced at the *New Haven Register*, which lay open on her coffee table. "Look, it made the front page."

KIDNAPPING ATTEMPT
BY HOSPITAL SOCIAL WORKER FOILED

Janice picked up the paper, looking totally horrified, and began to skim. "Why didn't you call me?"

"I didn't want to scare you."

"You were held hostage? Jesus, you should have called me!"

"It was so late when I got home. And he only had us for five minutes. What good would it have done to wake you and make you worry? I just really wanted a hug in person."

She hugged me hard.

"I spoke with our father this week too."

She drew back. "You what?"

"It was a beginning, that's all."

"The beginning of what?"

I shrugged. "I'm not sure. But I do know that fractured endings have a way of coming up over and over. And I'm sick of crashing into this one." I took her hand. "He asked about you."

"As he damn well might," she sniffed. The teakettle whistled as Brittany and her dog galloped back into the living room.

"Six times!" she announced. "We ran around six times! That's fifteen dollars!"

Janice kissed her daughter's forehead and smiled at me. "She hasn't learned her multiplication tables yet. Brittany, come help me fix tea for Aunt Rebecca. And I think we need cookies." They banged cheerfully into the kitchen.

I leafed through the rest of the paper while Janice and Brittany made tea, stopping abruptly in the obituary section.

> *Alice Miller Meigs, 49, Educator and Musician*
> *Alice Miller Meigs died at her home on Friday af-*
> *ter a long illness. She is survived by her husband,*
> *Detective Jack Meigs of the Guilford Police Depart-*
> *ment; her daughter, Caroline Miller; and two sisters,*
> *Lorraine Bradford of New York City, and Elizabeth*
> *Esposito of Miami, Florida. Mrs. Meigs was a math*
> *teacher at the Guilford High School until her retire-*
> *ment five years ago. She also sang in the Con Brio*
> *chorus and was an active member of the Guilford*
> *Garden Club. Services will be held at the Church of*
> *Christ in Stony Creek on Tuesday at 4 p.m.*

Alice Miller Meigs. *AMM*. Another one of Annabelle's mystery patients?

"Janice," I yelled toward the kitchen. "Can you hold the tea until tomorrow? I have to run up to see Annabelle and then get to a funeral." I tucked the newspaper into my purse and hurried out to the car.

I drove from Madison up Route 17 to the Gaylord Rehabilitation Hospital in Wallingford, where Annabelle was recuperating. She had been rolled out into the courtyard in her wheelchair, a hospital blanket tucked around her shoulders and a leftover lunch tray on the table beside her. She had her face tipped up to the day's last rays of spring sun. She looked thin, and sad, but so much better than she had in the hospital.

I kissed her and handed over a foil packet of homemade cookies tied up with a green ribbon. "Chocolate chip," I said. "The chocolate's a little soft from sitting in the car.

And don't you dare tell me you're on a diet. You didn't eat anything for a week."

She accepted the package and set it on her lap, lower lip quivering. "Victoria's favorite." She forced a smile. "Mine too."

"Was Polson your hated and hateful patient?" I asked gently.

She nodded. "You can't imagine how awful he was when they came in together." She wiped her lips with the back of her hand, the fingers still taped together. "Well, I guess you can. But I'll never understand why he shot Victoria."

"I'm betting she'd figured it out," I said, "that he'd put you in the hospital. Who knows, maybe she confronted him and he panicked?"

She gazed across the courtyard. "That's the kind of woman she was, fearless about consequences. She got a rush from stirring up trouble."

"And she loved you," I said softly. "Heather's a brave woman too."

Annabelle wiped her eyes. "We spoke this morning. She asked me apologize to you about the purse snatching. She thought you might have a way to get in touch with me, your phone or something . . ." She rustled in her sweatshirt pocket for a Kleenex.

"I wish you'd felt like you could talk to me about your sisters."

"That subject is so painful," said Annabelle, studying the package of cookies again. "I would have gotten there eventually. Isn't it funny that talking about it to Russ felt easier than to you, one of my dearest friends?"

"Maybe it's because he doesn't insist on dissecting relationships endlessly, like us."

She smiled warmly. "He's sweet that way."

Damn, sooner rather than later, I was going to have to tell her what I'd done to her boyfriend while she was out cold.

Annabelle blinked and yawned. "We all have secrets. You with your mother."

I felt myself blush. I'd lived with the history of my mother's suicide in Technicolor in my own mind for so long, it was hard to find a place to slip the facts into a new friendship. And then the moment passed and it just felt awkward. In the end, the shame held me back. Why hadn't my mother cared enough about her kids—me and Janice—to stick around? And what about my father? Annabelle probably felt the same shame—as though if she'd been a better sister, the ending would have changed. Victoria would be alive and Heather wouldn't be locked away in a psychiatric ward. And Meigs too—maybe if he'd been a more adequate husband . . .

"When you trust someone enough to let them in, anything feels lighter," Annabelle said with a small smile. "Wouldn't you think we two would understand that?"

"My mother died when I was four. She took her own life. I found her," I said. "My father disappeared soon after, leaving Janice and me with our grandparents."

"Rebecca, I'm so sorry," Annabelle said. "Can I give you a hug?" I crouched down beside the wheelchair and we embraced. An aide bustled over to collect Annabelle's tray.

"I'll leave the Jell-O, shall I?" she said to Annabelle. "You barely ate anything."

Annabelle grinned. "I'll try to do better next time."

"Hey, I met your Dr. Phipps this week too," I said, once the woman left. "I made a sand tray." I told her about the little girl turning away from the forest. "And I called my father. Maybe we'll get some things sorted out there. In time. But I'm afraid the romance with Good Old Bob went kaput."

Annabelle looked horrified. "I missed your spring dinner. How was the carbonara?"

"To die for. And I found these fresh baby artichokes and marinated them with asparagus for a couple of hours. That balsamic vinegar you gave me for Christmas?" I kissed the tips of my fingers and released them.

She stared mournfully at the puddle of green Jell-O wobbling on the table beside her wheelchair. "You'll make it again?"

I nodded.

"So we'll reschedule with the guys—you'll make up with Bob and we'll start fresh. They won't mind eating the same meal twice."

I cleared my throat. "Unfortunately, there was a minor snafu with the dinner. I'm afraid I wasn't much of a hostess."

"Not food poisoning?"

"No problem with the food. Everyone loved that." I coughed. "The Boggle game didn't go over so well."

"You made them play Boggle?" She snickered. "Russ went along with that?"

"For a while. But he seemed to take offense when we teased him about the three-letter words. Then he got the impression that I was accusing him of abusing you."

Annabelle's eyes widened. "Were you?"

I nodded, flinching in anticipation of her anger. "Your neighbor across the road said something about how no woman deserved to be beaten no matter what the guy said she did. I thought she was hinting about you and Russ."

"That was *her* story, Rebecca. Just like Mary Polson. *She's* the one who had an abusive husband. It took her thirty years to leave him."

"And then she said her black pug only barks at men . . ."

"Those dogs bark all the time," Annabelle said. "They don't discriminate against anyone."

I gulped. "I'm sorry—I seemed to have screwed up all around."

"What happened with Bob?"

"He got the idea that I wasn't ready for a relationship after I bailed out on his parents on the golf course."

"You're incredible."

"I can call Russ," I offered. "I'll grovel. I'll tell him he should give you another chance—not judge you by your wacky friends."

She burst out laughing. "Oh, don't be silly." A wicked grin played over her lips. "Besides, he called me this morning. He's bringing Chinese food over later."

"Wow, that's a load off." I smiled, and then paused before pulling the obituary page out of my bag. "Alice Meigs died."

Annabelle's smile faded. "The poor woman. She fought right up to the end."

I watched her carefully. "I can't believe you didn't say a word about any of this." I cleared my throat. "I guess I have to admire how you kept their confidences, even from me."

"You'll be late for the funeral," she said, squeezing my fingers.

Chapter 28

The Church of Christ in Stony Creek is possibly the quaintest structure in the quaintest town on the Connecticut shoreline. Stone steps lead up to a stone building with a turret on the left side and a row of stained-glass windows along the front. The Thimble Islands float just off the harbor, reachable only by boat. Some are inhabited by the richest of the rich, others by old shoreline families unwilling to surrender their crumbling cottages to the New Yorkers spreading through the area like kudzu.

Although the town's a zoo come summer, on this cool spring weekday, it was deserted. Just across the street, the harbor sparkled, dotted with kayaks in primary colors. A stocky fisherman called to his dog, busy nosing in the trash. "Mr. Wagner—come here right now!" The dog ignored him.

I lingered on the grass, hating the idea of facing the sadness inside the church. Only when I heard the first wheezing strains of the organ did I plod up the stairs to join the line of mourners waiting to sign the guest book. The place was jammed. By the time I'd scrawled my name in the book, I had to squeeze into a pew much closer to the front than I'd intended, pressed next to a woman wearing too much floral perfume. The congregation was struggling through a rather tuneless rendition of "The Lord Is My Shepherd," which is a lot prettier as a psalm than a hymn.

"We welcome you, friends and loved ones, to the celebration of the life of Alice Miller Meigs," said the minister, an older man with ruddy cheeks and a wispy white beard. I leaned around the burly man in front of me, searching for Meigs, and got a full view of his wife in her coffin instead. She was laid out on white satin pillows, the lower half of her body encased in the cherry casket. She looked small and peaceful.

A woman approached the coffin and with a nod to the organist began to belt out "You'll Never Walk Alone," which reduces me to gelatin under the best of circumstances. I rustled in my purse for a tissue and the perfumed woman beside me patted my knee. I pressed back my tears by focusing on the dark brown wainscoting that lined the ceiling and then the stained-glass windows on the far side of the church where a haloed Jesus ministered to a group of what appeared to be beggars.

"The death of a younger person feels different than when an old person dies," said the minister. He stroked his beard. "Alice lived with a terrible illness for too many years." The congregation sighed and sniffled. "When sickness lingers and death comes too early and yet too late, we can't help wondering about fairness and suffering. We can't help wondering where God is when bad things happen to good people."

He invited one of Alice's sisters to come to the podium, where she spoke in a voice that cracked about her sister's

love of flowers and music and children and the happy hours
she spent in her garden and raising her daughter. A former
mentor talked about Alice's gift as a teacher and particular
warmth with challenging teenagers. The a cappella choir
from the high school filed to the front of the church and
sang "Swing Low, Sweet Chariot." My Kleenex was soggy
and my sinuses clogged with stale perfume. Would the service never end?

At last, the minister approached the podium. "Alice
adored poetry. Christina Rossetti was one of her favorites,"
he said, and began to read "One Sea-Side Grave" from a
small, battered volume.

When he'd finished, he walked over to Meigs and pre-
sented the book to him. "Please accept these poems as a sign
and symbol of the love of your friends and family. We will
be with you always, but especially in the dark days to come."

Meigs looked at the minister, then down at the book, his
face blank. With the minister at his elbow, he rose from the
front pew and made his way down the aisle, Alice's other
relatives falling in behind.

I'd made up my mind to slip out the side door without
speaking to Meigs. I would write him a note later this week,
praising the lovely service and expressing my condolences.
But the crowd surged forward, pushing me out into the soft
afternoon light and releasing me just feet from Jack Meigs
himself. He had his hand on the back of a teenage girl. She
had glossy brown hair and a pale, narrow face that might
have been pretty if she was smiling.

"Caroline," he was saying, "it would be polite if you'd
stay here and greet the folks who came to support us."

She glared at him with a look of pure hatred. "Screw
you. You're not my father." She stormed down the steps,
trotted the length of the sidewalk, and hurtled across the
street toward the water. Meigs's eyes met mine.

"I don't seem to have Alice's knack for handling challenging teenagers." He flashed a lopsided smile that broke my heart.

"I'm so sorry about Alice," I said. "I didn't realize—"

"She went quickly at the end," he said at the same time. "Small mercy." He looked bewildered and exhausted, still clutching the volume of poetry in his left hand.

I took his right hand with both of mine and squeezed. He drew me a step away, seeming unaware of the line snaking behind me, waiting for him.

"Are you okay?" he asked. "I felt like a first-class jerk when they told me what happened. The juice ran out on my phone—"

"Please," I said, releasing my grip. "Don't even start. I'm fine."

He slipped the book into his suit jacket pocket, and pulled something else out. The small figure of a knight in armor lay in his palm. He looked at it, then back up at me.

"I forgot all about this," he said. "I only wear this suit for funerals." He put the knight back into his pocket. "I'm sorry I put you on the spot at Ms. Hart's place. Alice was seeing her in therapy and she met with us together sometimes too. She helped us through some terrible times."

I nodded, trying not to show what I'd guessed.

"At the beginning of last week, Alice asked Ms. Hart if she would bring her tray to our house," he said. "She couldn't make it up the steps to Ms. Hart's office anymore." His gaze shifted off to the right where his stepdaughter was flinging rocks into the Sound. "I thought maybe Alice had left a message for me in that tray. I thought you could figure it out."

"So *you* took the knight?"

He nodded.

"I'm sorry I couldn't help," I said.

"She didn't make the tray for me anyway," he said with a tired shrug. "I understand that now."

"Your wife was dying," I said. "Grasping at straws is perfectly understandable."

"That wasn't the only reason I asked you to come to her house," he said. "I didn't buy the robbery story either. I was worried the beating was connected to me. Pissed-off bad guys have a way of going after our soft spots. It's hard on a marriage. Poor Alice. It's not easy being married to a cop."

The couple next in the receiving line began to rustle and clear their throats.

"I should let you go," I said. "Your friends are waiting."

Squeezing his hand one last time, I turned and strode down the steps.

My cell phone rang as I reached my car. I glanced at the screen: Mark. I settled into the driver's seat, rolled down the window, and took the call.

"Angie told me what happened," he said. "What a nightmare. Are you okay? When can I see you? Dinner this weekend?"

I looked across the water and sighed. "I still love you dearly," I said. "And I'm really glad we worked together on this. It reminded me of why we got married in the first place. But I need—I'll call you in a couple of weeks, okay?"

I hung up with Mark, feeling just about as sad as one of Christina Rossetti's maudlin poems. The phone rang again: Connie Frazier.

"Dr. Butterman?"

"Rebecca," I said.

"Rebecca. I went to see Annabelle this afternoon. I couldn't stop thinking about the fish oil capsules. Remember she asked me about using them to treat bipolar disorder?"

"I remember."

"Like we thought, she was desperate for anything to stabilize Heather. I've promised Annabelle to help her find a treatment program. Meanwhile, Heather's psychosis is clearing."

"Great," I said, too tired to hash one more thing out. "Thanks for keeping me posted."

"I have a confession too," Dr. Frazier added before I could hang up. "I should have told you earlier, but it's embarrassing . . ."

"Go on," I said, tensing for something bad.

She paused. "I've been walking my golden retriever in Annabelle's neighborhood," she said finally. "I admire her work so much. I'm sorry if I scared her in any way. Or her neighbors. Do you think I should tell the cops? I wasn't stalking her, I was just walking the dog."

"You have a green car?"

"Yes."

I laid my hand on my chest and whooshed out some air. "Were you on Mulberry Point the morning he beat her up?"

She choked out another yes. "But I didn't see anything. I wish I had. I would have killed the bastard myself."

"I think you should tell the cops. And Annabelle too, once she's in shape to really talk things over. And find some other place to walk your dog."

Frazier coughed. "One more thing; about Craig Sebastian. I'm sorry I ever said anything to him about your competence. It was childish. I was annoyed that you were covering for Annabelle when I wanted to be the one helping her. I'm sick about it. I'm sorry."

My head felt like it had been stuffed with wet wool. Annabelle wasn't the only one who'd need time and space to process everything. "Apology accepted."

"Just be careful, okay? He's gunning for you."

I laughed. "Sebastian I can handle." I closed the phone and watched a pair of robins peck at the fringe of grass along the beach. My stomach growled and I started the car and pulled away. Spring, and a woman's fancy turns to supper.

Penguin Group (USA) Online

What will you be reading tomorrow?

Tom Clancy, Patricia Cornwell, W.E.B. Griffin,
Nora Roberts, William Gibson, Robin Cook,
Brian Jacques, Catherine Coulter, Stephen King,
Dean Koontz, Ken Follett, Clive Cussler,
Eric Jerome Dickey, John Sandford,
Terry McMillan, Sue Monk Kidd, Amy Tan,
John Berendt…

You'll find them all at
penguin.com

Read excerpts and newsletters,
find tour schedules and reading group guides,
and enter contests.

Subscribe to Penguin Group (USA) newsletters
and get an exclusive inside look
at exciting new titles and the authors you love
long before everyone else does.

PENGUIN GROUP (USA)
us.penguingroup.com